MY DARKEST NIGHT

K-9 SEARCH AND RESCUE BOOK 4

LINDA J. WHITE

Linda J White

WINDY BAY BOOKS

Cover Design, June Padgett, Bright Eye Designs.

First printing, August 2022

White, Linda J. 1949-

ISBN 978-1-7372356-2-0 (paperback)

ISBN 978-1-7372356-3-7 (ebook)

For Karen,
my reader, my role model, my advisor
my big sister.
Love always.

The light shines in the darkness,
and the darkness has not overcome it.

— JOHN 1:5

1

"SEEK, LUKE. SEEK!" I gestured with my arm and watched with pride as my German shepherd took off, leaping gracefully over broken concrete in the rubble pile, nose working, tail wagging, body strong, his coat glistening in the sun.

We'd been preparing for this day for months. A contact I'd made with Virginia Task Force-1, the FEMA disaster response group, had invited me and other volunteers from Battlefield Search and Rescue to take a field trip to their practice facility in Northern Virginia. Almost all Battlefield's searches took place in wilderness or residential areas. Responding to an urban disaster like a collapsed multistory building required different skills, and although we might not be called upon for a job that extensive, Buzz thought we might like to see how they train.

I not only wanted to see the place, I wanted to run the pile, so I began prepping as soon as we set the date. In wilderness or regular urban searches, Luke's normal indication—his signal that he'd found someone—was to run back to me, pull the tug on my belt, then run back to the victim. But you don't want your dog running back and forth over a rubble pile, so I'd taught him something we call "reward on find." As soon as I could tell from his body language that he'd found someone, he got his favorite treat in the world—baked liver. It was a new game and he loved it.

I set up practice equipment in my friend Nathan Tanner's yard. Nate helped me modify standard agility equipment, increasing its difficulty to more closely resemble what a dog might face in a disaster. So, for example, the elevated "dog walk" Luke had to cross was eight feet off the ground. The jumps were higher, the tunnel was a crawl-through, and the A-frame he had to climb over led to a wobbly surface that challenged his balance.

Luke and I practiced on that equipment in all kinds of springtime weather, along with my friend Emily and her border collie, Flash, and Bill with his black Lab, Ruger. On a chilly, beautiful day in early April, we arrived at the VATF-1 facility ready to test our skills.

My contact, Buzz, first explained to the six of us who'd come how the pile was built. Although it looked just like a collapsed structure strewn randomly with typical building materials, hidden inside were a series of tunnels in which "victims" could hide. Strategic cameras monitored the searches. The tunnels could be rearranged to create different problems.

"We make each search a successful search, one way or the other, to keep the dogs engaged," Buzz said. Then he introduced two VATF-1 handlers, one with a Lab and one with a shepherd. Each ran a search with a victim hidden in a different place in the pile.

After that demonstration, Emily took a shot. I stood with the sun warming my back watching Flash, who did well until he slid on a slippery sheet of metal. Then he froze.

Emily responded perfectly. She remained calm and patient and encouraged her dog until he was ready to proceed one foot at a time. Although he didn't find the "victim" hiding in the pile, he did continue to search. Then one of the VATF-1 handlers hid near the edge so Flash could get his reward.

Bill and Ruger went next and found the victim in about

fifteen minutes. Then Luke and I took a turn. I removed Luke's collar and vest—you didn't want anything to get snagged on the rubble.

My first step on the pile sent adrenaline through me in a hot rush. A slab of concrete slid under my feet, exposing a black void. My father had died in a hole like that on 9/11.

I shook off my gut reaction and pushed forward, determined not to let my search partner down. I climbed up the pile and just then, Luke began barking non-stop.

I shot my hand in the air to signal he had found someone.

"All right," Buzz called out, "good job! There's a victim in a tunnel a foot below him."

"Good dog, good dog!" I gave Luke his yummy reward, and we climbed down.

"You beat the best time of our dogs," Buzz teased. "Don't ever do that again. It's demoralizing."

I grinned at him, proud of my dog.

I WAS THINKING about that experience three weeks later as I brushed out my dog in the tiny backyard of the townhouse where I lived with husband, Scott Cooper. Scott, an FBI agent, had recently been cleared for regular duty after being shot last year. He had fought hard to regain his strength and fitness while doing deskwork at home, studying for his second master's degree, and completing the personal counseling mandated by the Office of Professional Responsibility.

Although Scott's focus on recovery had set back our plans to move to a house with more yard, seeing the look in his eye when he slipped his holster on his belt that first day going back to the office made it all worthwhile. I'd come so close to losing him.

"America is safe once more," I said, teasing him as I tucked his suitcoat around his gun and said goodbye that morning.

He cradled my face in his hands and kissed me tenderly. "I'm praying I never have to use it again." He hugged me. "Thank you for all you've done. I'll miss working from home."

"Well, unless you plan to spend your time arresting me and Luke, I think you'd better get back out in the world."

"I might take on Luke," he responded, "but you? No way. You're too tough." Then he kissed me again.

I smiled as I thought about that sweet moment. I loved that man.

I finished brushing Luke and patted him on the side. "Okay, buddy, you're done!" He shook, as if he had to fix his hair now that I'd messed it up. Then I saw his shoulder dip. "Oh, no you don't!" I said, grabbing his collar. I knew what he was going to do—roll, preferably in dirt, ideally in something stinky. "Come on, let's go."

As we started to go inside, my watch signaled a text. A callout!

I quickened my step and jerked open the door. I grabbed my phone off the kitchen counter so I could see the details more clearly. Battlefield SAR had been tapped to assist with a building collapse. *Wow,* I thought, *a first!*

"You want to go?" I asked Luke.

He went crazy, spinning and grinning and galloping toward the door.

I texted back that Luke and I would respond, ETA forty minutes.

We loaded up in record time. I checked my weather app: cloudy, high of seventy, chance of afternoon rain. Then I headed out.

I imagined what might be ahead. There are a lot of reasons why a building can collapse—earthquake, tornado, hurricane. I could rule all that out. Then there were gas leaks, structural problems, fire, or explosion of unknown origin. There'd also been a rash of incidents in the news in which an out-of-control vehicle slammed into a building and caused a partial collapse.

Whatever the reason, if people were trapped, I wanted to

help. Although I'd trained for it, I'd never worked this kind of situation.

I drove through streets full of April gardens lush with flowering azaleas and trees sporting bright green, new leaves. When I got to the scene, it was worse than I had imagined. The collapse was in a low-rise office park now glutted with fire trucks, ambulances, and police cars, all with their lights flashing and radios blaring. Smoke still billowed up from one part of the building. Bricks had been flung everywhere. Dust hung in the air along with an acrid smell. The firefighters wore protective masks. Most of the building lay in a heap of concrete, framing, glass, and debris. One section of the wall still stood.

I parked where I was directed and stepped out into the chaos. The temperature had just hit sixty-five degrees, so I could afford to leave Luke in the Jeep for awhile. I opened the back gate to give him some air, then I craned my neck, found Tom, the incident commander, and walked over to him.

"Thanks for coming, Jess," he said.

"Who else will be here?"

"Emily and Bill, within the hour."

"Nate?" Nathan Tanner was Battlefield's training director and a reliable source of wisdom, which I suspected we were going to need.

"Couldn't reach him. Left a message."

I pictured Nate sitting on a mower at the community college where he worked as a maintenance man. Or deep in the basement of a building using a nail gun. He would have responded to the callout text if he'd heard it.

I looked around. The office park had four rows of two-story buildings, brick with asphalt shingles. I'd seen about sixty different businesses named on the sign coming in. "What caused the collapse?"

"Some kind of explosion. One of the involved offices belongs to a dentist, an oral surgeon. They sometimes have volatile chemicals." Tom shrugged. "The dentist's office is next to a Social Security office, then a doctor's office. Second floor had a psychologist and an insurance office and the back office of Social Security. Oh, and there was a small post office at this end."

"Just two floors, right?"

"Two floors and an attic," he said. He gestured toward an undamaged part of the office park. "Just like those. Soon as we get clearance, we can go in. But they want us to stay away from that section where the wall is still standing until they take it down or stabilize it. They're waiting for a structural engineer."

"What time did this happen?"

"Nine-fifteen this morning."

I checked my watch—two hours ago.

"They think everybody got out," Tom said, "but because they didn't have an exact count of who was inside, they need us to double-check."

"Okay." I looked around. There was barely a scrap of grass to be found. "I'm going to walk Luke back there." I gestured toward a strip of woods beyond the last buildings. "Text me when we can go in."

I got Luke out of the Jeep, leashed him up, and began walking. I passed spectators clustered in little pods, police officers interviewing witnesses, rumbling fire trucks, and ambulances. I saw an EMT I knew and asked him if anyone had been transported.

"We've treated several for shock here on the scene and a couple went to the hospital with hearing loss."

"That's all?" I stared at the mound of collapsed walls, foundation, and a roof that was just beyond the first row of fire trucks.

"Surprised us too. One guy said the fire alarm went off before the explosion."

"That's weird."

"Yeah."

I had half an hour to think about that, sitting under the trees with my dog. Emily and Flash arrived, as did Bill with Ruger. We knocked around strategies for searching the building.

Finally, I spotted Tom coming toward us. "Heads up."

"All right, team," Tom said. "We've got the go-ahead. The fire captain believes from what witnesses said that everyone got out. They've checked the pile and haven't found any evidence of victims. But they'd like us to search anyway, everywhere but the part of the building where that roof section landed, next to the wall that's still standing. That area is unstable. Now, how does this sound?" Tom gave us our assignments. We'd search for an hour, then take a fifteen-minute break, and we'd stagger the breaks so at least two of us were always on the pile. Luke and I were up first.

I was glad. We were antsy. We would focus on the east end first, then switch to the west end, and Bill would take a breather. Every once in awhile, one of us would hide so a dog could "find" us and get rewarded.

That sounded good to me. I walked Luke over to the building. I checked the wind. It was coming from the southeast. I studied the rubble pile. There'd been no fire on this end, so I didn't have to worry about heat. I could see cinder blocks, torn up wallboard, plumbing, wires, framing, windows, HVAC ductwork, desks, office chairs, cubicle partitions, file cabinets, loose paper, computers, printers, copiers all jumbled together in a crazy heap. How in the world should we begin?

In the end, I let Luke decide. I took off his collar and dropped it on the ground with his leash. Then I said, "Seek!" and gestured toward our end of the pile. I followed him gingerly, taking care not to step on glass or fall. My dog was much more nimble than I, climbing over the rubble like a deer. *Lord, make my feet like hinds' feet on high places,* I thought.

That first hour went by in a flash. We came off the pile, took our break, then headed toward Bill's end to relieve him. As we were walking, out of the corner of my eye I thought I saw Luke raise his head momentarily. Wishful thinking. He kept walking.

We continued that way all day, with a longer break for lunch. It was a discouraging search. Luke had stopped, sniffed, and considered various places at both ends of the pile, but he'd never given an indication, and neither had the other dogs, except for the times one of us "hid." Luke must have been frustrated. I know I was.

Around four in the afternoon, the predicted rain showed up. We retreated to our cars. I put Luke in his crate with water and sat with the driver's seat rocked back. I wondered if the rain would further destabilize the pile. I checked the radar on my phone. It looked like the shower would last about twenty minutes.

As soon as the rain ended, we returned to our job, carefully working over the pile, which was now wet and slippery. We checked crevices newly opened by firefighters, and rechecked old openings, and we found exactly nothing.

As we approached the ten-hour mark, even I was ready to call it a wrap. The storm was long gone, the sun was dropping in the sky, witnesses had been dismissed, and all but one ambulance and two fire trucks had returned to their stations. The fire chief seemed anxious to begin pulling apart the rubble pile so the fire marshal could determine the cause of the explosion.

So Tom ended our search.

I called Luke off the pile, put his collar back on, and leashed him up. Then Emily, Bill, Tom and I gathered to debrief. The wind had come around, clocking 180 degrees from where it had been when we'd started. I could smell the acrid odor of the charred portion of the pile as I listened to Tom. A SAR group with human remains detection dogs, he said, would come in behind us to check for deceased victims. "I don't think they'll find human remains," I said confidently to Tom. "Luke didn't." My dog was cross-trained for both live finds and human remains detection.

We were in the middle of talking when I noticed my steel-toed boot was untied. I squatted down, dropping Luke's leash as I did. A jolt of shock ran through me when he took off.

"Luke! Luke, come!" I called after him.

He ignored me, heading straight for the pile, straight for the forbidden zone.

"Hey, hey!" the fire marshal yelled, gesturing toward my dog.

"I'll get him!" I ran after him, angry at first, then scared. He climbed onto that roof section, into the danger zone, leash bobbing after him like a freed anchor rope.

I stepped gingerly onto the pile just as he reached the top where the brick wall still stood. Then he stopped and began barking, looking straight at me.

I halted in my tracks. That was his indication. He'd found something. He'd found some*one*. And, heart pounding, I followed him.

"Don't go up there!" someone yelled.

I ignored the warning and kept moving toward Luke. I felt the pile shift, scrambled to keep my balance, and had to reach down and touch something to get right again. As I neared Luke, he began scratching at the piece of roof, scratching and whining and going ballistic.

He must have been bored after a long day with no finds, I thought. He looked like he'd gone crazy. The way he was acting made me reach down, grab a section of that roof, and throw it off.

When I looked down again, I saw a hand, a left hand, gray as death, covered in drywall dust. "I got someone!" I yelled. Luke's barking deafened me.

The ring on the third finger caught my eye. My heart jumped. I jerked off my glove, licked my thumb, rubbed it over the ring, and the wedding band's unique Celtic design came into view. My heart seized up. My head spun. "What are you doing here?" I cried out, panic shearing away my insides. "Why are you here?"

"Is he alive?" someone yelled at me.

I was a certified EMT, but I did not want to touch him. If I couldn't find a pulse, if there was no blood coursing through that body, my own life would implode right there.

"Hey!" someone yelled. "What are you doing?"

I had no choice. I grabbed a breath, reached down, and wrapped my fingers around Nathan Tanner's wrist.

"MEDIC!" I screamed.

2

"Medic! I need a medic." The tiny thumps of an artery in Nate's wrist indicated *life*. I yelled down to my SAR group, "It's Nate!"

I began throwing rubble off my best friend.

I shouldn't have done that. The pile was unstable. But I couldn't stop myself. Luke tried to help, but when I saw him digging frantically at framing with exposed nails, I managed to restrain both of us.

I heard a female voice below say, "Coming up!" An EMT, bag in hand, climbed up beside me. "Are you okay?" she asked.

I grabbed both of her arms. "Help him! Please!" I gestured toward Nate's exposed hand. The pile shifted under my feet again and an arrow of fear shot up my spine.

"Go down," she said, "slowly. We'll take care of him." She glanced toward the unstable wall next to us then spoke into her radio.

I obeyed, bringing Luke with me. Two firefighters and another EMT passed me on my way down. My Battlefield friends met me at the bottom. I heard sirens in the distance.

"Did you say 'Nate'?" Tom's eyes were wide.

"Yes!" I replied, tears blurring my vision.

"Nate Tanner?"

"I don't know why he's here!" I sobbed.

Emily started to wrap her arms around me, but I backed away. Instead, I dropped down and hugged my dog, burying my face in his black and gold coat. "I'm sorry, I'm sorry," I said to Luke. "You tried to tell me." That little sniff. I should have stopped right then and asked him to search.

Luke faced the pile, his body tense. He turned to slurp my ear. Dog slobber—the universal antidote.

I clung to my dog, breathing fervent prayers to God, until I heard someone begin asking questions about the victim.

"Jess is the one who knows him best," I heard Tom say. So I stood and faced the woman with the clipboard in her hand and answered her questions while my body trembled with fear. Over her shoulder I could see three people on the pile. One was bent over where I'd found Nate's hand, the others were pulling away debris.

My mind bounced around like a ping-pong ball. *Were they giving him oxygen? Fluids? Why was he in this place anyway? What would I do, what would we all do, if he died?*

I forced myself to refocus on Miss Clipboard. Name, date of birth, address, next of kin, medical history ... Nate deconstructed and reduced to blanks on a form.

Oh, he's also courageous, wise, loving, and the most authentic Christian I've ever known. He'll give his life for you. He'll tell you the truth when you're messing up, and he'll keep on loving you anyway. He's a faithful husband, a steady friend, a brilliant dog trainer, a natural leader ... fit that on your form. And save this man because we need him. We all need him.

After Miss Clipboard left, I tried calling Nate's wife, Laura. Her cell went straight to voicemail. I left a simple message: *Call me.* Then I called Scott, my husband. Again, I had to leave a voicemail.

Time seemed to stretch like a balloon about to break. Were the rescuers moving slowly or was it just my imagination? My stomach was tense with fear, my knees like jelly, and I had to remind myself to breathe.

I thought about the textbook consequences of entrapment: crush injuries, hypovolemic shock, kidney failure, pneumothorax, and numerous other medical issues. I imagined the horror of being trapped. I thought about Dad, who died in the rubble of the World Trade Center, for the millionth time.

Then another wave of panic hit me. Sprite. Where was Sprite? Nate's springer spaniel went everywhere with him.

I had to find Sprite. "I'll be right back," I said to my friends, and bringing Luke with me, I began searching for Nate's red Tahoe in the parking lot. Could Sprite have been in that car all day long? Would she have survived the heat? Was she, right now, cooking in a hot car because of my stupidity?

After ten minutes of desperate searching, I finally found the Tahoe—or what was left of it—peeking out from under a pile of burned rubble right next to the building. I stood stunned, imagining little Sprite caught in what had obviously been an inferno.

Luke whined. *Did he smell her?* Sick to my stomach, I put Luke on a down-stay and moved toward the pile, now soggy wet from the rain and the fire hoses. I put a gloved hand on a two-by-four.

"Hey, miss! What are you doing?"

I turned and saw a firefighter. I closed my eyes momentarily, bracing myself for a fight. "I need to see in that car," I said. "There may be a dog in it."

"No dog in there, no live dog, anyway," the guy said.

I bit my lower lip, forcing back tears. "I need to see. My friend," I gestured toward the place where workers were trying to free Nate, "he'll need to know."

"It's his dog?"

I nodded. The tears I'd tried so hard to suppress dripped down my cheek. "He took her everywhere."

The firefighter gave a small, decisive nod, turned, and began pulling debris off the Tahoe. Window frames, soggy wallboard, charcoaled two-by-fours, a burned metal file cabinet—we threw all of them aside.

The Tahoe was completely destroyed, burned almost beyond recognition. Seat covers gone, steering wheel melted, and on the dashboard, Nate's sunglasses were a lump.

The firefighter, whose name tag read "Lof," took a piece of wood and probed the pile of ashes in the back seat. He turned to me. "I don't see any bones."

"Can we get to the cargo area?"

We moved more stuff, and he checked the ash and burned materials in the back cargo area. I saw some things I recognized —carabiners, clamps, Nate's tool chest—but nothing that looked like animal remains. I looked at Mr. Lof. "Thanks for helping me."

"Yes, ma'am." He smiled. "Maybe just this once he left the dog at home."

My throat closed. I managed to nod.

I GATHERED up Luke and began walking back to my SAR group, I tried calling Laura again and got the same no answer. "What's taking so long?" I asked my friends, nodding toward the rescue site.

"I got no idea," Tom said.

I handed Luke's leash to him. "Would you hold him?" Then I got down close to my buddy and said, "Luke, stay." He barely took his eyes off the pile.

I walked over to where a cluster of fire department people stood. I saw the fire marshal's eyes narrow as I approached. I avoided him, sucked up my gut, and went straight to the fire chief. "I'm Jessica Cooper. My dog is the one who found him. And I'm a friend of the victim. Can you update me?"

He grimaced, indicating he was not at all happy to see me. A short man, he was wiry like Nate, with a full head of graying hair and a thick moustache. But for all his posturing, I saw kindness hiding in his gray eyes.

I lifted my chin, thankful the walk had stopped my shaking. "Sir, I'm an EMT myself. Can you tell me what's going on?"

He sized me up, took a deep breath, and said, "The victim is receiving oxygen and fluids. There's no massive bleeding that we can see, but he is still unconscious. He's trapped by one leg—"

"Which leg?"

He blinked, then spoke into his radio. "Left," he said to me.

My heart thumped. "I can help with that if you let me go up there."

He cocked his head, asked me how, and when he heard my answer, he agreed. "Go that way." He pointed toward a path the firefighters had made. "Wear a helmet."

I borrowed a helmet and within minutes I was up at the rescue site.

Nate lay on his back in the rubble, eyes closed, face and clothing all a deathly gray. My gut clenched at the sight. A small oxygen tank pushed air into a mask on his nose, a brace stabilized his neck, and an IV delivered fluids. All his body but his left leg lay exposed. A rescue basket waited nearby. I fought to control my emotions, setting my jaw, focusing on the job at hand.

The chief had radioed up that I was coming to help. "Let me get where you are," I said to a dark-haired EMT. He moved. I carefully took his place. I felt Nate's thigh until I found the juncture I'd been hoping for.

"Scissors," I said, holding out my hand.

Someone slapped a pair in my palm, and I began cutting Nate's trouser leg off. Then I reached in and probed. Nate, an amputee, wore a pin and lock prosthesis, something most EMTs would be unfamiliar with. But I knew it well. I'd been with him the night he lost that leg, and with him through his rehabilitation.

I pressed the pin that would release the leg. Jammed. I looked up at the EMTs. "I need you to push his upper body down toward his legs. Gently."

They followed my instructions and the pin released. Nate's artificial leg detached. I slipped the sleeve off his stump and cut the rest of the way through his trousers. Nate was free.

Breathing a silent prayer of thanks, I stood and watched as they transferred my friend to a rescue basket. I saw his chest rise and fall. I saw very little blood. His body looked intact. I hoped I was right.

I followed them off the pile. I could hear Luke barking all the way.

"Good work," the fire chief said.

"Where will you take him?" I suppressed a shiver.

"The trauma center in Charlottesville. There's a chopper waiting a mile from here at an elementary school."

"If you can retrieve that prosthetic leg, he'd appreciate it." I handed him my business card. "Let me know. I'll come pick it up."

That seemed like a crazy thing to say, but those things are expensive, even with insurance.

As I jogged back toward my SAR friends, my phone rang. Scott. My voice broke as I filled him in. "I don't understand. Why was he here?"

"What's in the building?"

"An oral surgeon, insurance agent, social security, a small post office ..."

"Hmm ..."

"I left Nate there for ten hours—ten hours!—because I didn't follow through."

"On a sniff?"

I could hear the skepticism.

"Did any other dog alert there?"

"No. We had nothing all day. And we were told they thought everyone had gotten out."

"So it's not your fault. Stop blaming yourself. Be glad you found him when you did. Before they brought the bulldozers in."

I shivered.

"What's the possibility of other survivors at this point?"

I told him what I knew, that people routinely survive forty-eight hours after a collapse, and even up to two weeks if they can get water. Then he asked if I'd called Laura.

"I've tried, but I can't reach her! She's with her mother in Monterey. Nate told me cell service is iffy up there." I paused and took a deep breath, trying to calm myself down.

"Monterey's in Highland County, right?" Scott asked. "What's her mother's name?"

"Elva," I said, "but I don't know her last name."

"What was Laura's name before she married Nate?"

A logical question. "McCoy."

"I'll call the sheriff and ask for some help," he said.

Hope surged in me. "Thanks, babe!"

"You follow Nate, I'll find Laura."

I clicked off my phone and turned to Tom. "I want to go to the hospital. Nate's wife is out of town. Scott's trying to get in touch with her, but in the meantime, I'm his emergency contact."

He nodded. "If they ask us to go over the pile again, we can handle it."

LUKE and I leaped in my Jeep and headed south, toward Charlottesville and the UVA hospital's trauma unit. We hadn't gone two miles before Scott called me.

"Hey," he said. "Amanda's going to Nate's. She'll take care of the horses. And Sprite, too, if she's there, as long as she needs to. So if you want to drop Luke there ..."

Scott's daughter had done a complete turnaround over the last year, seeming to mature overnight after a terrifying close call. "I'll head that way now."

3

THIRTY MINUTES LATER, I pulled into Nate's driveway. My stomach felt queasy. Would we find Sprite? What if we didn't?

But Luke's enthusiasm as we arrived at the house encouraged me. Sure enough, Sprite was waiting for us inside. Whatever Nate was doing at that building, he'd decided he couldn't take his dog.

"Hey, girl, hey, Sprite! What's going on?" I blinked away tears. Her little stubby tail wagged like crazy. "Why are you here by yourself? Where'd Nate go?"

She didn't answer. "C'mon," I said. "You need to go out." The two dogs played like the best friends they were. Then Sprite sniffed around while I hosed Luke off. Who knows what contaminants he'd been exposed to?

As we were about to head inside, I saw Amanda coming up the driveway in Scott's old black Nissan Rogue.

"I'd hug you but I'm full of dust," I said as she got out of the car.

"Go shower. I'll take care of the dogs," she responded.

So I grabbed my go-bag from my Jeep and took the quickest shower ever. Clean and redressed, I started to walk out into the great room, brushing out my hair. Then I had a thought. I went into Nate's room, into his closet, and grabbed his old artificial leg, thinking he'd need it.

"So what's the latest?" Amanda asked me. Tall, lean, with striking long blonde hair, she could have been a model. Instead, she'd accelerated her studies and was now attending the community college where Nate worked. She'd recently told her dad she wanted to pursue pre-law. I thought his chest would bust open from pride.

I filled her in on Nate, my throat closing with emotion. "He'll make it," I said. That was more hope than promise. "Are you okay to handle things here until one of us gets back?"

"No prob," she responded.

I said goodbye to Luke and took off toward Charlottesville, anxiety increasing with every mile. What would I find at the hospital? Was Nate alive? Impaired? Would he survive one more trauma?

I flipped on the news to distract myself. I shouldn't have. "Authorities say one person has died at a building collapse in White Spring," the newscaster reported.

My stomach dropped. He was wrong. He had to be wrong. Nate was alive when he was transported. Surely ...

I switched my car's media center to a playlist on my phone and spent the rest of the drive listening to worship music. I tried to sing along but couldn't. My throat was too tight.

YEARS AGO, before he was married, Nate had made me his emergency contact for SAR purposes. I leveraged that now to get past the reception desk at the trauma unit. I guess it also helped that I was carrying his prosthetic leg.

I headed for the exam room number the receptionist gave me. Just as I approached it, a man stepped in front of me. "Are you here for Nathan Tanner?" he asked.

My heart jumped like a scared deer. "Yes."

"I'm Dr. Markham."

"How is he?"

He studied me for a second. "In entrapment cases, we are always worried about crush injuries and kidney problems. Mr. Tanner doesn't appear to have any, not that we've found so far anyway."

"So he's alive?"

He frowned. "Yes, of course." He looked at me like I was crazy.

"The news said ..."

"I don't know about that. Mr. Tanner is alive but unconscious."

"Unconscious?"

"Yes."

I wanted to collapse in tears of relief. Instead, I straightened my spine.

He continued cataloguing Nate's condition. "The force field generated by an explosion can cause concussion or brain injury which can cause unconsciousness. He has a lot of dust in his lungs and eyes, and both eardrums are ruptured so his hearing is impacted. We're taking him back for additional scans. If you'd like to see him first—"

"Yes!" I said. "Yes, please."

Dr. Markham pushed back the curtain to Nate's exam room. I was surprised to see the head of his bed elevated. I quickly realized that was to help him breathe. The dust had been washed off his face and out of his beard and despite the clear, plastic oxygen mask he looked better, so much better I had the courage to touch his hand. Tears came to my eyes when his hand closed around mine.

"You're okay, Nate. You're going to make it. The docs are taking good care of you." I rubbed his arm with my left hand.

I got no further response from him.

A transport tech came in, ready to take him for scans. "You can wait here," he said. "He'll be back in a few minutes."

I texted an update to Scott and Amanda. Scott texted back, *OMW ETA 90 min.*

Then Emily texted: *They pulled an elderly woman's body out of the rubble.*

Identity?

UNK. Unknown. An elderly woman—that was the fatality.

The tech's "few minutes" turned into more than an hour. Nate still wasn't back when Scott and Nate's wife Laura walked in. She had on olive-green trail pants and a light blue shirt. Her dark, braided hair hung down her back. Wisps framed her face.

I hugged her, expecting her to cry in my arms, but she didn't. "Thank you," she said, "for finding him."

I felt my face grow hot with guilt. "It wasn't me. It was Luke."

"I'll buy him a steak."

"A hamburger is fine," Scott said, smiling. "He works cheap."

"He works for love," I said, folding myself into my husband's arms. I told them everything the doctor had told me, then added, "But they haven't found any of the more serious crush injuries."

"Good," Laura said.

"I can't figure out why Nate was there."

"Me neither. I just don't know." Laura looked as puzzled as I felt.

What a mystery. We heard a noise behind us, and a tech rolled Nate back into the room. I watched Laura looking over him, mentally assessing his condition as I had done. When the tech left, Laura kissed her husband's forehead, ran her hand over his head, and stroked his jaw. I could almost feel the love flowing between them.

A nurse came in and Laura peppered her with questions about the monitors, Nate's blood pressure, the IV fluids, and where he might go from here. When she'd learned all she could, she pulled a chair close to the bed, took Nate's hand, and settled in. She looked over at me.

"You must be exhausted. Why don't you go home?"

"No," I said. "I'm not leaving you." As sensible as I knew Laura to be, she might need help making decisions or, if the worst happened ...

I couldn't complete that thought.

Scott said, "Why don't we go to the waiting room? Laura, you can text us if you need us or if there's an update. I'll come back and check on you after awhile." That was smart. Realistically, the trauma room was too small for the three of us plus the bed and all the machines.

The nurse adjusting Nate's fluids stopped and looked at us. "I have a better idea. They're going to move him to ICU as soon as the scans are read. Why don't you go to the ICU waiting room? It'll be a lot quieter."

So we left and found the ICU waiting room. We were the only ones there. We claimed a comfortable couch and sat down together. Scott put his arm around me and asked about the search. I started giving him an objective, clinical version of the story, but when I got to the part where Luke ran away from me, onto the pile, my emotions swamped me. "Nate was there. ... He was there all along. ... I just left him because I didn't believe Luke." I sobbed.

"You said you weren't supposed to search there."

"That's right."

"You can't blame yourself. Luke just sniffed. That must have seemed like an outlier."

"But if I— "

"Stop, just stop. You're beating yourself up."

I tried processing his words.

"Jess, you condemn yourself. Why do you do that? You set an impossible standard for yourself, then berate yourself when you fail. Why?"

I didn't know. I really didn't.

I snuggled close, and as I began to relax, I asked him about his day, and he started telling me. I dozed off, comforted by the sound of his voice and exhausted from tension.

When I woke up a couple of hours later, I was stretched out on the couch, my head on Scott's leg. Across from me, I saw Laura sleeping as well. When I looked up, I saw Scott staring intently at his phone. I recognized the look in his eye.

"What's up?" I whispered as I rose.

He kissed the side of my head. "Work stuff."

"Like what?"

He knew I'd persist until he told me. "Somebody blew up that building intentionally. ATF is getting involved because of the social security office and the post office. " He kissed me. "Go back to sleep. I'll go check on Nate."

Sometime later, male voices awakened me. I opened my eyes and saw two men in long-sleeved shirts and cargo pants standing in front of Laura. I sat up. ATF? Already?

"Mrs. Tanner, why was your husband in that building?" I heard one ask.

"I don't know."

"He didn't tell you?"

"No. I was out of town."

"You don't know of any reason why he would be there?"

"No."

"Where were you?"

"In Monterey at my mother's."

"Did your husband have a claim with social security?"

"No."

"Was he scheduled for oral surgery? A doctor's visit?"

"No. Our doctors aren't in White Spring."

"He was a veteran, right?"

"Yes. Iraq and Afghanistan."

"He came back wounded?"

"Yes."

"Was he bitter about that?"

"At first."

"And did he have episodes, like PTSD?"

She answered him honestly. "Occasionally he had nightmares. Still does."

"And he knows about explosives."

The fog in my brain cleared in a snap. They weren't looking at Nate as a victim. He was a suspect!

I shot a quick text to Scott, then I stood and walked casually across the room, inserting myself between the two men. Somebody had to shift the balance of power. "I'm Jessica Cooper, a close friend," I said, answering their unasked question.

One of the men nodded, then went back to his notes. "Was your husband a member of any groups?"

"A Bible study."

I flinched. Recently some right-wing extremists had called their group a "Bible study" as a cover for their anti-government activity.

"Was he frustrated with the government? Politics?"

"Not especially," she answered.

I could see from the look on her face she hadn't yet caught on to the trajectory of their questions.

"Would you mind if we take a look around your property?"

I'd seen the mess law enforcement could make of a house while searching it. Furthermore, I knew Nate had guns, ammunition, and maybe other things ATF might see as suspicious around the house and barn. "Do you have a search warrant?" I said.

"Well, no, but ..."

The older agent seemed to want to back off that topic quickly. "Had your husband purchased explosive materials lately? Practiced with them around your property?"

Laura looked stunned. "Are you saying ...? Nate would never bomb a building. Never!" She set her jaw.

Just then Scott walked in with three cups of coffee and a bag of food in his hands. Our eyes met. He put all that stuff down and approached the men. "Scott Cooper, FBI," he said, extending his hand.

I knew enough about inter-agency rivalry to know they weren't going to instantly back down just because Scott was with the Bureau. Still, they shook hands and turned toward him, which left Laura and I out of the loop. They told Scott what they were investigating, and he told them Nate wasn't the perpetrator.

"We have to check every lead," I heard one of them say. "His fingerprints were on the fire alarm."

"So he saw it was about to blow and pulled the alarm. That was smart," Scott said. "Look, I appreciate what you're doing but you're on the wrong track. Nate's not your guy."

The two agents looked at each other, then one turned his eyes on Laura.

The older one pulled out a business card and handed it to Laura. "Call us when he's awake. We'll need to interview him."

As they walked out of the room, I looked at Scott, so angry I thought my head would explode. How dare they suspect Nate. And ignore Scott! Those jerks. I started after them.

"Jess!" Scott said. "Don't even think about it."

I stopped moving, my heart pounding.

He squatted down in front of Laura, who was crying. "Don't worry about them," he said, holding both of her hands. "They're just doing their job. There's no way anything's going to stick to Nate."

I paced over to the big window wall in the ICU waiting room. It overlooked the main lobby. I stood there watching those two ATF agents leave the hospital, my anger still running hot. Behind me, I heard Laura ask, "What should I do if they come back and you're not here?"

I turned around. "Admit nothing. Question everything. Ask for proof," I snapped.

Scott shot me a look, blocking me from going further. "Tell them you're not comfortable answering their questions without a lawyer present," he said more helpfully. "Then call me. Do you have a lawyer? You or Nate?"

She shook her head. "Not really. Just the one who drew up our wills."

"Call me. I'll find you a lawyer." He touched her shoulder. "Don't worry about this. They don't have anything on Nate. They're just fishing."

I turned back to the window, my heart drumming, my question nagging me like an unanswered prayer. Why was Nate at that building?

4

WE CONSIDERED it a near miracle Nate hadn't been crushed to death. "He must have been in a void," the doctor said, by which he meant the beams, framing, and rubble had fallen just right, leaving Nate in a space that allowed him to breathe.

But while Nate avoided serious injuries, he did not avoid being hurt. He had corneal abrasions from dust and couldn't open his eyes for four days. When he finally could see, we discovered he couldn't hear. The explosion had deafened him, rupturing both eardrums. We had to write notes to him on a whiteboard. That's when we found out he couldn't remember anything. Not one thing. That whole day was a blank for him. He didn't remember leaving the house or driving to the building, and he had no idea why he was there. He asked about Sprite. He was relieved to find out he had left her at home.

The force of the explosion had caused a concussive brain injury, doctors told us. Maybe his memory would come back and maybe it wouldn't. Meanwhile, they said, try to keep him from getting agitated. Give his brain a rest and time to heal.

Then Nate developed pneumonitis, an inflammation of his lungs caused by the dust he'd inhaled. He'd wheeze. Any exertion caused him to gasp for air, to go into what looked to me like an asthma attack. The docs gave him steroids, but it was still bad. Scary at times.

Despite his trouble breathing, the doctors wanted Nate up and moving to keep him from developing pneumonia. It was a good thing I'd brought that spare leg.

SCOTT HAD to go back to work, so he wasn't there when the two ATF agents showed up again. Fortunately, Laura spotted them coming down the hall and refused to let them in the room.

"He's not supposed to be agitated," she told them, "and I'm sure you'd do just that." A passing nurse backed her up, and the investigators retreated.

I was proud of her.

About a week into it, I could tell Laura was exhausted. So I volunteered to spend the night with Nate. By then, he was out of ICU, and I guess she felt comfortable leaving him, so she accepted.

That evening, I stood in Nate's room at the window watching the evening skies grow dark and the streetlights pop on, thinking and, yes, praying.

"Jess ..."

I turned around and took his hand.

Nate continued in a raspy, hesitant voice:

"in your book were written, every one of them,
the days that were formed for me,
when as yet there was none of them."

He squeezed my hand.

My eyes widened. "You're quoting Scripture? Now? You're comforting *me*?"

He couldn't hear me, but he smiled softly. He motioned for

me to sit in the chair next to the bed, and he pushed himself up. Gesturing, I asked if he wanted to sit up straighter. He nodded yes, so I raised the head of his hospital bed and then sat down again. It turns out he wanted to talk and for that, he needed breath.

"I didn't want to upset Laura none," he said. "You and me, we can keep this between us, okay?" I nodded and then he began to tell me what it was like to be buried in that rubble pile. "I weren't unconscious all the time, but I couldn't see, couldn't hear, didn't know if I was dead or alive. Like floating in the dark." He reached for my hand, laboring over every sentence. "I figured if I were dead, I'd be seeing something—Jesus, or angels, or something. Nothin' hurt, but it was weird, bein' like that. I kept waiting for fire, pain, noise. There weren't nothin'." He shook his head. "So I started praying, praying for Laura, for you, for Scott, for the folks working that pile. Praying for myself. I weren't ready, Jess. I didn't want to die. I got Laura to take care of. Sprite. So I prayed."

He shifted his position, pausing to catch his breath. I was keeping one eye on the monitor above his head, watching his blood pressure and his heart rate and listening to his breathing. *So far, so good,* I thought, so I let him keep talking.

"I felt him draw close ..."

By "him," I knew he meant God.

"... felt that peace. You know what I mean."

Again I nodded.

"It went on for awhile, like a warm cloud hovering around me and through me, and then, then I saw somethin', Jess. It scared me."

My heart thumped. I cocked my head to indicate I was listening.

"You kin understand me, right? 'Cause it's weird not hearing myself."

I nodded and squeezed his hand.

"It was like I was watching from up high, like I was in a helicopter. I saw myself down below and up ahead, standing in a field, watching the sunset. It was beautiful, all gold and red and orange and white and yellow. And I was standing there just drinking it in, glory all around me. But behind my back, something dark was building, rolling toward me like a storm, a huge black cloud all swirling and billowing like a giant wave moving across the plains, picking up dirt and growing stronger.

"I willed my other self to turn around, to see it, so I could run or drop to the ground. So I could save myself. But my other self didn't turn. It kept looking straight ahead, watching the sunset, payin' no mind to what was coming at me." He paused for what seemed like five minutes.

"What happened?" I couldn't wait any longer.

He knew what I'd said, even without hearing my words. "I couldn't watch. I knew something terrible was about to happen. I squeezed my eyes shut. Braced myself. And when I opened them again, it was gone. I was back to just ... nothin'. Blackness."

A deep chill went through me. I shivered.

Nate gazed off to the side, frowning, then looked back at me. "I got no idea what that was."

"What did you do then? How'd you calm down?" I gestured.

"I prayed. Psalm 23. 'The Lord is my Shepherd, I shall not want.' I said it over and over."

I PONDERED what Nate had told me after he drifted off to sleep. But after that, neither one of us mentioned Nate's hallucination or vision. It was something we just tucked away, like a random thought or a bad dream.

After a few days, the doctors released him to go home. At that point, they said, he just needed time, time for his hearing to come back, for his lungs to clear, for his brain to heal. Time so the deep vaults of his mind could begin to release the memory of that day.

But what would happen when he remembered?

. . .

I HELPED Laura get Nate home. Luke went crazy when we rolled him into the house. He turned in circles, whacking Nate with his tail, a silly grin on his face. He kept glancing at me, like, "See, see, I told you he was there!" There is something so goofy about an eighty-pound German shepherd lying on his back, his tongue lolling out, begging for a belly rub from his second favorite person in the world.

Of course, Nate obliged, bending over until he nearly fell out of the wheelchair. Then Sprite had to get in on the act. We about had to make the dogs go lie down to get Nate to stop petting them and catch his breath.

One of the first things Nate did when he got home was ask me to hand him his guitar, which hung on the wall in the great room. He could tell by the way the strings felt it wasn't in tune, so he fiddled with the pegs until the tension seemed right. Then he played his music, fingering soft and gentle tunes, his hands coaxing that instrument to play what he could not hear. I sat and listened while the deaf man filled the house with music from his heart.

THE DOCTORS HAD SAID within two to three weeks, Nate should see improvement in his hearing and his lungs. When that time came his memory was still a blank, leaving the rest of us still wondering why he'd been at that building.

A clue came from the oddest place. A newsletter from the community college lay buried in the pile of mail that had accumulated on one end of the kitchen countertop at Nate's. In it was a memorial column about the widow of a former college president who died suddenly in a building collapse. She was the only victim, the article said. Amanda showed it to me, then to Laura, and the three of us discussed it.

"I mean, like, how many building collapses have there been in the last three weeks?" Amanda said. "I think we should ask him if he was with her."

"But what if it upsets him?" Laura asked. "Do we risk it? I hate it when he can't breathe!"

I bit my lip as I thought. "What if I investigate a little further? I mean, let me look into why she was there. Nate could have met her at some point if he knew Henry Thorpe." Thorpe was the late president of the school. "It'd be just like Nate to help her out. Maybe she had a dental appointment or an insurance problem."

We agreed that I'd check out the connection before mentioning it to Nate. I was, after all, a private investigator. I'd recently renewed my license and had started taking cases. Why not Nate's?

5

I STAYED a couple of nights at Nate's to make sure Laura and Amanda could handle things on their own. Then Luke and I drove home to our townhouse. I couldn't wait to get back. I missed my husband.

That fact alone amazed me. I'd been single, emotionally detached even from my family, for so long. First Nate had begun to breach the self-protective fortress I'd built around me. He taught me search and rescue and offered me a steady, safe friendship centered around our mutual love of dogs. He helped me find God by living his faith in front of me.

As the walls around my heart began to crumble, I included Scott in my small circle of friends. Eventually, I fell in love with him. No one was more surprised about that than me. (Well, maybe my mother.)

Scott and I married in the hospital about a year ago after he almost died. Some friends gave us a great wedding gift—the whole month of September in the house they own on Chincoteague Island, off the coast of Virginia. At first Scott was reluctant to leave his daughter, Amanda. After all, she'd been abducted and nearly lost to traffickers. He'd nearly lost his life saving her. Of course, he was still protective.

But Amanda had bonded well with Nate and Laura, and after setting some boundaries to keep her safe, we all were able to convince him to leave.

Chincoteague had everything we needed—privacy, the beach, a small town to enjoy, good physical therapists not too far away, and access to horses at the nearby Hope Ranch. That was for Scott. He's a horse person.

We loved our month there. We focused on Scott's rehab, finding a comfortable rhythm to married life, and learning to fight. Fight? Yes—duh! We're human! He's pretty OCD and I'm, well, independent. He calls it "hardheaded." So we had to learn to fight. We're still learning.

We spent long, lazy hours on the beach, we swam in a neighbor's pool, and I ran with Luke on the sidewalks and trails and kept up his SAR skills. Scott did physical therapy and started rebuilding his strength. We volunteered at Hope Ranch several times a week, helping with their equine therapy program. We spent our evenings cooking, watching sunsets, and reading, sometimes out loud to each other. Who knew how romantic that could be?

Over time, the salt air and the rhythms of the sea washed away the tension that had us in its iron grip for far too long, making room for love and peace and joy to flow in. By the time we drove over the causeway and back to real life, we were as relaxed as we'd ever been. We vowed to remember that feeling, to purposely cultivate moments in our married life that brought us back to that peace, despite our stressful jobs and individual quirks. Until now, we'd been pretty successful.

THE TOWNHOUSE where Scott and I lived was neat as a pin when I got home, of course, since Scott was so OCD. I couldn't wait to mess it up ... the kitchen at least. I'd stopped at a store on the way home and bought steaks, a good wine, sweet potatoes, and a salad. I skipped dessert—we usually did except for special occasions. By the time Scott walked in the door, the house smelled wonderful.

I heard him whistling as he opened the door from the garage. He came up the stairs quickly. My heart beat fast. Our eyes met. "Jess," he said, and took me in his arms. He kissed me, and said, "I missed you."

"I missed you too," I murmured.

Over dinner, we caught up. I told him about Nate's progress and finding out about Helen Thorpe, and he told me about work. He was excited because a friend of his recently transferred to the Washington Field Office and had stopped by to see Scott in Quantico.

"Name's Mike Perez," Scott said. "We went through the academy together. Haven't seen him in years."

"So you had a lot to catch up on."

"Which is why," Scott said between bites, "I want him to meet you. Last he heard I was wallowing my way through a divorce."

"Is he married?"

Scott shook his head. "No. The nicest guy though. Really. Funny and smart. Can we have him over? Or take him to dinner?"

"Sure! He's working here now?"

"Yes. Living in an apartment in Fairfax."

"Where'd he transfer in from?"

"Austin. Hopes to get his ticket punched at headquarters eventually."

Our conversation evolved as we talked about politics, crime, and his daughter, Amanda. She was trying to decide which four-year school to transfer to. Scott had definite opinions about that, which I gently suggested he temper a little when he talked with her.

Happy, we took a long walk and went to bed, secure in each

other's arms, grateful for the life we'd found, blissfully unaware just how short-lived our peace would be.

THE NEXT DAY, I dropped Luke off at Nate's house and drove down to the community college where Nate works so I could follow up on the lead Amanda had uncovered in the newsletter.

I showed up, identified myself as a private investigator, and asked to speak to the president. Of course, they handed me off to an assistant. But when I explained what I wanted, she excused herself, saying, "I'll be right back."

Moments later, President Lashawn Morgan greeted me and invited me into his office. Over six feet tall, he had the stride and the build of an athlete, and sure enough, his office wall was covered with his football pictures.

"Clemson?" I said, nodding toward the wall.

"Four years in Death Valley," he said, grinning broadly. "Now what can I do for you?"

"I'm trying to find out why Nathan Tanner was in the building that exploded in White Spring," I said. "I know he works here. I need more information."

Morgan leaned forward. He picked up some three-by-five cards on his desk and straightened the stack, turning them on their edges. I could tell he was calculating his move. Finally, he looked at me. "You with a law enforcement agency?"

I frowned. "No. I'm a PI. My client is Laura Tanner, Nate's wife."

Morgan sagged back in his chair, his body telegraphing his relief. "I got a call from the feds. I don't know what they're thinking, but they got the wrong idea about Mr. Nate."

"I know that!" I pressed further. "Can you tell me? Had he taken leave that day?"

"That would be in his personnel records, which are private.

But I'll say this: If he were playing football, I wouldn't have thrown a flag."

Which meant he was not AWOL. "Did he know Helen Thorpe?"

He pressed his lips together. "I got no idea. But he was working here when Henry was president ..."

Which meant Nate could have known Henry's wife.

"... and it'd be just like him to help her."

I asked a few more questions, but it was soon clear Dr. Morgan didn't know any more than he'd told me. I thanked him, and he walked me to the door of his office. With his hand on the doorknob, he paused.

"I got kids asking me every day how Mr. Nate is, when he's coming back, can they go see him. Some folks think this," he gestured toward his office, "is the most influential job on campus, the chance to shape lives. But I got nothin' on Mr. Nate. No sir. He's the real big deal around here."

I WALKED out to the parking lot, lost in thought. I had just pressed the unlock button on my key fob when I heard my name being called. I turned. "Amanda!"

Scott's daughter jogged in my direction. She had on denim shorts and a pretty bandanna print top. Her black backpack hung on her left shoulder. She could have been a model for a back-to-school ad campaign. "What'd you find out?" Amanda was my secret backup plan.

"I went to the secretary who works in Nate's shop. I said I had this book he loaned me, and I needed to return it."

I smiled. Very smart.

"She told me that Nate had been hurt, helping out a friend, and she didn't know when he'd be back. I asked some more questions and guess what? It was Helen Thorpe he was helping!"

"Good for you!"

"She was having a problem with social security, and he said he'd take her to the office. She was old, you know, like eighty-something."

"Amanda, that's awesome!"

"Nate talked to the secretary the day before. Told her he'd be in late and told her why."

"Good work!"

She smiled. "People love to gossip."

"Hey, do me a favor," I said as she turned to leave. "Don't tell Nate about this yet. I want to see how he reacts."

"Okay!" She began to jog off. That's when I saw a guy standing about twenty feet away. He was tall and dark-haired. Looked a lot like her dad. I realized he was waiting for Amanda. She turned back to me. "And you don't need to tell my dad about this, okay? I don't want to see how he reacts!"

I smiled and waved. *A boyfriend? Amanda?* Scott would have a fit.

So Nate was at the building helping Helen Thorpe resolve a problem with her social security. I was mulling over that when Scott called. "Hey," he said, "guess what?"

"What?"

"ATF thinks that bombing may be linked to a couple of others up west of Winchester."

"Really! I don't remember buildings collapsing up there."

"Smaller bombs. Mailboxes."

"Why does ATF think they're linked?"

"Materials. I don't know more than that."

"If we can prove Nate wasn't anywhere near Winchester around those dates, he's clear."

"Unless they try to link him to a group."

"What group?"

"A far-right extremist group would be the most likely possibility. That explosion happened on April 19."

"April 19?"

"The anniversary of the raid on the Covenant, Sword, and Arm of the Lord militia compound in the Ozarks. Then there's Waco and Oklahoma City. A big day for the far right, anti-government groups." He changed the subject. "Hey, can we have Mike over for dinner tonight?"

I checked the time. "Yeah, if he won't mind something quick."

"Steak is quick."

We'd just had steak. "Maybe salmon," I suggested.

"Or steak." Scott laughed. "Really, whatever we can put together."

"I'll come up with something. I'm headed for Nate's now. I'll aim for dinner at seven."

"You're the best."

"I know. You're so lucky."

Of course, I was kidding him. I was the lucky one. Scott—broken down, rebuilt Scott—was the best husband. The trauma from last year had forged new depths in him and had both softened him and strengthened him.

When I pulled up to Nate's house, I could hear Luke barking. "Hey, buddy," I said, opening the door.

"Jess! Nate heard him bark. It's the first thing he's heard in three weeks," Laura said. Joy and hope filled her eyes.

"That's awesome!"

I greeted my dog, then walked in to see Nate. He gave me a thumbs-up. "I heard it," he said. "I heard that dog bark."

I hugged him. "Can you hear me?" I gestured that thought. Nate shook his head. "It's okay. It'll come."

"You can text him," Laura said. "I bought him a smart watch so he could read texts even without his phone."

"That was a good idea."

Just then, my phone went off. So did Nate's. We exchanged

looks. A callout! The volunteer search-and-rescue group we both belonged to, Battlefield SAR, was being activated.

I checked the text. A jogger was missing from a resort about forty minutes away.

Nate gestured. "Go."

I could tell he wanted to go himself. He wasn't well enough. I covered his hand with mine. "Someday soon, Nate, you'll be back in the game."

I caught Laura's eye. She followed me out to the car, where I grabbed my go-bag. I told her what Amanda had found out about Nate. "So apparently, he'd offered to help her with a social security problem."

"Well, that's a relief," she responded.

I also told her about the mailbox bombs west of Winchester.

"So ATF should lose interest in Nate," she said.

"You'd think." I didn't put anything past them. "Look, I'm going to respond to this call out. I'll be in touch."

She glanced back to the house. "He hates not being able to go."

I touched her arm. "He'll be back. I know he will. He's got plenty of life left." I heard a car coming up the driveway. "Who's this?"

"That's a seven-year-old named Harper. A friend's foster child. I'm introducing her to horses."

"Since when?"

"Since today. She's having some adjustment problems. She's not speaking. I thought horses might help." Laura smiled.

"Scott would agree with you on that." I gave Laura a quick hug, picked up my bag, and went inside to change. Luke picked up on my excitement. When I emerged in my SAR clothes, he began turning in circles and barking. From the living room, Nate gave me a thumbs-up. "Be safe!" he said.

6

I HAD CALLED TOM, the incident commander, to tell him I'd respond to the call out. He said he'd heard from Carol, a deputy I'd met on a previous search. She was off that day and wanted to respond as a walker. Awesome, I told him, and then I called Carol to see if I could give her a ride. Soon we were making our way up into the mountains. It was great to have company on the drive—like the old days with me and Nate.

The resort was actually a campground built around a lake up in the mountains. It catered to RVers, so it had paved roads, electricity at each site, and a lodge with a snack bar, a game room, and a large lounge overlooking the pool.

"Not exactly what I would call roughing it," I said to Carol. She agreed.

The missing man, Paul Hodge, fifty-three, was an experienced trail runner, Tom had told us when I called him on the way up. He'd gone for a run at seven thirty that morning. His wife expected him back around nine. When Carol and I arrived at three, he was still missing. Deputies had searched the trails on ATVs. The thinking now was that Hodge had gone off a trail or fallen. Perhaps he was hurt and couldn't respond to the whistles and calls of searchers.

My friend Emily and her border collie Flash had responded to the call out, along with a new member, Alex, with his black-and-tan shepherd, and a couple of trainees who needed the field time. So there would be three dog-handler-walker teams, and Tom would coordinate from base.

He handed us topographic maps of the area showing each of the five trails. The shortest trail, just one mile, went around the lake. Emily would cover that plus the other easy trail. Alex and I took the more difficult runs. We'd see who would take the final trail when we'd finished our first assignments.

Mine was the longest assignment: a seven-mile loop that ended in a two-mile uphill climb. The day was hot for early May —about 80 with 80 percent humidity. I packed extra water for both me and Luke, and I warned Tom I wasn't going to push because of the heat. I'd seen people and dogs get heat exhaustion, and I had resolved not to let it happen to Luke.

"You ready?" I asked Carol.

"Ready." She had dressed wisely in strong hiking boots, tough cargo pants, a hat, and a long-sleeved shirt. She carried extra water in her pack. Both of us had sprayed insect repellent on our clothes when we got out of my Jeep.

I puffed a little baby powder. There was virtually no wind. "Mark our starting point," I said to Carol, who manned the GPS.

"Got it."

I paused, said a quick prayer, then leaned down and unclipped Luke's leash. "Seek! Seek, Luke!"

He took off, happy at least to be doing what he loved. He ranged back and forth across the trail, pausing now and then to sniff a particularly interesting place, then pressing on. I watched with admiration.

Some dogs are born to be companions, others are guardians,

guides, or hunters' helpers. Luke was born to work, to be useful, to rescue. First he rescued me when I was lost in a pit of despair. Now he worked to rescue those who were physically lost, and he let me come with him. The joy with which he fulfilled his purpose was infectious.

Naismith's Rule (William Naismith was a Scottish mountaineer) once said to allow twenty minutes per mile of hiking on a good trail, plus an extra hour for each two thousand feet of elevation you climb. In other words, going uphill takes longer, a fact that everyone but Luke understood. Using this calculation, our seven-mile trail alone should take two hours and twenty minutes. Adding in the ascent, I estimated it would take between three and four hours. Add in another half hour at least for heat and humidity.

The trees at this altitude, about three thousand feet, were relatively short—maybe sixty feet tall. Blooming mountain laurel provided a white, lacy underlayment to the forest. The trees—mostly oaks and poplars—were completely leafed out and formed a cool canopy over the ten-foot-wide trail. The trail, maintained by the campground, was constructed of dirt with a thin layer of gravel.

I'd run on trails like this before. The loose gravel could be dangerous. What's more, I wondered if Hodge would really choose a trail that began with a downhill and finish with a steep climb. He was fifty-three after all. But then, his wife said he was a marathoner.

"How's Scott?"

Carol's voice jarred me out of my own thoughts.

"Scott? Oh my gosh, Scott!" I suddenly realized I hadn't told him I had a call out. "We were supposed to have someone over for dinner tonight!" I jerked my phone off my belt while crafting apologies in my head. Of course, there was no signal.

"Oh, boy!" Carol said, laughing.

I sent a text and hoped it would go through. Meanwhile, Luke ranged up ahead, his black and gold coat glistening in the dappled sunlight. We reached the bottom of our trail, and I called a water break. Luke didn't want to stop, but I made him. We sat in the shade near a rocky outcropping, looking out over a valley. A hawk soared in the cloudless sky, catching thermals as it watched for prey. Behind us, a mockingbird chattered, annoyed we had invaded the neighborhood. I heard a pileated woodpecker nearby banging apart some dead tree in search of bugs.

All these things—my dog, the hawk, the mockingbird, the woodpecker, the forest, the mountain, the valley—testified to me the creativity and glory of the Creator. I inhaled the beauty of it like a tonic, and I wondered how I could have missed it for so many years.

Carol drew back my attention, asking me how long it took to train Luke. While we sat and talked, I studied the trail. I saw a place nearby where it slanted toward the drop-off. Could Hodge have stumbled there? Lost his balance? Curiosity overcame me. I snapped on Luke's leash, handed the end to Carol, and told my dog to stay. "I'll be right back."

I walked over near the edge, dropped onto my belly, and peered over the hundred-foot drop. Below me, I saw a few scrub trees, fallen rock, and some bushes, but no body, living or dead. I felt a slight updraft on my face. I wondered, could Luke smell Hodge if he'd fallen down there?

If he was dead, yes, I decided. If alive, I wasn't sure.

"Hello!" I yelled, hoping for a response, but there was none. I pushed myself to my feet, dusted off my clothes, and returned to Luke and Carol. "I'm going to walk him near the edge," I said. "Hang tight."

I walked Luke over toward the cliff, then made him lie down. I got on my belly next to him, and together we army-crawled to the drop-off. He thought it was a fun game. When I got to the edge, I kept a good grip on his leash. "What's down there, buddy?" I asked. "Anything?" His nose worked hard, but I could tell from his demeanor no interesting scents were wafting up on the breeze.

So we returned to Carol. "Nothing. Let's press on."

We marked that spot and set out again. Soon we were on the uphill climb. Four-wheel-drive Luke could go faster than Carol and me, even though we were both pretty fit. He kept returning and looking at us impatiently, then taking off again.

We were about half a mile from the campground. Luke ranged up ahead, and I had my eyes peeled, looking for signs of our missing runner—broken bushes, footprints, a dropped item. Suddenly, I heard a noise, then growling. I looked up to see Luke and what I thought was another dog fighting! They were on the ground, rolling, dust flying everywhere, snarling, teeth snapping.

"Luke!" I screamed, running toward him. "Luke. Hey, Luke!"

The two separated and the other dog raced off down the hill to the right. Luke stood up, shook off, and came running back to me.

I clipped his leash on. "Are you hurt, buddy?" Heart pounding, I went over him with my hands.

"Is he okay?" Carol said.

"I think so." I inspected him again. "Wow, I've never had that happen. Where'd that dog come from?"

"I don't think it was a dog," Carol said. I stared at her. "I think it was a coyote. Maybe a coy-wolf. He came trotting out of the woods," she gestured toward the left side of the trail, "and ran into Luke. Honestly, I think they were both surprised."

A coyote? Wow! "What'd he look like?"

"Gray and brown. Rangy. Tall, but thinner than Luke. They tangled for just a minute. Maybe you should rinse his mouth out just in case he got a piece of that guy."

"Great idea." I took Luke's water bottle and gave him a good rinse. I didn't see any blood or fur in his mouth, a good sign.

"Do you think you'd better keep him on leash just in case?"

I thought about that for a minute then made a decision. "He

can't really search on leash. He isn't prone to fighting, and he came when I called. I think we'll just shake it off and go on and trust Mr. Coyote won't return."

"Luke had a good thirty pounds on him. That should discourage him."

I checked Luke one more time, running my hands through his coat, inspecting his feet and his head, and then I had him heel, just like at the start of a search. I unclipped his leash, gestured forward, and said, "Seek, Luke. Seek!"

I have to admit I was nervous as he went forward, then swung right, sniffing. But almost immediately, he swung left again, then proceeded as if nothing had happened. Twenty-five minutes later, we emerged back at the campground. We walked over to Tom. I shook my head. "Nothing. No sign of Mr. Hodge."

He nodded. "Take a break. The campground said we can cool off in the lodge."

"They probably have Wi-fi," Carol suggested.

She was thinking about Scott, which was a good thing, because I wasn't.

I went by my Jeep, got Luke some water, and then walked over to the lodge. The sun was dropping in the sky and the daylight was mellowing. I suddenly wished I were home, spending the evening with my husband, instead of here, on a mountain, after an unsuccessful search and a brush with a coyote.

They did have Wi-Fi at the lodge and a good cell signal. As I accessed the Wi-Fi, I got a text Scott had sent hours before: *Need to cancel tonight. Something's come up.*

So I guess it didn't matter that I was on a search. We'd have to reschedule dinner with his friend anyway.

Standing at a wall of glass overlooking the pool, I called my husband. Below me, kids were playing a version of water volleyball. They were elementary school age, boys and girls, and I suddenly felt a familiar pang.

Scott was so broken, physically, at the beginning of our

marriage that we focused on his rehab. We didn't even talk about whether to have kids. Maybe he thought I was on the pill. I wasn't. I don't know what I was thinking. I was just letting things happen, but nothing had. And now every once in awhile, I felt an emptiness I hadn't anticipated.

My call finally went through, breaking my train of thought. "I'm so sorry! I forgot to tell you I had a callout," I said to Scott.

"I just got five text messages from you!" he responded. "When I couldn't reach you, I called Laura, and she told me about it. Did you find the guy?"

"No, not yet. Sorry we'll have to reschedule with your friend."

"Well, we both got caught up in other stuff. Remember I told you about the link to those previous bombings?"

"Yes."

"They're forming a task force and want me on it."

My mind began racing. "Do they know you're friends with Nate?"

"Nate's not a valid suspect."

"By the way, guess what we found out?" I told him about the connection with Helen Thorpe, the deceased victim. "Apparently, he was helping her with a social security problem."

"That explains a lot. What'd Nate say?"

"Haven't told him yet. I got that callout."

"Oh, right. You coming home tonight?" Scott asked.

"I'm not sure what the plan is. We're cooling off in the lodge." I looked down at Luke, who lay sprawled on the clean tile floor. "I'll call you when I know."

"Okay, Mike's coming over later, but he's not expecting dinner."

As I CLICKED off the phone, I saw Tom approaching. Carol, who'd been sitting nearby, came over to hear the news.

"Sheriff wants to call it off for tonight. He says these mountains are too dangerous to search after dark. It's only going down to sixty-eight degrees, no rain, so Hodge's survivability isn't an issue."

"So are we spending the night here at the campground?"

Tom shook his head. "We have fresh legs coming in the morning. You all go home."

I HATED walking away empty-handed after a search. But on our way down the mountain, Carol and I cheered ourselves up talking about dogs. She was ready to go all in on volunteer SAR now that her kids were virtually grown.

I encouraged her. "When it comes to picking a dog, you want one with high play/prey drive," I said. "Some people go to shelters and find what they're looking for, a well-balanced dog who loves to play. Others go to breeders looking for the same thing. Smart but energetic."

"Where'd you get Luke?" she asked me.

I edited that long story. "He was a tactical police dog that wouldn't bite," I said. "Another officer began training him for SAR. He died, and I inherited Luke."

I told her about my early days with Luke, about discovering he was cross-trained, and about the time I took my SAR pack and left Luke behind, and he was unhappy. "He ate the rug, the doorframe, scratched up the door ... it was a mess!" I laughed. "It's funny now, but I was upset then."

"My husband is looking forward to having a Lab."

"Choose wisely."

She hesitated for a minute. "How do you make sure your dog doesn't run off? I mean, when you're working off leash, there's a lot of time when Luke is out of sight. How'd you train him to always come back?"

"Consistency."

"I'd be so scared of losing my dog."

"It's about developing your relationship with the dog. I mean, once when I first had him, he was chasing a ball and didn't come back when I called. He ran out of sight. Crossed a railroad track just as a train was coming by. Scared me to death! But when the train went past, there he was sitting on the other side, grinning at me. I worked with him on recall after that, and our relationship has grown. I'm confident he'll always listen to me now."

"A lot of dogs would have chased that coyote."

"You have to build that bond."

Looking back, I was so sure of myself, so in control. I failed to factor in the possibility of calamity.

We kept talking dogs as I drove down the mountain. The dark night enveloped us, yielding only to the intrusion of my headlights. The road twisted and turned and reminded me of another road I was on when guilt and shame overwhelmed me and beckoned me into the black abyss of despair. I would have driven into a tree to end my pain had I not had my dog with me. Luke saved my life that day.

I dropped Carol off and continued home, alone with my thoughts. I imagined Paul Hodge lost, possibly injured, spending the night on the mountain by himself. I thought about my Fairfax PD partner's widow and son left alone after he died on duty. I thought about Nate, poor Nate, trying to help someone and now trying to recover from one more trauma. I thought about Dad, dying on 9/11.

So much sorrow, so much pain. Sometimes, the amount of suffering in this world overwhelms me.

It was after eleven by the time I pulled up to our townhouse. I was disappointed to see a strange car in the visitor's spot. I really did not feel like socializing. Tired, dirty, and sad, I parked, let Luke out, grabbed my pack, and trudged up the walk, bracing myself for cheery voices and happy talk inside.

That's not what happened.

Scott met me on the porch. He wrapped his arms around

dirty old me and gave me a kiss. The darkness, some of it, slunk away. "I'm glad you're home," he said. I relaxed into his arms. "What can I do for you?" He kissed my ear.

"Your friend?" I needed to know what I was facing.

"He left half an hour ago. It's just you and me."

I glanced toward the strange car. "Who's that?"

"Must be visiting a neighbor."

And I was glad.

7

Scott looked around the walnut table in the conference room at the FBI office. Eleven experts from the FBI, the Bureau of Alcohol, Tobacco, Firearms, and Explosives, state police from two states, fire chiefs, and local police occupied the black leather chairs. A twelfth was on the way.

At the last minute, Scott's friend Mike Perez slid into the seat next to him. "Hey, man!" Scott said. They did a slap-grab handshake. "Why're you here?"

Mike grinned. "All I know is they said to keep an eye on you."

Scott rolled his eyes. As Supervisory Special Agent Malcolm Caldwell called the group to order, Mike leaned over and whispered, "I worked the Austin bomber."

Scott nodded. A couple of years prior, someone had planted bombs around that Texas city. Scott couldn't remember the details, but he knew people had been killed, and for awhile the hunt for the serial bomber had been intense.

"... three bombs," Caldwell was saying as Scott tuned in. "The first, here." Caldwell pointed to a place in West Virginia, near Winchester, where a small bomb had damaged a homeowner's mailbox. “The second one here.” He pointed to a suburb twenty miles away where another mailbox had been destroyed. “And the last one here.” The bomb that had leveled the building where Nate was had detonated about twenty miles from that last location.

“You can see for yourself the escalation. The components that caught our attention are these burner phones used as detonators and this type of wire.” Caldwell held up a piece of it.

“That stuff’s pretty common, isn’t it?” a guy up front said.

“Yes. The burner phones are sold at Walmart. They move thousands of them a year, but they also keep good records. As for the wire, the bombs were wired together exactly the same way, same technique, same number of twists. In this last case, we had one person dead, one badly injured, and a few others treated for shock and hearing loss.” Caldwell looked around the room. “The first two, no one got hurt, but again, the technique suggests it’s the same bomber.”

Someone Scott couldn’t quite see raised her hand. “What about the office building? What do we know?”

A guy with a two-hundred-dollar haircut sitting next to where Caldwell was standing raised his hand. Scott recognized him—James Hitchens from ATF. He’d been assigned to BAU for a while as a liaison. He worked in a different group than Scott, but he’d seen him around.

“Hitch?” Caldwell said, calling on him. “Introduce yourself first.”

“I’m James Hitchens, ATF, currently assigned to BAU. I responded to the Deer Park bombing, arriving at 1500. There were approximately sixty people in the building. Most got out because someone—maybe even the perpetrator—pulled the fire alarm just before the blast. The deputies who responded interviewed everyone who was there except the victim pulled from the rubble. No one reported anything unusual.”

"What about the trapped victim?"

"His hearing has been impacted, and so has his memory. As of now, he has no recollection of the event, in fact, nothing of that day."

"And the deceased victim?" someone asked.

"Helen Thorpe, eighty-nine. A widow who lived about twenty miles from Deer Park. We believe she had an appointment with social security. Her late husband was the president of Rivanna Community College, which is where the surviving victim works. Is there a connection? We are pursuing that."

Heads-up, Nate, Scott thought.

Caldwell continued, outlining the framework of the Deer Park investigation. All the witnesses were to be reinterviewed, and security camera footage from a five-block radius captured and analyzed. Every hardware store within a hundred miles of the blast would be contacted and records reviewed for nail, phone, and wire purchases. Likewise, gun stores for smokeless black powder.

The background of every person who had been in the building would be reviewed. Did someone know Mrs. Thorpe had an appointment and decide to kill her? Did someone have a grudge against one of the businesses or against social security? Did anyone from a nearby office building observe anything suspicious? Were any of the tenants in financial trouble and looking for insurance?

On and on Caldwell went, listing the questions investigators needed to answer. There'd be more, too, as evidence accumulated.

"Fragments of a backpack were found, and the FBI lab is working to identify it," Caldwell said. "As well as the specific brand of nail and BBs found at the scene. The first responders did not manage the scene the way we would have. From now on, we will respond to any explosion in Virginia or West Virginia in a radius of two hundred miles." Caldwell pointed to a slide with

White Spring in the middle and a large red circle outlining the target area. "If we are called, I expect the designated team members to be on site within two hours."

Caldwell looked around the table. His eyes fell on Hitchens. "Hitch, you're ATF. How about you take charge of logistics and report directly to me."

Hitchens nodded. Scott thought he looked pleased.

Caldwell continued. "Hitch is your team leader. We'll have initial assignments in ...," he looked at his watch, "ninety minutes."

Chairs rolled back as the investigators prepared to leave. Mike looked at Scott. "Want to grab some coffee?"

Scott checked his watch. He really wanted to call Jess but waiting a few minutes wouldn't hurt. "Sure. I got time."

They walked up to the cafeteria, fixed themselves coffee, and found a quiet corner. "Are you settled in?" Scott asked.

"I'm a bachelor," Mike said. "There's not much to settle."

"No tiny china cats?"

"No foo-foo at all. Just me, my boots, pants, jackets, shirts, guns, and a fridge full of beer." Mike grinned and took a swig of coffee. "You must remember what that's like."

Scott did remember. The word that came to mind was "lonely." "Thankfully, the two women in my life, my wife and my daughter, come locked and loaded. Not a cat in sight. But there is a dog."

Mike grew serious. "So how's it working out for you, Scott? You got married, what, a year ago?"

Scott nodded. "Yeah. And it's great. Almost getting killed has a way of clarifying priorities, you know?"

"You fully recovered?"

"Pretty much. My hip hurts if I do too much."

"No nightmares? Flashbacks? That kind of thing's pretty common when you've been shot."

Scott paused, taking a long drink of coffee, calculating how much he wanted to share. He swallowed, then said. "Having Jess to talk things out with has helped a lot." Before Mike could ask anything else, he changed the subject. "So tell me about Austin."

The look on Mike's face indicated he'd recognized the evasion, but he didn't press it. "This kid in his twenties, he put bombs on people's porches. Tied one to a CHILDREN AT PLAY sign. Killed a couple of young men. One of them was a gifted musician."

Scott nodded. "What kind of bombs?"

"Package bombs, trip-wire bombs. One went off at a FedEx distribution center. and we found another at a different FedEx facility. We defused it. Five bombs total, two dead, five injured, and the whole city panicked."

"How long 'til you caught him?"

"It was quick—twenty days."

"What led to the kid's arrest?"

"Oh, we never got to arrest him. Cops pulled him over, and he blew himself up."

"Wow."

"Injured a cop in the process. But all the bombs used nails as shrapnel. We investigated a boatload of hardware and home stores—found an unusually large purchase at a Home Depot. We matched that sale to security camera footage and saw a kid with a hat and a long blond wig. When he left the store, we could see his license plate. From then on, we had him; it was just a matter of time."

"Why'd he do it?" Scott asked.

"We still don't know. He was a quiet kid, a loner, home-schooled, from a very conservative Christian family. They were shocked." Mike drained his mug. "If you ask me, you can take religious stuff too far, you know? Push kids over the edge."

Twenty thoughts sprang into Scott's head all at the same time. None came out of his mouth.

Mike pushed his chair back. “Gotta run.” He held out his hand. “Looking forward to working with you, brother.”

“Me, too,” Scott said, shaking his friend’s hand. “See you.” He took the last swig of his coffee as he stared at Mike’s retreating back. Then he walked outside, got in his car, and called Jess.

8

SCOTT HAD LEFT EARLY in the morning for a meeting. By the time I rolled out of bed, the outside temperature already read eighty degrees. Luke, lazy as I was, yawned and stretched as I stepped over him on my way to the bathroom. When I returned, I had to ask him twice if he needed to go out. Of course, he did. He just didn't want to make the effort.

Standing outside, waiting for him to empty his bladder, I checked my phone. No word from Tom about Paul Hodge. I wondered if we'd be called back to search more.

Just in case, I loaded my SAR pack with fresh clothes. I threw the ones I'd been wearing yesterday into the wash and started the machine. I fed Luke, then decided to work on my PI cases while the laundry ran.

There were only two cases—a background check for a daycare center and an inquiry from a lawyer whose client believed she was being cheated out of her inheritance by her father's second wife. I quickly dispatched the background check —the potential employee didn't even have a traffic ticket. The second case took a lot more digging. I hit a wall, then decided to take Luke on a short run through the steamy Virginia day. By the time we got back, I'd thought of another angle.

Sure enough when I pursued it, I could find no record of that second marriage. There'd been a date, a ceremony, a reception, a honeymoon, and taxes filed jointly for over a decade, but the marriage was never officially recorded that I could find.

Curious! But also crucial. Virginia doesn't recognize common-law marriage. If the guy's second marriage wasn't officially recorded, Wife #2 wasn't entitled to anything. She wasn't really a wife.

I had a contact in Virginia's Vital Records Department, a friend who did SAR with another group. I called her, and she said she'd expedite a deep search. To back up my request, I sent an email on my official PI letterhead. "Give me ten days to two weeks," she'd told me.

With that case on hold, I decided that once my laundry was done and my pack reloaded, I'd drive to Nate's. I wanted to tell him what we'd discovered about Helen Thorpe and see if that jogged his memory.

WHEN I PULLED up to Nate's house, I saw Laura out working with the horses. I waved to her and went inside. Sprite was right there, ready to greet us, and she and Luke began wrestling immediately. Nate appeared at the kitchen door, walking with a cane. He was using his spare artificial leg, but I guess he figured he needed to steady himself.

I gave him a hug. "Let's talk on the front porch," he said.

That was so the dogs could play. I knew that. I held up my finger, indicating I'd be there in one minute. I poured a couple of glasses of Nate's ever-present lemonade and took them outside, then walked back in to retrieve the small whiteboard.

"How's your hearing?" I asked, pointing to my ear.

"Comin' back slow," he said. He rubbed his hand over his

beard. "Still feel real cut off." He took a long swig of lemonade. "On the other hand, gives me lots of time to think."

Nate's house was a log cabin from a kit, which he mostly built himself. It sat on a rise overlooking his garden and pasture for the horses. The porch spanned the entire width of the house. We'd had many deep conversations there.

He reached over and took my hand. "How do you feel?" I asked him, mouthing each word.

"Breathing's better. Got measured for a new leg." He squeezed my hand. "I guess I'm okay."

"Do you remember anything yet?"

He took a deep breath. "No."

I pulled a picture of Helen Thorpe out of my pocket. "Do you know her?" I pointed to the picture, raising my eyebrows.

His eyes brightened. "That's Helen. Helen Thorpe. Widow of Henry. Used to be president at the college." He looked at me, the next question in his eyes. "Why?"

I pulled up the whiteboard and wrote, *When's the last time you saw her?*

He frowned. "Henry died two years ago. I saw her at the funeral, and I been out to the house now and then to cut grass and clean out her gutters." He looked at me. "I call her once in a while, but the last time I seen her was maybe a month ago. She's all alone, no kids. I check in on her." His blue eyes were bright. "Henry, he was good to me. Let me bring Sprite to work. Made sure I had good equipment. We went fishing now and then." He blinked. "She okay?"

I watched the dogs for a minute as I edged our conversation out onto thin ice. "Nate, she died."

"No! What happened? Was she sick?"

I didn't want to write the whole story on the whiteboard, so, silently offering up a prayer, I showed him the obituary from the newsletter and watched as he read it. I saw tears come to his eyes, then he sat back, letting the obit in his hand sag to his lap. He closed his eyes, and I knew he was praying. I put my hand on his shoulder.

He looked at me and gestured with the obit in his hand. "She was there?"

I nodded.

"With me?"

"Do you remember?"

"No." He shook his head emphatically. "No, I don't." He rubbed his hand over his face, then a new level of alarm forced his eyes to widen. "She was trapped?"

I shook my head and wrote on the whiteboard: *The ME thinks she died right away of a blow to her head.*

Small comfort, that's what that's called. But at least it was something.

Nate pulled the handkerchief out of his back pocket and wiped his eyes. "Why were we there?"

Problem with social security. You were helping her, I wrote.

"I don't remember nothin' about that day." He looked at me, checking to see if I believed him.

I nodded. "I know."

Nate leaned forward and dropped his head into his hands. I put my hand on his back and started praying out loud. That's what he would have done. After a few moments, he turned his head and looked at me.

"Thank you," he said when I finished. Had he heard me? Doubtful. Did he feel vibrations in the air? Sense the sound waves? Did he look at me by chance?

I didn't know. He was comforted, that's all.

"I'm sorry, Nate."

"Funeral's done?"

I nodded.

He pulled his empty pipe out of his pocket and stuck it in his mouth. Below us, the dogs were wrestling on the ground. Sprite's head was in Luke's mouth. It amazed me how they always knew how to have fun without hurting each other.

I touched Nate's arm. "What are you thinking?" I asked, gesturing.

"I want to go up there to that building. Will you take me?"

"Sure. Let's see if Laura wants to go."

"We'd need two cars."

He was right. My Jeep had been modified for SAR and could only carry one passenger.

I heard a noise and the front door opened. Laura joined us on the porch. "Nate wants me to take him to the building. Do you want to come?"

She frowned and moved in front of Nate, squatting down to face him. "Are you sure?" she asked, speaking slowly so he could decipher her words.

"I need to see it."

Laura glanced at me. Like Nate, she had beautiful blue eyes, clear as a mountain stream. "Do you need me?"

"Not for this," he said, and then he kissed her.

"I'll stay home," Laura said.

"Okay if I leave Luke here?" I asked.

Of course, it was fine.

FIFTEEN MINUTES LATER, I pulled my Jeep out of Nate's driveway and onto the road.

Nate sat in the passenger seat. It was weird, driving with Nate and not talking. We made a few aborted attempts at conversation, but soon Nate bowed to his frustration, pulled out his unlit pipe, and stuck it in his mouth. End of discussion.

While we were driving, I got a phone call from Tom. Paul Hodge, the jogger we'd searched for up in the mountains, was found dead. A drone spotted his body sixty feet down a mountain, off the trail Alex had searched. A rescue worker had rappelled down and confirmed his death. They were retrieving his body now.

Nate had been watching me while I took the call. "What?" he said.

I glanced over and shook my head. How could I convey the message while driving? I couldn't.

He must have understood. He reached over and patted my shoulder.

Some of our searches are fruitless, and a few end by finding the victim dead. The news that Paul Hodge had died felt heavy. Could Luke and I have found him if we'd taken that trail instead of the one we did? Would we have found him injured and been able to get him help?

Rationally, I doubted it. Luke might have caught a whiff of his scent from up on the trail, but I didn't have rappelling gear with me, so it still would have been a while for rescuers to come.

Emotionally, it was a different story. Failure is a bitter pill.

Ten minutes later, I forced myself to put that aside. I pulled into the office park. The collapsed building was cordoned off with temporary chain-link fencing. The rubble pile was still there, waiting I imagined for the insurance company.

I parked near the fence, and we got out. I showed Nate the front of the building first, pointing out where the social security office was. He asked me where they'd found him, and I pointed in the general direction. I watched him carefully for signs of stress and trouble breathing. He looked pensive leaning on his cane, his brow furrowed, his eyes squinting in the bright sun.

When we'd seen all we could see in the front, I took him around back. I anticipated a more emotional reaction at the rear of the building, especially if his Tahoe was still there.

It was. He took one look at the burned-out car and shook his head. "Me and that car been through a lot," he said. "I'm sorry to lose her." He turned away, focusing on the rubble pile. "You said the bomb was in the back?"

I showed him approximately where the source of the blast was, not far from his Tahoe.

"And Helen. Where was she found?"

I pointed out that location. That area was still smoking when we were searching. That's why Luke didn't find her.

Nate stared at the rubble, then down at the ground. "There was a red fire-alarm box," he said.

"You remember!"

He nodded.

I pointed at him, then toward my fingertip. I said, "Your fingerprints were on it." I gestured like I was pulling the alarm.

Nate's jaw shifted. "I pulled it?"

"Yes."

"Well, I'll be."

Then Nate turned to look at the still-standing buildings. "Think we can walk through one of them?"

I immediately realized what he was doing—trying to retrieve more memories. "Let's drive around," I said, "and pick one out."

"We want one that's laid out the same, not the mirror-image."

"Right." I made my way through the office park, probing my memory for what I'd seen when searching the pile, which would give me a clue about how that building had been laid out.

Nate gestured. "Let's try this one."

I stopped the Jeep, got his attention, and gestured. "Large office on the left," I said, spreading my arms wide, "smaller ones on the right. More upstairs."

He nodded, and we got out of my Jeep. "Come up with a story in case someone stops us," he said as we walked up the front sidewalk. "And take some pictures, okay?"

"Okay." I tugged open the front door. Inside stood brown and beige tile stairs leading to the second-floor offices. A decrepit-looking elevator sat beside it. Down the hall to the left I could see a door leading to a large first-floor office and, at the end of the hallway, restrooms. To the right were smaller offices. So we had the right floor plan.

I took pictures on my phone while Nate walked around. I kept thinking, *This place needs updating.* The floors were worn brown and beige linoleum tile, and hallways matched—brown on the bottom, beige above. Ugh.

A directory in the lobby listed the occupants: a travel agent, a management firm, a life coach, and a survey company on the first floor, a computer repair shop, temp agency, psychologist, and a cleaning service on the second floor. I documented that.

While I was reading the sign Nate wandered down the hall to the left, peering into the travel agency, then returning to the lobby. "Let's go upstairs," he said.

I started toward the elevator.

"No, the stairs," he said.

I frowned. "Your breathing!" I said, putting my hand on my chest and taking a deep breath to demonstrate what I'd said.

He pointed toward the stairs.

Okay then.

Up we went. We had to stop on the landing so he could catch his breath. I shot a picture of the stairway. We made it to the second floor. He pointed to a red fire-alarm box at the top of the stairs. I took a picture of it from several angles. We looked around, and then he saw a door with an EMPLOYEES ONLY sign on it. He tried the knob. It turned. He glanced at me, opened the door, and walked in.

"Hey!" a man's voice called out.

I jumped. Then I reached in and grabbed Nate's arm. "Dad, you have the wrong door!" I shouted in his ear. Then I turned to the man, who was dressed in khaki workman's clothes. "Sorry, he gets confused."

The man chuffed his response. I closed the utility room door and pretended to guide Nate down to the men's room, all the while hoping the man would go away.

He did.

Nate disappeared into the men's room, waited a couple of minutes, then came back out. He looked at me. "Dad?"

"You heard that?"

He grinned.

"Let's just go before you get arrested!"

We walked back down the stairs. I was ready to leave by the front door, but Nate made a U-turn. *What now?* I wondered, following him.

Behind the stairway was a door leading out to the parking lot. Thankfully, it wasn't alarmed because while I stood by, he pushed straight out of it and walked outside. He looked around, then reentered the building. It took me a minute to realize what he was doing—trying to recreate the day of the bombing. He and Helen might well have come in that back door. It would have been near where he parked the Tahoe.

Nate came in the door, walked to the main hallway, and took a right turn, acted like he was going into the big office down that hall, then stood staring at the door, trying to figure out what he'd done next.

Apparently, no answers came, and finally he was ready to leave. On the drive home, I kept glancing over at him. Nate sat staring straight ahead, searching for memories hidden deep inside.

9

I COULDN'T WAIT to tell Scott about our trip to the Deer Park office site and to find out about Scott's meeting. I'd been assigned to a multiagency task force once when I was a Fairfax County police detective. We were trying to find a serial rapist, but I swear we spent more time jockeying for position and fighting turf battles than making progress on the case. By the grace of God we found the guy, but looking back, I actually think it took that—God's grace.

So I could imagine Scott coming home emotionally worn out. I planned a special dinner—chicken piccata, pasta, garlic bread, and salad with a nice dry Riesling. I could see us relaxing afterward in front of a movie, reconnecting as we snuggled on the couch.

Yeah, not so much. The chicken piccata was nearly done and the pasta water boiling when he called to say he had to work late, and they were going to grab dinner on the run. "Sure! Okay," I said, mentally shoving my inner June Cleaver back in the pantry. "See you when you get home."

I flipped off the stove burners, slid the chicken into a glass storage container, and put it plus most of the salad in the fridge.

The garlic bread sitting on the baking sheet stared at me. Resisting the temptation to bake it and eat the whole thing myself, I slid it back into its foil bag and threw it in the freezer. "C'mon, Luke," I said, "we're on our own."

I slipped into running shorts and shoes and a navy-blue T-shirt. I clipped on Luke's leash, and we headed out the door.

The townhouse community we lived in worked well for Scott when he was single. It was convenient. The house was easy to maintain and had a garage where he could keep his Bucar.

I hated it. Seriously. If I didn't love Scott so much I wouldn't have put up with it. I'm a woods-and-fields type of person, a country girl even though I was raised in the suburbs. Give me mountains or give me the beach, I don't care, just get me away from people.

We'd been looking for a place to move on and off (mostly off) for months. Every time I was about to insist we move, something happened. Now I guess it was going to be a serial bomber.

Maybe I should just look on my own, I thought as I jogged down the sidewalk. I admit, I was irritated.

I crossed a street, Luke running on my left. Ahead of me I saw a guy with a Labrador mix. Labs are usually pretty chill, but this one was reactive. As soon as he spotted Luke, he started lunging and barking. Out of courtesy, I moved out into the parking lot on my left. I thought putting a row of parked cars between the two dogs would be enough.

But no. Just as we went by, the guy lost control of his dog. The Lab jerked the guy off his balance. He fell and dropped the leash. Over my shoulder, I saw the Lab charge toward us. I turned toward the threat and put Luke behind me.

"No!" I yelled, holding up my hand in a *stop* gesture. The dog kept coming. "Hey, get your dog!" I yelled.

The man let loose a stream of profanity. Luke thought I was being threatened and pushed in front of me, stiff-legged, hackles up. Just as the two dogs were about to tangle, the man dove for the end of the leash and yelled—at me! "Watch your dog!"

"Me? Me? Me watch my dog? Are you kidding?" I can't remember the last time I was so angry at a stranger. "You'd better get some help with that dog!"

He told me exactly what he thought of my suggestion. I wanted to punch him. I stood with my fists clenched, Luke standing by my side, glaring at the guy. No way was I going to turn my back on him. Finally, he walked away.

When they were at a safe distance, I gave Luke a tug. "C'mon, buddy." I desperately needed to run off the crazy.

We continued in the direction we'd started, ran through Scott's neighborhood (I refused to call it mine) and into a park. The sun had set, and the sky was a deep blue. One lone star peeked out, testing the evening like a dominant puppy. I inhaled the cooling air, letting it fill my lungs. I hoped it would diffuse the tension, but honestly, it didn't.

By the time we got back to the house, I was still tied up in knots. I slouched on the sofa while Luke cooled down. Before I could stop myself, I sent Scott an angry text. *We have to move!*

I had no right to expect an answer, but Scott texted back. *We'll talk later.* Then I got a second text, an afterthought. *You okay?*

I wouldn't respond. I jerked to my feet, fixed Luke his dinner, then sat in the kitchen watching him devour it. Twenty-eight seconds. That's all it took. *I really need to look into those bowls that slow dogs down,* I thought. I opened the door and let him out into our tiny (and I do mean tiny) backyard. The sky now had just a hint of color, but more stars had popped out. They were like diamonds sitting in a jeweler's tray, catching the light and tossing it to me. The mother-of-pearl moon creeping up over the row of houses behind us awakened my conscience.

There's beauty and there's ugly, a voice in my head said. *Don't add to the ugly.*

Remorse flowed through me in a hot stream. *I'm fine,* I texted my husband. *I'm sorry.* I added a heart emoji to make up for my rudeness.

I got a heart back.

I showered and went to bed, letting Luke climb up next to me, a practice frowned upon by my generally dog-tolerant husband. As I stroked my dog, half-listening for the sound of Scott's car entering the garage, I prayed. I prayed first for my own soul, given to critical anger, especially when it came to other people and their dogs. I prayed for Scott, for Amanda, for Nate, for Laura. I prayed for our nation and the world. Somewhere in the middle of praying, I fell asleep.

My phone woke me up two hours later at eleven thirty. I jerked myself up in bed and looked toward Scott's side. Empty. I grabbed my phone. "Hello?"

A callout. A teenaged girl, angry at her mother, had stormed out of the house at eight and was still missing. The house was in the mountains next to a lake. The sheriff had asked for help, possibly for a water search. I shoved Luke off the bed.

"Nate's going," Bill, the incident commander said.

"Nate! Why's he responding?" I swung my legs over the bed.

"You'll have to ask him. Are you in?"

"Yes!"

Luke recognized that word and started doing his happy dance. Bill would text me the details. I clicked off the phone and went to call Nate, then remembered his hearing was still gone. So I texted him. *Why are you responding?*

I know that family.

Wait for me. I'll pick you up, I texted back.

I threw on SAR clothes, laced up my boots, and grabbed my pack. Within fifteen minutes, we were in the car headed for Nate's, my mind racing. Five miles in, I remembered to text Scott. (I can be taught.)

The look on Laura's face when I got to Nate's said she wasn't at all happy he was responding. "I'll take care of him," I said, putting Nate's pack in my Jeep.

"I know you will." She kissed him goodbye, hugged me, and we set off.

At the end of Nate's driveway, I stopped. "How are your lungs," I asked, gesturing.

"Better," he said. Then he gestured for me to turn right, using exactly the hand signal we use to send dogs in that direction, and stuck his empty pipe in his mouth.

I shook my head and grinned. *Nate's gonna do what Nate's gonna do*, I thought. End of discussion.

It was almost two in the morning when we arrived at the search location. As soon as I got out of the Jeep, I saw the concern. There was just enough moonlight to see an empty canoe floating in the middle of the lake.

I grabbed a clipboard so I could make notes for Nate, and we walked over to where Bill was talking to the sheriff. "She and her mom had a blistering argument. Mom took away her cellphone, and Lacey stormed out. The mom expected her to come back after an hour or so, but she didn't."

"Where's her dad?" I asked as Nate read my notes.

"On a business trip. Atlanta. Travels a lot, according to the mom."

"Who else is responding?" I asked Bill.

"We've got four more people on the way."

I didn't write that down. Nate nudged me with his elbow, protesting my omission. I held up four fingers.

As I looked around, I could see the lights of one or two other houses around the lake. Otherwise, this place was pretty remote. *How do you know them?* I asked Nate, writing on the clipboard.

"Oldest son is a student at the college. He's a vet. We talk." Just then a motorcycle roared up. Nate turned. "That's him." He took off toward the bike.

"You heard that!" I said, jogging to catch up. Admittedly, the bike—a Harley—was loud. Maybe Nate felt the rumble.

I caught up to them when they were hugging. "He can't hear," I told the young man. "He was in an explosion."

Nate gestured toward the young man. "Connor," he said.

"Hey, Connor, I'm Jess." I shook his hand. "Tell me about your little sister."

He put his helmet on his bike. "She's a handful. Got ticked off at my mom, apparently."

"Did she hike around here? Use the lake?"

"We all did. Swimming, hiking, canoeing, camping. That's what the fight was about. Lacey wanted to go camping with her friends. Mom didn't want her to, at least not 'til Dad gets home."

"She's off for the summer?"

"No summer school, that's for sure. She's too young to work. Maybe babysits now and then. But you can see, she's pretty isolated, and Mom, well, Mom can be overprotective, especially when Dad's gone."

"That your canoe?" Nate gestured toward the lake.

"Could be. We have one like that." He glanced toward the sheriff's car. "Look, I got to go see Mom." Nate nodded. "Thanks for coming."

"How much of that did you hear?" I asked Nate as Connor moved away.

Nate shrugged. He gestured toward my clipboard, so I mapped out the gist of what Connor had said. "Sounds like that girl is just out sitting in the woods, cooling off," Nate said.

The canoe? I wrote.

His jaw shifted. "I'll bet you anything she just shoved that thing into the water to scare her mom."

Yeah, I thought. *That's the kind of thing I would have done.*

Bill came up to us. "Emily's here and Paul Turner." Paul had a border collie I liked a lot. "Frank is on the way." He looked at me.

"You're the only one water certified. The sheriff wants us to search the lake."

"Is there another boat?"

"One of his men is bringing a jon boat."

Oh, great. A small boat. Tiny. I told myself to buck up. "Okay. Have they called for divers?"

"They'll be here at first light. They're asking us to do a preliminary search."

"We can do that. It'll have to be just me, Luke, and the helmsman." *And he better know how to steady a boat.*

I sketched this out for Nate on my clipboard. *You stay here,* I gestured. *Sit in my car if you get tired.*

He nodded. "Take this," I said, handing my clipboard to Bill. "You can write stuff to Nate. There's nothing wrong with his brain, just his hearing. He can help."

I GOT my life jacket and Luke out of the Jeep and walked him around. He was ready to go, bumping me with his nose, like, *come on!*

The night was clear, the air about seventy degrees. The moon had begun dropping in the west and soon would disappear behind a mountain rising beyond the lake. I could hear frogs in the swampy area near us, including a big bullfrog. I took a deep breath, smelling pine and humus, fresh water, and cars. It could be worse. It could be raining, or cold, or snowing.

A pickup truck pulling the boat on a trailer drove up. The deputy driving navigated around until he could back the boat into the water. There was no dock, no dry way to get into the boat. Oh, well.

Nate walked over. I knew what he wanted. I could see it in his eyes. "Let's pray," he said. Of course. So we did.

I walked toward the boat, remembering the first time I tried a water search. We almost capsized. I got thrown into the water. I knew my heavy boots would be a liability if it happened again, so I took them off and put them by a tree, walking barefoot to the boat. I buckled on my life jacket.

The boat owner's name was Bryan. "Your dog bite?" he asked.

"Are you a steak?"

He laughed. "What's his name?"

"Luke."

"Okay, put him in, then you and me'll push the boat out."

Luke happily jumped into the boat. I moved him toward the front and told him to settle. Bryan and I pushed the boat out further. I hopped in, and he got in behind me.

The boat had a small electric outboard motor on the back, and Bryan fired it up and moved us away from the shore. "How do you want to do this?" he asked.

I'd been thinking about that. "Let's go out to the canoe and then make concentric circles around it, widening our search field as we do."

"Okay. If I start going too fast or too slow, just tell me."

We started moving toward the drifting canoe. Luke had no place to lie down, but he knew what he was supposed to do. He leaned over, sniffing the water. He was very still, and I was grateful for that.

When we got to the canoe, Bryan pulled alongside. Empty. "No paddle," he reported. "Either she lost it when she fell overboard or ..."

"... or she launched the canoe from shore," I said. "A paddle would float."

"Most likely."

I shined my flashlight around the water. Nothing. Not even a stick.

We began traveling in circles over the mirror-still water. I actually began to relax.

We made about eight circles around the canoe, then started a zigzag course toward the shore. We remained silent. Except for me encouraging Luke, the sound of the water lapping against our boat was the only noise. It was almost peaceful.

"You want to call it?" Bryan asked me. We'd been out on that lake for about ninety minutes.

"Let's take a break. I want to find out how the lake is fed and if there's an outflow." Currents matter, especially when it comes to bodies. "I want to know how the canoe drifted out there."

But none of that proved necessary. We were about twenty feet offshore when we heard a general cheer go up. I grabbed my radio. "She's been found. She's fine," Bill told me over the radio.

"Take us in," I told Bryan. "They've found her."

"Let's get the canoe." He increased the throttle and we started moving faster. We came alongside the canoe. Bryan tied a rope to a place on the bow, and we started back to shore.

I wondered—had Emily found her? Paul? Frank?

We pulled up near the shore. Bryan and I jumped out to pull the boat up. Luke decided that was a good idea. He hit the water, swimming joyfully. Nate met us, collecting Luke as we dealt with the boat.

"She just walked out of the woods," Nate said.

"Nobody found her?" I asked, gesturing toward the searchers.

"She showed up herself."

Wow. I hadn't expected that end to the evening. At least she was alive and unhurt.

Nate handed me Luke's leash and my boots and walked toward the group gathered around Lacey. As I laced on my boots, I saw him hug the mom, then the girl, and shake hands with the brother, the motorcycle guy. I heard Nate say to the girl, "You'll figure out along and along that runnin' don't solve much." He glanced toward me, and I felt my face grow hot.

Nate walked back toward me. "Take Luke over yonder. I'll hide near the lake. That boy needs a reward for his work."

10

THE SKY WAS TURNING light in the east as we drove home. Nate and I were both tired, but I was so happy that girl turned up. I think I chattered all the way home, even if Nate couldn't hear me. He sat in the passenger seat, his pipe in his mouth, glancing over at me once in awhile, a satisfied look on his face.

I dropped Nate off and got to our townhouse at about 8:00 a.m. Scott had already texted me that he was leaving for work so I knew he wouldn't be there. I entered the front door, intending to walk straight through to the backyard so I could hose off Luke. I got stopped by the dozen roses and the note on the kitchen table.

I miss you. I love you. I hope you found the girl. You are my hero. Scott

Awww.

I gave Luke a bath in the backyard, then showered and crawled into bed. I put the roses on my night table so I could see them every time I woke up. I plucked a couple of petals and put them on my pillow so I could smell them as I slept.

I love that man.

. . .

SCOTT and I were able to have a nice evening together the day after my search. He told me a little bit about the task force, about the lines of investigation and about some of the people involved, and about the inevitable jockeying for power that occurs whenever strong-willed investigators try to work together.

The head of the task force, Malcolm Caldwell from the FBI, didn't have a lot of experience with serial bombings. He was relying heavily on Hitch, who seemed to know what he was doing. Scott was okay with the way things were going. The bright spot for him was reconnecting with his friend Mike Perez. He was, in Scott's words, "a stand-up guy." I still hadn't met him.

Mostly we talked about me—the incident with the unruly Lab, my search, why I wanted to move, and where I wanted to move. "At least an acre," I said. "I don't care about the house, just the yard and the community. I need more space!"

"No," he said.

My eyes widened.

"At least five acres, preferably ten."

"You want room for a horse."

"Maybe two." He grinned.

"It's going to be a lot harder to find a place with that much acreage that we can afford," I said.

"Well, let's pray about it," Scott responded.

I was about to make a snap remark about passivity when I realized this was what I'd wanted—a husband who trusted God. I blinked and shut my mouth. I can be so complicated.

"We can start seriously looking as soon as we get this bomber," he said.

Didn't catching the Atlanta Olympics bomber take five years? The Unabomber twenty years?

Somehow I managed to keep my mouth shut. Still, Scott must have read my mind. The next morning just before he left he brought up house hunting again. "Tell you what," he said. "You check your apps. If you see a property you want to look at, set it up for 7:00 p.m. tonight."

"Really?"

"Yes. I think I can leave by six."

Yay!

As soon as I heard him drive off, I began checking my apps. I found two properties I was interested in and called the real estate agent I'd talked to before. We made an appointment for seven. Done and done.

I FELT happy and excited driving down to Nate's that day. I couldn't wait to tell him and Laura we were going to start looking for a house.

When I pulled up, I saw a car I didn't recognize.

Laura welcomed me at the backdoor. "Come on in!"

"I hope I'm not interrupting something," I said. "I need to work Luke on the equipment."

"No problem. Crissy brought Harper over for a little horse therapy. Nate's inside."

By "inside" I knew Laura meant in the living room. I said a few words to Crissy as I walked through the kitchen, surprised Harper wasn't with her.

I found the little girl snuggled up next to Nate on the couch. He was reading a book to her. She barely glanced at me as I walked in.

Harper was a tiny girl, with dark hair and equally dark, shy eyes. If you'd asked me, I would have guessed she was five, not seven.

Laura had told me Harper hadn't spoken since she was removed from her neglectful home. Her mother had died, and her father couldn't care for her, at least according to social services. The little girl loved animals, so Laura and Crissy wanted to see if the big, silent, gentle horses could help Harper find her voice again.

I dropped down into the leather chair, waiting for them to finish. As I looked around, I realized that this was where my inner GPS read "home." The honey-colored logs, the tall ceilings, the river stone fireplace, the bookshelves. Could Scott and I find a log house like this, I wondered? I would love that so much.

I heard the words "The end." Nate glanced at me. "Mornin'," he said.

"Don't let me interrupt."

"We're just finishin' up here." He jostled Harper. "This here's my friend Jess," he told her. She hid her face in his side in response.

"I'm going to work with Luke outside." I gestured as I said that. Nate's hearing was starting to come back. He could hear words now, but it sounded like he was under water.

"Yep," he responded.

I paused going back out through the kitchen. "What's up with that?" I said, gesturing toward the great room and Nate.

"She adores him," Laura said. "He can't hear so she doesn't have to speak. So no pressure. She latched right on to him as soon as she met him."

"That's so funny," I said. I'd watched Nate charm adults and teens but seeing him with a little kid was new.

I went into the yard and set up the high plank, the weave poles, and the tunnel. The next time I turned toward the house, Nate emerged, walking toward the barn with his cane in one hand, and holding the little foster girl's hand with the other. Harper was scuffing her feet in the dirt, kicking up little dust puffs as she did. Sprite trotted behind them. Laura and Crissy lagged by about twenty feet.

I told Nate once I thought he'd make a wonderful father. "Maybe now I would've," he'd replied, "but not before. God had to soften me up. He had to break down the younger me pretty good."

Maybe God was still breaking me down. Maybe that's why I wasn't pregnant.

Sprite emerged from the house following Nate, and immediately rushed over to meet her BFF, Luke. I gave them some time to play, then I clipped on Luke's leash, told Sprite to go find Nate, and we started working, first on basic obedience, then on the equipment. Up on the high ladder, between the weave poles, then through the tunnel, over and over. Luke did well and got his play reward in return.

During a water break, I looked back toward the barn and pasture. I saw Nate standing next to Abby, Laura's horse. He had Harper in his arms, and Laura was holding Abby's lead rope. As I watched, Harper reached out tentatively, touched Abby, then pulled her hand back quickly. Nate stroked the horse's neck. When I looked back twenty minutes later, Harper had her arms around Abby's neck, hugging the horse.

Ah, the persuasive power of Nate.

Half an hour later, I was ready to quit. Luke's tongue was lolling out of his mouth. I gave him water from the hose, and when his panting had slowed, I took him inside to cool off in the air-conditioning. Nate and Laura joined me a few minutes later. I heard car tires crunching on the gravel driveway. Crissy and Harper were leaving.

"Let's sit down," Laura said, gesturing toward the kitchen table. "I haven't had a chance to catch up with you lately."

So the three of us sat and sipped some lemonade and talked. I heard all about Harper and the horse, and I told them Scott had agreed to start house hunting. When I mentioned he wanted five to ten acres, Laura smiled. "For a horse?"

"Horses, plural," I said. "We have an appointment to look at a couple of places at seven," I added, looking at my watch. "Speaking of which, I'd better get going."

I stood up and Nate followed suit. I hugged him and Laura and started to walk away. My phone vibrated. I pulled it out of my pocket. A text from Scott.

Explosion in a mail truck near Winchester. Got to go. I'm sorry! Won't be home tonight.

I looked up. So did Nate. Our eyes met.

11

Postal carrier Dwayne Richardson was standing on the front porch of a rural customer's house when the bomb exploded. He reacted, accidentally pushing his customer inside and onto the floor.

"Are you hurt? Martha, are you all right?" he said, concerned about the eighty year old. The package he'd been handing her and another five pieces of mail lay splayed over the blue carpet where he'd thrown them when he reacted.

"I reckon I am." She struggled to right herself. He gave her his hand and helped her to her feet. "My goodness, Dwayne! What happened to your truck?"

He turned to look, horror gripping him. The doors of his little white delivery truck lay on the ground. The windows had shattered, the backdoor flung open, and mail was scattered everywhere. Smoke rose from the interior.

Dwayne turned to Martha. "My boss is gonna kill me."

Scott Cooper got the call about the mail truck bomb when he was leaving the office with Mike Perez to interview another person present when the Deer Park bomb detonated.

"You good to go?" he asked Mike.

"You want to change?" They were dressed in business suits.

"No, Hitch wants us there ASAP."

"Okay."

They headed out Route 66 toward the western edge of Virginia. Scott, who was driving, used voice-to-text to tell Jess they'd have to look at houses another day.

AN HOUR LATER, Scott held his creds out of the window and eased past the roadblock on the tiny two-lane rural road. When they got close enough to see the flashing lights of the emergency vehicles ahead, he moved forward, then pulled his Bucar, a black Suburban, off the road.

"Did you see this place is called Woodchuck Heights?" Mike said, grinning.

"Nowhere, Virginia. Just the kind of place my wife and I would like to live. How far are we from the site of the first bomb?"

"Twenty miles. I'd say the drive's about forty minutes. The roads go along the lines of the mountains."

Scott opened his door. "Let's go."

They left the car and walked past the fire trucks, ambulances, and police cars that lined the two-lane road. The hill rose sharply on the west side of the road and dropped off just as sharply to the east. Everything was green—it looked green, and it smelled green, that is until they got within range of the blown-up vehicle. Then Scott could smell the explosive.

"Black powder," Mike said.

"No question."

The little truck sat by itself on the edge of the road cordoned off by crime-scene tape.

"There's Hitch," Scott said, pointing to a cluster of men halfway up a driveway on the west side of the road.

They had to jump a ditch and wade through some brush to join Hitch. The bottom of the driveway was cordoned off. Hitch looked up as Scott and Mike joined the crowd of police officers.

"Good," Hitch said, "you're here. We're still waiting on the bomb squad and the postal inspector. Scott, you go up and interview the postal worker and the old lady." He gestured toward the small white house up the hill.

"Okay."

"Mike, you organize evidence collection outside the perimeter. Make sure all these cops know what we're going to do and how. I don't want anything missed."

"Got it."

"The evidence team will be here soon."

Scott walked up the steep driveway. *Mike's got his work cut out for him.* Papers, envelopes, and fragments of packages were scattered all over. He saw one paper fluttering in the branches of a tree.

The driveway was seriously rutted. Most of the gravel had washed down. Scott stepped over the muddy places, wishing again he had his boots and his field gear on. A deputy stood on the small front porch. Scott showed him his creds.

"What's her name?" he asked, nodding toward the house.

"Crandell, Martha Crandell." The deputy opened the front door.

The inside of the house was dark. It didn't feel air-conditioned. There was no foyer. The front door opened straight into the small living room, which contained an overstuffed chair, a couch, and a large TV. Scott could see through to the kitchen, where an EMT stood.

Scott walked on back. "Hi, I'm Special Agent Scott Cooper, FBI," he said, showing his creds. "Mrs. Crandell?"

"That's me, honey. I don't reckon I ever expected the FBI to show up in my kitchen."

"No, ma'am." She was at least eighty, Scott figured, with wispy white hair, a couple of missing teeth, and blue-framed glasses. She sat at a small kitchen table across from a man in a postal service uniform. He was drinking a bottle of water. His hand was shaking.

"How are you feeling, Mrs. Crandell?" Scott noticed a second EMT stood near her with a blood pressure cuff in his hand.

"Like I want to keep my shotgun handy. We coulda lost Dwayne here, 'cause of some dang fool. It better not be his boss that done it. I know where he lives."

Scott turned to the postal worker. "Sir, you are?"

"Dwayne Richardson."

"How long have you been with the postal service?"

"Fifteen years now. Never had nothing like this happen."

Mrs. Crandell interrupted. "If I hadn't been asking about Alice—"

"—she's my wife," Richardson said.

"... if I hadn't asked about his wife, he'd've been back in that truck and blown to bits, body parts all over my yard," Mrs. Crandell said.

"Yes, ma'am. I'd like to talk with both of you, one at a time. Are you both feeling up for that?"

"Yep."

"Yessir."

"Mr. Richardson, why don't we go into the living room?"

Scott led the mailman and the EMT with him to the other room. "Pick your seat," he said, gesturing. That's when he saw the cats—a black cat next to the television, a white cat on the overstuffed chair, a calico curled up under the coffee table.

Great.

Richardson sat on the couch. Scott scooted the white cat off the chair. He tried not to think about the cat hair he was collecting as he sat down. "So tell me, Mr. Richardson, what happened today?"

The postal worker leaned forward, resting his elbows on his

knees, the bottle of water in both hands. Scott guessed he was about forty-five. His shaggy brown hair caught under his collar, and he had a scar right near his lip. His eyes were dark, and he focused on that bottle of water while he spoke.

"I was runnin' my route, as usual," Richardson said. "Miz Crandell, she had a package and, you know, I wanted to get it up to her. I could see it was from her daughter, and I knew she'd want it. So I parked my truck ..."

"Why didn't you drive up the driveway?" Scott asked.

"Well, that would have been terrible, wouldn't it?" He looked at Scott, wide-eyed. "I mean, we're alive because I didn't."

"Did you suspect something was wrong in the truck?"

Richardson blinked, like he was trying to understand the question.

"Did you see a suspicious package or something strange about the truck?" Scott waited. "Is that why you didn't drive up to the house?"

"Why no! It were the ruts. Last month, I got stuck backin' down, which we ain't s'posed to do anyhow. Had to get Martha's tractor to pull my truck out. Made me late, and my boss got mad. So no, I ain't goin' up that driveway again!"

"Turned out that was a good thing today, wasn't it?"

Scott continued asking questions. Did Richardson load his own truck? Did he notice any odd packages? Anything oddly addressed ... an unfamiliar recipient or bizarre writing on the package? Was his truck unattended at any point?

That last question prompted a ducked head and evasive look. Scott pressed the point.

"Okay, look," Richardson admitted. "I did go into the Walmart. I needed somethin' and, you know, it ain't near home."

Scott saw Richardson redden. Clearly that was not something he was supposed to do. "I understand. Hey, it happens, right? We all got stuff that comes up." He rubbed his jaw. "Which Walmart?"

Richardson looked up. "The only one 'round here. Over by town."

"Winchester?"

"Right."

"How long were you in there?"

"Maybe twenty minutes. But I was making good time on my route. It weren't gonna run me late."

"Did you lock your truck up?"

"Sure!" Richardson was looking like he was putting a scenario together. "I think so."

Walmart would have good security cameras on the parking lot.

"What time were you there?"

Dwayne frowned. "News just came on. Must've been noon. Yessir, noon."

Scott made a note. "Did you leave your truck any other time?"

"No, sir! I didn't."

"So you didn't get out to deliver any other packages?"

"Well," Richardson stalled. He took a deep breath. "I did deliver to old Joe Thornton. He's got a bad back and just can't make it to his box."

"Were you out of sight of your truck?"

Richardson nodded slowly. "Yes, sir. I guess I was."

"How long did you talk to him?"

"Maybe ten, fifteen minutes? We go way back. His son and me, we're huntin' buddies."

Scott nodded. "I understand. Give me Joe's address, okay?"

"Yes, sir."

"Mr. Richardson, anybody have a grudge against you?"

"Me? No, sir!" He ran his hand over his chin. "My father-in-law, he ain't a fan, but he wouldn't do nothing like this."

"You and your wife having problems?"

Richardson looked at Scott like he was crazy. "Me and Alice? No, we're good."

"Why'd Mrs. Crandell suggest your boss could be behind this?"

"My boss? Oh, everybody knows Ev's mean but he's okay, really."

"Ev?"

"Yeah," Richardson started laughing. "His name's Evelyn. He's always mad. We say it's because of his name. You know, like that Johnny Cash song? 'A Boy Named Sue'? Ev got stuck with a girl's name. Takes it out on all of us."

"So not just you?"

"No. Everybody. And no way would he blow up a mail truck. Do you know what kind of paperwork he'd have to do? Besides, he loves his trucks. No, Ev's not behind this."

After a few more questions, Scott moved on. He found Martha in the kitchen, stroking the white cat sitting on her lap.

"Honey, kin I git you some sweet tea?" she asked as Scott entered.

"No, but thank you. Do you feel like talking?"

"My old man said I could talk the bark off a tree. Yessir, I feel like talkin'. Anytime."

Martha told the same story as Dwayne. He'd brought the package up to the house. "I sure did 'preciate that," she said. They were standing on the front porch talking when the mail truck blew up. "He jumped. Ran into me. Knocked me right flat on my back. Both of us laying there shocked. I swear, I don't know what kind of fool blows up mail."

"Yes ma'am." Scott cocked his head. "Why'd you wonder if Mr. Richardson's boss was behind it?"

"Oh," she gestured like she was throwing something away, "Ev ain't your man. I know he's been givin' Dwayne a hard time, but Ev, he wouldn't blow up one of his own trucks. That little man is so proud of his empire."

Scott asked more questions. How long she'd lived in the area, how long had she known Dwayne, how did she know Ev. Any reason to suspect someone had a grudge against Dwayne. Who the bad actors in the community were.

When he thought he'd gleaned everything he could from Mrs. Crandell, he thanked her.

"You gonna catch this guy?" she asked.

"We are."

"Better do it soon. Christmas'll be here afore you know it. Don't nobody wantin' to be scraping Christmas presents off the road."

"Right."

"Dwayne, honey," she called out, "you come in here and we'll have some tea."

12

WHEN I GOT that text about the mail truck bombing and our eyes met, Nate asked, "What happened?"

"Bomb."

"Come on," he said, waving me toward the great room.

There, I wrote on the whiteboard the specifics. Nate's brow furrowed. "Scott's going?"

I nodded. "Yes."

He grimaced and shook his head. "Social security. Post office. Somebody got a grudge against the government?"

I wrote two words, *Mailboxes first.*

"Practice rounds?" Nate said.

I shrugged. "Who knows?"

I ADMIT I was bitter Scott had been called away. Again. I kept the real estate appointment anyway by myself. Well, with Luke.

The properties were awful. (I know. How could I be mad because Scott couldn't show up for what turned out to be a useless appointment?) One of the houses was a rundown cracker box. The other was okay, but there was a lot of old junk in the decrepit outbuildings, and everything was being sold as is. I couldn't imagine how long it would take to clear the barn and sheds, much less fix them.

So the real estate agent said she'd keep looking for us. *Great*, I thought. *Maybe we'll find a place before I'm dead.*

I knew it wasn't Scott's fault that he got called out on this case. Of all people, I should understand that. At least his sudden absences were part of his job, the job that was paying most of our bills. Still, I was hurt that he'd missed our appointment. It felt like something I really, really wanted was way down on the list. *I* was way down on the list.

Nate told me one time that marriage reveals our self-centeredness.

Check.

LATE THAT NIGHT, I felt Scott slide into bed behind me. I opened my eyes just long enough to see the time—12:13. *He must be exhausted.* I felt the warmth of his body. I smelled his woodsy shower soap. I nestled toward him, and his arm came around me, pulling me closer. I imagined his fatigue, his tension, melting away in our embrace, along with my irritation.

One of the great gifts of marriage is sleeping close at night.

I woke up early the next morning, intending to make Scott a good breakfast. To my shock, his side of the bed was already empty. I jumped out of bed just as he came back in the room, dressed and ready to go.

"You're leaving?" I said.

"I'm sorry, hon." He kissed me. "Hitch wanted me to spend the night up there. I told him I had to go home, but that I'd be back early."

I glanced toward my watch, still charging on my night table. 5:45. "You've only slept a few hours."

"But I slept with you. That made it worth it." He held me in his arms and kissed my ear. I would have given anything for him to be able to stay.

"I was going to fix you breakfast!"

"Thank you. We just need to get through this, then I'll take some time off." He kissed me again. "We'll find that house."

"Please be careful," I whispered.

I CRAWLED BACK INTO BED, listening as he left. I heard the garage door go up, heard the engine on his Bucar start up, and heard the garage door close again. I'd be lying if I didn't admit tears came to my eyes.

A few minutes later, Luke came in. I guess he'd decided it was time for me to drag my carcass out of bed. I stroked his beautiful face, then swung my legs over the side of my bed and sat up. As I did, my eyes fell on a white mug I'd recently bought myself: *Be grateful* the beautiful, flowing script read.

I squeezed my eyes shut. *I'm sorry,* I whispered. Ingratitude was one of my most frequent sins. I started to mentally list all the wonderful people and things in my life, chief among them my excellent husband and faithful dog and my good, close friends, and I thanked God for them.

I had a roof over my head, plenty of food to eat, clean water, comfortable clothes, and people (and a dog) who loved me. I was rich. Why did I so often live like I was lacking?

To be honest, the loss of my father on 9/11 had left a hole in my heart that neither Scott nor Luke could completely fill. What's more, we all walk around with God-shaped holes. That's what Nate taught me. We try to fill those holes with work, food, drink, relationships, sex, but nothing will fit except God, and we perversely resist him.

I'm amazed God puts up with us. Me, especially.

. . .

LUKE and I went for a run, about four miles. The day was cloudy and humid, and the weather app predicted thunderstorms in the afternoon. As sweat rolled down my neck, I wondered if I should start doing mountain races again. I'd run several fifty milers before Scott and I got together. I hadn't even thought about them lately. Was I getting old? Too settled?

I'm restless, I thought. *I need to work.*

So after I got back and showered, I opened my laptop.

Being a private investigator involves less shoe leather and more computer work than in the old days. First of all, people are so stupid about what they post online. Second, for a small fee I could find out an awful lot about a person, from college degrees to addresses to parking tickets to shopping preferences.

Like there was one guy whose wife suspected he was having an affair. Sure enough, I found he had a parking ticket issued on the same block as the woman suspected to be his mistress. Then there was the woman whose boss thought she was embezzling funds. She was clever, funneling money in small chunks to several family members. But when one of them bragged online about her third exotic vacation "thanks to Mom," I told my client, and he confronted the woman. She collapsed like a house of cards.

Some of it was kind of fun I had to admit. Other cases were just downright sad.

I sent out a bunch of emails to lawyers, a source of a lot of my work in the past. I emailed my friend at the Virginia Vital Records office to see if she'd found anything on that case I sent her. Then I started browsing around looking at the Wife #2's other information online, including her social media.

I hit a wall after forty-five minutes and resigned myself to waiting for my vital records friend to get back in touch with me.

Then another thought grabbed me. I went down into the basement room—supposedly a family room, but we used it for storage. Rummaging behind a bunch of weights, an extra chair, and a twin bed, I pulled out my old whiteboard. In the past, it had held a list of possible leads in a divorce case, an SAR training calendar, and a murder board. Now, I would use it to help solve a mystery.

I carried it upstairs, found the dry-erase markers, and wrote "Who's planting bombs?" at the top. I drew four columns, one for each of the bombings so far: mailbox, mailbox, building, postal truck. I made the "building" column wider. I knew more about it.

Then I wrote down everything I had learned, including everything Scott had told me, about each of them.

I quickly realized I needed to narrow my investigation. Solving the mailbox bombs, and possibly the mail truck bomb, would center on how the bombs were built, and that information wouldn't be available to me (unless I grilled Scott, which I wasn't about to do). So I'd focus on the building explosion, the one that had trapped Nate, the one that killed Helen Thorpe.

My whiteboard was reversible, so I turned it around, wrote DEER PARK OFFICE EXPLOSION at the top. Then I checked the office park's website, which thankfully had not been updated, and copied down all the offices that had been in that building. I went to each of their websites, found a contact name, and created a file on my laptop with that information. Then I took a deep breath and started making phone calls.

I admit I lied a little. I said I was working on behalf of one of the victims. I'd have to check with Nate later and collect my usual one-dollar fee from him.

None of the first three offices I called proved helpful. The psychologist and insurance agent had moved to other offices in the same office park and reported no problems with clients or threats. Same with the post office.

The oral surgeon, whose equipment was all destroyed, had not yet relocated, but I did manage to get in touch with his office manager, who was angry that the bombing hadn't been resolved.

"No one's been arrested or charged, and the insurance company won't pay up until we know who did this."

Did the insurance company suspect the dentist? I wondered about that, and I did ask some other questions but didn't get a firm answer. I wondered if the doc was in financial trouble and that's why the insurance company hadn't paid.

The back-office of Social Security didn't have a number, so I decided to stop in there. I'd make an appointment to find out how my friend (Nate) could apply for disability.

A week later, I walked into the agency's new office located about five miles from the old one. This building was definitely an upgrade. It looked like a repurposed grocery store. All on one level, partitions separated the waiting room from the representatives. A new security door defined the office space, and an armed, uniformed guard stood inside. A sign read NO FOOD OR DRINKS. About twenty people sat silently in aqua plastic chairs, placed in rows, all facing the same direction. High on the wall, a TV showed rotating informational videos explaining different types of claims and warning of fraud.

Was it fraudulent to ask questions?

My number was finally displayed on the TV, directing me to Window 5. I sat down in the chair, a Plexiglas window between me and the agent, a middle-aged woman with curly brown hair whose name was A. Scalino, according to the nameplate.

I explained why I was there. "A friend asked me to explore social security disability, how to apply, and if he was eligible."

"This information is all on our website," she said. "Why did you come in?"

"I thought you could explain it better," I said, sounding as wimpy as I could. I didn't mean to raise her suspicions right off the bat.

"What's wrong with him?"

"He lost a leg, and he's deaf."

She frowned.

"He hasn't been able to work, and I don't know if he'll be able to go back."

"How'd he get deaf? Born that way?"

"He was in an explosion."

Her eyes widened. She leaned forward. "We were too! Right here." She pointed to her desk. Of course, she didn't mean "here" here, like right in this spot. She meant at the social security office.

"In your office? Oh, wow. Did you get hurt?"

She shook her head. "Let me tell you, it was a miracle. Took down the whole building!"

"How'd you avoid getting hurt?"

"Fire alarm went off right before. We evacuated and *boom!*"

"Holy cow. Was it a bomb? Or a gas explosion? What have they told you?"

"Oh, honey, the rumors are flying. They haven't told us nothing, but it was a bomb, we know that."

"Who would do that?"

She waved her hand dismissively. "Who wouldn't. Between us we had about a dozen clients crazy enough or mad enough to have set off a bomb. We keep waiting for the police to ask us."

"Wait," I said. "The cops haven't asked?"

"Not that any of us know of. I mean, Jason Breyer, he's the manager, and maybe he gave them names, but we sure didn't." She glanced around and then continued. "We've got one guy comes in here wearing a helmet all the time. Helmet Man. That's our name for him. He's scared someone's going to hit him. Kill him, maybe. I think he carries a gun."

I glanced back toward the door. "There's no metal detector?"

"Nope, just Donnie out there. Helmet Man comes in on Tuesdays, Blanket Man every other Friday."

"Blanket Man?"

"Always has a blanket wrapped around him. Who knows what he's got under it? And those two are the tame ones. We got folks furious because they're not getting what they think they deserve, or other folks mad because they can't keep collecting after their mother dies."

"That's sad. Did any of your coworkers see anything suspicious that day?"

"Tom, he went out for a smoke. When he came back in, he saw a man racing up the stairs."

"What'd he look like?"

"Tom said he was tall and pretty thin. Shaggy hair. Had a black backpack."

"Had you had any threats," I asked.

"We get threats all the time. I mean, *all* the time. But nothing about a bomb. Mostly about guns and shooting."

"Did anyone die?"

"An old lady."

"Did you see her?"

"I didn't, but Donnie the guard remembered her coming in. She was kind of frail. Had a man with her, maybe her son. He was helping her."

Nate.

Ms. Scalino looked around again. "Honey, I'd better finish. We get timed, you know. I'll get you the forms for your friend, but let me tell you, get that man some money to help in the meantime. Disability takes forever to process."

I WALKED out of there with an application for social security disability in my hand and questions swirling around in my mind. Why in the world did the investigators not interview every employee in that office?

I couldn't wait to talk to Scott.

13

SCOTT WANTED to check the security cameras at the Walmart Dwayne Richardson had mentioned first thing that morning, but Hitch had other plans. Task force members and sheriff's deputies had gathered in the gym of the local elementary school and listened while Hitch handed out assignments. He wanted a door-to-door conducted along Richardson's route - every house contacted, every resident interviewed.

Scott calculated that must be over two hundred homes, and in his mind, it was a waste of time. The houses were very spread out. At best, only two houses could have seen or heard the explosion. Most of the residents would probably be at work. He doubted any useful information would come of a door-to-door.

He held his tongue, but by the looks on other agents' faces, he wasn't the only one feeling skeptical. Mike caught him leaving the meeting. "You going trick-or-treating too?"

"Yeah, but just twenty-three homes. I hope I can wrap it up quickly. The guy told me he'd left his truck in the parking lot when he went in to Walmart. I really want to check those videos." He squinted at Mike. "You still on evidence detail?"

"Yes, but now that the Evidence Response Team is here, I'm not sure why."

Scott clapped him on the shoulder. "We're just the foot soldiers. We do as we're told."

"See you this afternoon." Hitch had told them to regather at three.

SCOTT WALKED TO HIS CAR, determined to attack his assignment straightaway. He wanted to check out Walmart. He wanted to have dinner with Jess. He wanted to sleep at home tonight. Twenty-three houses were in the way of all that.

It was nearly noon by the time he finished. He'd connected with ten residents. He'd been harassed or at least barked at by eighteen dogs. Three times he'd been greeted by a resident with a shotgun. Life in the country.

Of the ten residents he'd been able to interview, only five knew the mail carrier's name and none expressed any grievance with either him or the postal service.

Like I said, Scott thought, *a waste of time.*

He drove to the Walmart and walked inside. The manager was at lunch. He'd be back at one.

So Scott grabbed a sub sandwich and a Coke and sat in the parking lot and called Jess. He about spit out a mouthful of lunch when she told him she'd gone to social security. "You went there? Do they know who you are?" She said she'd given an "alternate name."

"You shouldn't have done that!"

"Why not?"

"Because if they find out you were asking questions and you're my wife, it looks bad."

"I wanted information. I was curious."

Scott's heart drummed. He took a deep breath. "Look, it's bad enough that I know Nate. But if you get in there and they make the connection between you and me, well, it'll look like I'm playing both sides of the field. Like maybe I'm leaking information. Or you're obstructing justice."

"That's ridiculous."

"Not really."

"Okay, but listen to what I found out. The employees weren't interviewed."

"What?" Scott exploded.

"Yeah. The ones who deal directly with the public haven't been asked questions. How stupid is that?"

And here he was, driving around the country, bothering people who didn't have a clue what was happening. Scott worked to calm down. "That's good to know, Jess. I'll check into it. But please, don't get involved in this. For my sake. Please."

"I want you home," she said.

"I know. But not this way."

AGGRAVATED, he hung up and finished his lunch, then grabbed some gum to banish onion breath, and went back inside.

The Walmart manager cooperated. Came up with the security footage. And there was Dwayne's mail truck, sitting alone and unbothered in the parking lot for twelve long minutes.

A dead end. However the bomb got into his truck, it wasn't at the Walmart.

Scott sighed. He had an hour left before the afternoon meeting. He checked the map for places someone could buy black powder. There was a gun shop, two of them in fact, in Winchester. Did he have time to check them out? No, he decided. Instead, he called Dwayne. "Hey, I thought you'd like to know no one bothered your truck at Walmart," he told the mail carrier.

Dwayne let out a sigh of relief. "Well, thank God. I mean, I'm in enough trouble as it is."

"What trouble?" Scott asked.

"Getting my truck blown up. Ev is fit to be tied."

"Did you do it?" Scott figured he might as well be straight.

"No, sir! I wouldn't blow up my own truck. But he's still mad."

"Have you talked with the postal inspector?"

"She came by the house last night. Talked to me for 'most an hour. Told her just what I told you, no more no less."

"And you haven't had any other thoughts since then, nothing else you remembered?"

"No, sir. Nothing."

"Okay, keep in touch, man. If something else comes up, you call me," Scott said. He clicked off his phone. There was one other place Dwayne had left his truck unattended. Scott headed there.

Joe Thornton was at home. He remembered talking to Dwayne that day. "Well, Dwayne, he had his back to his truck the whole time we was talking, facing me. But I had a clear view of it. It and the road. Ain't nobody come up or down that road while we was at it. I'd've remembered that. Nobody drove by, and nobody walked by. Nobody fooled with that truck, not here anyhow."

With that taken care of, Scott drove back to the elementary school. It was a low-rise, one-story, brick building, and he'd guess it was maybe twenty years old. Had a colorful playground off to the side and ball fields. A huge FBI command center van sat parked before an overhang leading to the front door. Scott steered to a space in what he guessed was the teacher's parking lot and went inside, where he ran into Mike. "You got a second?" he asked.

"Sure."

Scott checked his watch. 2:50 p.m. Ten minutes. "I need to know if anyone interviewed the social security employees at that Deer Park bombing site."

Mike's eyebrows raised. "I'm sure they did."

"I need to know."

Information on the bombings was being collected in a database. Secure computers in the command center would have that information. As far as Scott knew, no secure lines had been run into the elementary school.

The two men walked out to the command center. Both pulled out their creds, but it didn't matter. "No one gets in but Caldwell and Hitchens," the agent at the door said.

Mike tried to get past that, but the agent stayed resolute. So he and Scott turned and walked back inside. "So what, we're gathering the information and someone else is analyzing it? That doesn't put us much higher than admins, does it?" Mike said, clearly miffed.

Scott bit the inside of his cheek. "I'll find out eventually."

"Just ask at the meeting."

Scott didn't say anything. He wasn't sure he wanted to do that.

Mike turned to him. "What makes you think they didn't?"

"Friend of a friend," he said. Then he tried changing the subject. "How's the evidence collection going?"

"We got everything packaged and shipped to the lab," Mike said. "I'd like to go through the weeds one more time." He gestured toward the gym. "Let's go see what he has for us."

They walked in and found seats in the gym. Caldwell was there, and Scott felt glad about that for some reason. He spoke to the group about what the higher-ups had been told and what they were asking, took some questions from the crowd, and then turned it over to Hitchens.

Hitchens outlined the progress they'd made that day. Scott listened as he checked off the boxes: evidence bagged and sent to the lab at Quantico; 137 interviews conducted; coordination with the postal inspector, FBI, ATF, state and local police; background checks on the postal workers; search of the post office; interviews with postal workers; reviews of security camera footage; yada yada.

The question about social security nagged at Scott like a loose thread, but he decided to keep his mouth shut. He didn't know Caldwell or Hitchens, didn't know a lot of the people in the room, and he liked playing his cards close to his chest, especially after last year.

A question drew Scott's attention. A guy in ATF gear asked if this bombing had been positively connected to any of the others. "Not yet," Hitchens replied, "but the lab has made this top priority, and I expect something on that soon."

"Do we know anything about the type of bomb?" the man asked.

"From the pieces we've collected it looks like six-inch galvanized pipe in an eight-by-eleven cardboard box, which we're tracing now. We didn't find enough of the box to identify either the recipient or the sender, but we're hoping the lab can help with that. The explosive was black powder."

"Detonator?"

"Standard blasting cap, but we're not sure how it was triggered."

"Any signs of the burner phone used in the other bombings?"

"Not yet."

The ATF guy seemed to settle back in his seat, satisfied with the information Hitchens gave him.

Hitch went on to describe additional lines of investigation, including some Internet chatter from some far-right groups. Then he said, "Most of you can go home. We'll reconvene at the Quantico office in two days. Thirty-four of the houses on the door-to-door have not yet been surveyed. I want four of you, Adams, Taylor, Perez, and Cooper, to stay over and take care of those. The names and addresses are in your email."

Scott felt his face redden, anger coursing through him. He could see Mike staring at him out of the corner of his eye. *Not right. Not what I want to do.*

Under other circumstances, he would have protested, or at

least begged off. But something told him to keep a low profile. So he tightened his jaw and stayed silent.

Mike, however, didn't. "Hitch, will we have full access to the database once we're back at Quantico? It's hard to investigate blindfolded."

"You'll have access to anything you need," Hitch said. He turned away.

Mike persisted. "One other question," he said, raising his hand. "Were all of the social security employees at Deer Park interviewed?"

Scott looked sharply at Mike.

"I'm sure they were. Of course," Hitch said.

"I heard they weren't."

Scott felt his face grow warm again. *Drop it, Mike.*

Hitch's eyes narrowed. Then his face relaxed, almost like he was forcing himself to look friendly. "I don't know what you heard or from who ..."

Did Hitch glance at him?

"... but I have the supervisor's report right here, and I'm quite sure we interviewed the other employees. I mean, why wouldn't we?" He looked over the crowd. "Anything else?"

There was a general murmuring and shuffling of feet and people got up to leave. Scott stayed seated, frustrated and angry. He couldn't afford to get angry. Not on the job. Anger management. That's why he'd been in forced counseling for the last year.

"Hey, you okay?" Mike asked.

Scott rose to his feet. "Yeah. Just had plans, that's all."

Mike stared at his phone. "Let's knock these out together. We can do some before bed and finish up in the morning. C'mon, it'll be fun."

Fun?

14

Nate sat in his chair in the living room, reading, drinking a cup of coffee. The book in his hand, *Providence,* was thick and deep.

He heard a car coming up the driveway and assumed it was Amanda coming home from class. But then Sprite raised her head and gave a low growl. He got up and looked out the front window. He saw a man get out of a black SUV. He was medium height and slim, wearing a black suit, white shirt, red tie. And he was walking toward the front porch.

Nate stepped out, the heat and humidity buffeting him. He closed the door behind him. Sprite, barking, came out with him. "Afternoon," he said.

"Are you Nathan Tanner?"

"I am."

"Mind if I come up?"

The bulge under the guy's suitcoat didn't get by Nate. He was a cop. "Come on," he said. He turned to Sprite. "Enough." Grumbling, the little springer spaniel moved away and slumped down near the porch railing.

"Robert Carmichael, ATF," the man said, showing Nate a business card. "You have a few minutes to talk?"

"Have a seat." Nate gestured toward the chairs on the front porch. It would be cooler inside, more comfortable. That's why he offered the man a seat on the front porch.

"Whew, warm one," Carmichael said, sitting down on the far chair.

"Yep." Nate angled his chair more toward the man. He wanted to be able to see him.

"You were at the Deer Park Office Park bombing."

"Yes, sir."

"The one trapped in the rubble."

"Yes, sir."

"You lost your hearing?"

Nate nodded. The man had deep brown eyes, a wide forehead, and his hair was dark brown. Maybe black.

"But it's better now?"

"'Bout 80, 85 percent. Still missin' some high frequencies."

"Why were you there? At the office park?"

Nate shifted his jaw. "Near as I can tell, I was helping an elderly friend, Helen Thorpe. I only know that from what other folks have told me. Apparently, I told my work that's what I was aimin' to do. I don't remember."

Carmichael frowned. "You don't remember anything?"

"I don't remember why I was there. I do remember one thing. A red fire alarm, one of those boxes that say PULL." Nate gestured with his hand.

"Where was that box?"

"I don't know."

"Did you pull it?"

"I don't know."

"Why might you have pulled it?

Nate frowned. "Why would anyone pull it? Only reason I can think of is if I saw a fire, or some other reason why we should evacuate."

"But you don't remember anything."

"No, sir."

"What do doctors say about your memory?"

"They don't know when or if it will come back." He shifted in his chair. "Believe me, I wish I could remember. It's weird losin' a day like that. It bothers me."

"Hypnosis can help bring back memories. We'd like you to consider it. We have a practitioner ..."

"No, sir, I'm not doing that."

"Why not?"

"Don't believe in it."

Carmichael raised his eyebrows. Then he sat back in his chair and looked out over the land spread before them. Nate's garden took up about half an acre. He'd fenced it off to keep deer out. Beyond that lay the bottom part of the L-shaped pasture he and Scott had built for the horses. "Nice place you got here."

A sudden, deep, irrational thought ran through Nate—a cold and dark fear. What if he got charged with something that would cause him to shell out more for a lawyer than he had? What if he lost this place! His mouth went dry. *I shoulda called that lawyer Scott gave me.*

The next question from Carmichael snapped him back. "You build this yourself?"

"Yes, sir. The house is from a kit, but me and some buddies, we put it together."

"And cleared all that?" Carmichael gestured toward the garden.

"Most of it. Bottom land, where the pasture is, that was clear."

"Did you ever use dynamite to blow out stumps?"

Nate's heart thumped. "Sure. When I was a kid up in the country. But here, we used my friend's front loader. Less chance of losing a hand."

"So you don't keep any here?"

"Dynamite? No."

"You hunt?"

"I did, 'til I lost my leg."

"Regular rifle?"

Nate felt irritation building. "Bow. Rifle. Whatever I had time for."

"Black powder?"

"I shot a black powder rifle once. Don't own one. Don't care to."

Carmichael nodded. When he did, Nate noticed a gray patch in his hair at the top of his head on the left side. "Where do you work?"

Nate told him.

"You lose your leg in the military?"

"No, sir, that happened later." Nate pulled up his shirt. "This was from the military." He saw the shock in Carmichael's eyes as layer upon layer of burn scars came into view. "And this." He pushed up his sleeve to show the scars that ran from his shoulder to his wrist. "It was hard," Nate said, "but I'm proud I served my country as a Marine."

Carmichael's eyes shifted away from the scars, away from Nate's story.

"Mr. Carmichael," Nate said, "you didn't come out here to shoot the breeze with me. What is it you really want?"

The agent dragged his eyes back and met Nate's gaze. "Mr. Tanner, we want to know everything about that day. Why you were there. What you saw. Who you saw. What you did. So far you're not helping us much."

"I tol' you, I don't remember. If I did remember, you feds would be the first to find out."

"Did you initiate that bomb?"

"Of course not." Anger rushed to Nate's face.

"How do you know? You don't remember anything."

"I know myself. I have no reason to do that."

"You weren't angry at the government? At Social Security?"

Nate cursed. "No, sir. And if I was, which I'm startin' to be, I'd never handle it that way."

"What would you do?"

"Assert my rights, which I'm gonna do right now. I'm done talkin'. I'd like you to leave. You got anything else to say to me, call my lawyer."

That was a bluff. Nate couldn't even remember the name of the guy Scott had recommended.

"Okay," Carmichael said. "We will get to the bottom of this." He got up, went down the steps, and walked to his car. He paused with his car door half open. What was he looking at?

Nate walked as casually as he could to the end of the porch, anger pulsing in his hands. Following Carmichael's gaze, he saw Laura leading her mare, Abby. Harper was sitting in the saddle.

He looked back at Carmichael, ready to charge down the steps if that man made a move toward Laura.

He didn't. He got in his car and drove off.

"C'mon, girl," Nate said to Sprite. He went back inside, taking one last look at Carmichael's car as it crossed the creek and disappeared into the trees. "Lord," he said, "I'm sorry I cussed. I'm so mad right now I could spit. Alls I ask is, protect us from that man and his false accusations. I trust you. I don't trust that man. And I don't trust myself to act right if he comes here again."

15

SCOTT CALLED to say he wouldn't be home that night. I missed him. I had a nice dinner planned ... *again.* I was tired of being alone. I wanted to hear about his life.

"Isn't the Evidence Response Team there? Why do they need you?"

He made some vague explanation, but the bottom line was, "They asked me to and it's my job."

I didn't want to argue.

"Look Jess, I hate having to stay up here tonight. But I'll be home as soon as I can. In the meantime, please don't go back to Deer Park."

Scott was not my enemy. I hitched up my big girl pants. "I understand. I won't. I love you."

"I love you too."

I clicked off my phone.

Another empty evening and another empty bed stretched before me. "C'mon, Luke," I said. "Let's go for a run."

I snapped on his leash, and we stepped outside. The air felt thick with humidity. Dark clouds gathered in the west. I checked the weather app. We still had time before the storms hit. So I started the timer on my watch and off we went, Luke and me, running off the crazy.

I prayed and ran, prayed and ran, my feet setting the cadence for my prayers.

We crossed the edge of the community and entered the park. Few people were out; it was dinnertime. Hot, humid, and storms were on the way. I glanced down and saw Luke's tongue hanging out, dripping, and reminded myself not to get him overheated.

As I ran I tried to figure something out. I was okay, for the most part, as an independent single woman. Yes there were lonely times, but I did okay. I worked and had Luke. Nate came along and became the closest friend I ever had. Then I met Scott. Eventually, we fell in love. So why was it that I now felt so .... What? Dependent?

I felt my phone buzz. I stopped and pulled it out of my pocket. My sister. "Hey, Brooke!"

My sister is eleven years younger than I am, a product of my mother's second marriage. As a kid, I resented her intrusion in my life, and even now I had trouble feeling close to her. She initiated most of our interactions. "Jess!" she began, her sunny personality raining on my gloomy parade. "Guess what?"

"Tell me."

"I'm getting married!"

"You're what?" I stopped running. I knew Brooke had been dating a guy. She was a paramedic and so was he. I had no idea they'd gotten serious.

"I'm getting married! Me and mom are going shopping for a wedding dress at the outlets tomorrow. Want to come? I want you to be my matron of honor!"

What, what? ... She was talking so fast I could barely keep up. "This is big news," I said. I cradled the phone in my shoulder, knelt, and cupped my hands so Luke could get a drink from a dog-level fountain. "Who? When? I'm excited for you?"

"Jason, of course. And we want to do it soon—in September."

"Why so quick?"

"I'm pregnant!" she said, joy lifting her voice.

Shock. *Of course you are.* I stood up and wiped my hands on my shorts, tears hot in my eyes. "That's wonderful, Brooke." My heart sank. *Why can't I get pregnant? What's wrong with me?*

"Can you see mom as a grandmother?"

I swallowed hard. The lump in my throat wouldn't budge.

Brooke continued. "Hey, what day did you and Scott get married? Maybe we could choose that day! Then we'd have the same anniversaries."

Nausea. "No, Brooke," I said, "you'll want your own special day." *And so do I.*

"Yeah, I guess so. Can you come with us?"

My mind raced to find an excuse. "Hey, sorry. I've got something planned. But you and mom have fun!"

After saying goodbye, I clicked off my phone, fought off my tears, and began running again, my feet furiously pounding the pavement, my head tight with tension.

The storm broke when we were still half a mile from home. Buckets and buckets of rain poured down on my head. Thunder rumbled and lightning cracked around us. The shorter trees in the neighborhood, Bradford pears and crepe myrtles, shook their heads violently in the wind. Soon my feet were splashing through puddles, and I was soaked through.

The temperature dropped about twenty degrees. Blinded by the driving rain, I fumbled with my keys at the front door. *Brooke's pregnant,* I thought. *Pregnant.*

Finally, I managed to slip my key in the deadbolt. I unlocked it, transferred my key to the doorknob lock, and pushed the door open.

The second we stepped inside, Luke shook, and water went everywhere.

. . .

IT RAINED all night and all the next day. I muddled around the house in my sweats and slippers, forgoing our walks and letting Luke out only when he needed to go. He got as lazy as me, stretching out on the carpet in whatever room I was working.

By "working" I meant sending emails to lawyers, advocacy groups, and corporations trying to drum up business for my PI work. If Scott was going to be gone a lot, I should keep busy. I summarized my education and background and highlighted some of the types of cases I'd worked before. Then I invited them to ask about fees and availability.

The good news was I got a call from my vital records friend. There was no evidence of Wife #2's marriage on file. None. She'd cross-checked, looked for misfiles and misspellings, and basically had done everything she could to find those records. Elated, I called my client, the lawyer for the deceased man's daughter, and conveyed the news to him. "Vital records is sending you a letter to that effect," I told him.

He was thrilled. He hadn't thought to question the validity of the marriage. "You're a genius!" he said.

Uh, not quite.

SCOTT CALLED TWICE A DAY, at noon and 10:00 p.m. After checking out the additional witnesses on the postal truck bombing, the task force sent him to a large mail processing facility to interview workers.

"Feels like I'm spinning my wheels," he confessed.

I decided to stay upbeat. Supportive.

Scott told me there were about two-hundred investigators working on the bombing case now. "It's odd," he said. "So far we can't see a motive or even a rationale. The only connection is the way the bombs were made."

"And the government."

"Well, yes. There is that," he said.

After we hung up, I couldn't help it. I started researching bombers. Just online. I promised him I wouldn't go to Deer Park. I didn't promise I wouldn't read about the general topic.

I found information about the Unabomber, the Atlanta Olympics bomber, the Austin bombings, the Boston Marathon bombing, and several more. I learned what I could about motives and methodologies. I read a former FBI profiler's analysis and studied bomb-making components, including the many ways of triggering the devices. While rain continued to pound on our roof, I became educated on bombs and bombers. At least I'd be able to talk with Scott intelligently.

The rain finally cleared the next day. When Luke and I went for a run early the next morning, the sun was so hot water vapor rose in wisps from the wet ground. Sweat soon soaked my T-shirt.

I got back, showered, and checked my emails. I hadn't had any responses to my PI solicitations, so I decided to drive down to Nate's. There was always something to do at Nate's, with the horses, or his garden, or even just hanging out.

On the drive down, I wondered what he and Laura were doing for income. He couldn't work, and she'd quit her job at the library. Scott's daughter Amanda was living with them to help out, and I knew Scott sent Laura money for Amanda's food. But that certainly wasn't enough for everyone to live on. Plus, I was sure Nate must be getting restless.

I pulled off the road and onto Nate's driveway. As I drove through the woods that shielded his house from the road, I thought about what this place had become for me and so many others—a home away from home, a place of peace, a house of healing. No matter how ragged I was, how messed up, how broken, I knew I could come here and find grace. And I was not the only one.

Nate's driveway sloped down as it went through the woods, then crossed a small creek, before rising up as it entered the cleared area in front of the house. He owned about ten acres. He and Scott had built the L-shaped pasture for the horses that dropped down from the stables and across right in front of the woods.

I was surprised that day to see how high the creek was. Yes, it had been raining, but I'd never seen the creek so high. I hesitated to drive through it, but then, my Jeep sat well off the ground and it was four-wheel drive, so I decided to take a chance.

We made it and continued up the driveway and parked near the ramp in the back. Nate opened the back door, letting his dog Sprite out to play with Luke. "Wow," I said, adding gestures to my words, "I've never seen the creek that high."

"Rain gauge shows seven inches in the last few days. Everything's wet," he responded. Then he hugged me. "Come on in."

We went inside, leaving the dogs to play. I'd noticed Amanda's car was gone and so was Laura's. "Where is everybody?" I asked.

"Amanda's at school. Laura's got a job interview."

"Really? Where?"

"Down at Childers' House."

The women's shelter. "Great!" I smiled.

"Scares me some. Don't want some violent husband hurtin' her."

"Yes, I understand that."

I'd gotten pretty good at communicating with Nate as a deaf man. But he shared some good news. His hearing was coming back better now. He could actually understand the conversation. "They're thinkin' another month, and I'll be right again," he said.

I was afraid to ask the next question, but I did anyway. "What about your memory?"

His mouth twisted, and he shook his head. "Can't remember for the life of me." He rose to his feet. "Want to muck some stalls?"

I grinned. "Yes!"

. . .

We went out to the barn and worked together for about an hour, mucking stalls, cleaning grain bins, and using saddle soap on the tack. Nate was in a talkative mood. He told me he was hoping to go back to work soon. "I got to make some money."

"Are you out of sick leave?"

He frowned, so I repeated the question.

"People been donating it to me. I still got some left, but my Laura, she's been hanging out with little Harper a lot. Got a hankering to adopt her."

Shocked, I raised my eyebrows.

"I tole her I was too old."

"You are not!" I know he heard that because he laughed. "She's what? Seven? You are not too old!"

"Tell that to my arthritis." He grinned. Then he shook his head. "That woman's already talking about getting her a pony."

"Oh, my goodness." I smiled at the thought of Nate and Laura as parents. They'd be wonderful! Then practicality snuck in. "What about her biological parents?"

"Mom died of an overdose, Dad's into drugs and alcohol. Somethin' happened about a year and a half ago and she quit talking. Social Services is worried it had somethin' to do with the dad, so they took Harper away."

"She was okay before that?"

Nate nodded. He had stopped working so he could concentrate on our conversation. "Quiet and shy, but she could talk."

"And they don't know what happened?"

"No." His jaw shifted. "Whatever it was, it traumatized that little girl."

Trauma. Post-traumatic stress. No wonder Nate's eyes were shining. He could identify.

So could I.

"What's her last name?" I asked.

"Lee."

"Harper Lee? Like the author of *To Kill a Mockingbird*?

"I know. It's kinda literary." Nate shrugged. "It's weird."

I DECIDED to sleep at Nate's that night. I couldn't face my empty house. I missed my husband and for some reason, I felt sad.

I lay in bed staring at the ceiling thinking about what it would be like for Nate and Laura to adopt little Harper Lee. They would be a Godsend to her, giving her love, teaching her, guiding her. She'd grow up with horses and dogs and good food and the best schools, and most of all, love. And she'd learn about Jesus.

I could not imagine a better childhood. So what was the negative feeling lurking like a feral cat just around the corner in my mind? Was it concern for Nate and Laura? I mean, Nate already had a lot of challenges with the loss of his leg and now these latest injuries. And despite what I'd said to Nate, neither he nor Laura were particularly young. Could they keep up with a little kid? Could they afford her? Was I jealous because secretly I wanted a child? Was it because "everybody" (meaning Nate and my sister) was adding a child to their family?

I tried on different options. None seemed to fit.

I heard the rain start up again, beating like a military tattoo on the metal roof of Nate's cabin. The sound of it was a comfort to me, a reminder that I was in a safe, protected place, a place that had become a refuge. No matter how hard the rain beat down, I had a place where it was warm and dry, where people loved me, where I could get centered again when I went a little crazy.

And that's when I realized the name of that feral cat stalking me—fear. Fear that I'd lose my place in Nate's life, fear that Harper would usurp me in his and Laura's hearts, fear that I'd be cut off from this house of healing and have to try to restore my sanity on my own. Fear of being alone.

I was embarrassed to admit all this, even to myself. So I started to pray. And as I confessed my fear to God, I remembered another rainy night, lying in the mud on Assateague Island with a knife in my side, when I thought I was dying. Suddenly, peace overwhelmed me, and I knew I was not alone, that I would never be alone. And that perfect love casts out fear.

As I affirmed those truths in my prayer, I remembered something else, something Nate told me once: True love never subtracts, it multiplies. Like loaves and fishes.

I'd learned so much from him.

I finally began to relax. The beating of the rain on the roof had about lulled me to sleep when Scott called. They'd found another bomb.

16

THEY FOUND the bomb before it exploded in a backpack in front of a post office in Winchester. Someone had stopped the cop Scott was with to tell him about the backpack. "It could be some kid just left it," the citizen said, half-apologetically, "but it's odd."

"Thanks for telling us."

Sure enough, it was a bomb.

This time, Scott had been able to stay and watch the bomb squad diffuse it. According to ATF, it was made exactly the same way as the others, same number of turns on the wire, same detonator, same nails inside the same pipe. "That's what makes them believe it's a veteran, somebody with professional experience, who's done this over and over," Scott told me.

"What do you think?" I asked him.

"The longer I stay on this case, the less I know. It's chaotic."

Chaos. Interesting word choice.

"How's Nate?" Scott asked, changing the subject.

"He wants to head back to work." Then I blurted out the whole story about adopting Harper Lee.

"Wow," Scott said. "That's a big step. Is he up for it?"

"He thinks he is."

"His hearing?"

"About 80 percent."

"And his memory?"

"Nothing," I said. "Nothing about that day."

A silence grew between us. "I miss you, Jess. Are you okay?"

I swallowed, tears welling in my eyes. "I miss you too. I'm praying you catch this guy soon, and that you'll be safe. Please stay safe."

"I will."

"Are you sleeping? Eating? How's your hip?" He still had pain from his shooting incident a year ago.

"I never sleep well anymore without you. The rest of it's okay."

That meant he was in pain, eating erratically, and yeah, not sleeping. I tried to make light of it. "How is it we both lived single for years and years, and now we can't sleep without each other? No one told me this was part of marriage!"

He laughed. "What can I say. I'll be home soon as I can, Jess. Give the big guy a treat for me. I love you."

I clicked off the phone. Luke sat at my knees, staring up at me. He'd heard Scott's voice. "Did you hear him say 'treat'?" I asked my dog. He stood up and wagged his tail. "Come on," I said, and I walked to the kitchen to find them.

I want Scott home, I want a new house, I want Nate restored, I want all my needs met ... I want ... I was a virtual desire factory.

Not my will, Lord, but yours. Nothing more, nothing less.

Oh, I'm not that mature. I was reading it from a plaque on the wall in Nate's kitchen. I swallowed it like a vitamin. Vitamin G.

I BARELY HAD time to tell Nate about Scott's call the next morning. He and Amanda were headed for the college. She had two classes, and Nate was going to make a pitch for returning to work.

As I chattered away, Amanda grabbed a yogurt and left the

house. Nate glanced toward the door. "She's my ride," he said apologetically. "Tell me more later."

"Where's Laura?" I shouted at his back.

"Already gone."

And there I was, alone in the house.

I slipped on my hooded rain jacket and took Luke and Sprite out. We walked down the driveway. Nate's creek was muddy, but not quite as high as the last time. Both dogs stepped in it, Luke wading around, chomping at the water, and little Sprite following him. The temperature was in the high 70s, going up to 80 today, and the humidity was high. *This rain is ridiculous,* I thought. *It just won't stop.*

I whistled for the dogs, and we walked back up the hill and into the barn. I let the horses out. They didn't care about the rain. In fact, it kept the flies away. The pasture grass had grown well, and soon they were chomping away at it.

You make me lie down in green pastures. The words formed automatically in my mind. How hard it is for me to rest, to stop the cravings in my soul, cravings for action, for movement, for the next good thing. *I want Scott home, I want a new house, I want Nate here, I want ... I want God to hear me, to answer my prayers, to speak clearly into my life ...*

Really, is all that too much to ask?

We walked back to the house, and I hosed the mud off both dogs. I grabbed some old towels from the laundry room and dried them as best I could, then we went back inside.

I fed the dogs. I knew I should eat, but I didn't feel like it. I grabbed a Kind bar and some cheese and poured myself a cup of coffee. I retrieved my laptop from my bedroom and sat down at the kitchen table. I read a few emails, sent out some more letters to lawyers, and printed off some copies.

Nate and Laura's printer was in their unfinished basement. Nate had moved their office down there to make room for Scott and me when Scott was recovering from his injuries last year.

I could hear the printer working as I flipped on the light and headed downstairs to pick up my printouts. Of course, the printer had spit out the pages all over the floor. I gathered them up and used the desk to neaten the pile. As I did, my eyes fell on a note on the desktop in Laura's handwriting—information about little Harper Lee. Her date of birth. Her father's name. Her address.

My heart thumped. My mouth went dry. And then I crossed a boundary—I picked up a pen from the desk and copied down those facts.

I'm a curious person. It's part of what made me a good detective, and now a good PI. I think Laura would have readily shared all that information with me had I asked, but hey, it was right there, and she wasn't, and well, I took advantage of it. Which was wrong.

Back upstairs, I started cyber-sleuthing Harper Lee's family. It really was not that hard. I started with her birth certificate. Then I looked up her address.

Her father lived in a small, one-story, 1950s-era house outside of Winchester. Using Google, I found it. I could see it was built into a hill, so the front porch was off the ground enough that there was storage underneath and eight or ten steps going up. I could tell there was some sort of a basement, too, with an outside entrance. A driveway led around the right side, and there were no other houses in sight.

Harper's father's name was Charles Edward Lee. It wasn't hard to find things on him—a couple of DUIs, minor drug offenses, and hunting out of season. I couldn't help but wonder if Charles Lee's family was hungry, and so he headed into the woods. The last census listed him as a "handyman."

Ciara (which I think is pronounced "Kee-ra") Ahearne Lee was Harper's mother. Hers was a sad story. She had a college degree in English from a small college in West Virginia. There, it seems, she got pregnant and married Charles. Harper was the result. But something went south with Ciara. She had arrests for heroin, a court-ordered stay at a rehab center, more arrests, this time for opioids, and then she died of a meth overdose when Harper was five.

Sad, sad, sad.

But I thought the whole meth thing was old news. Why was she using meth? I looked it up and found that while the first wave of the meth epidemic died down after 2006 when DEA began controlling sales of decongestants, a second wave, featuring purer, cheaper meth from Mexico, had begun in 2014. It started in the west and spread east. By 2016, West Virginia had the highest meth death rate in the nation. And West Virginia was a stone's throw away from the area where the Lees lived.

So Harper's mother was a meth addict and died when Harper was five. But what happened that made the little girl stop talking?

I noodled around some more on the Internet but found nothing to answer that question.

Now I had an even bigger question: What would I do with this information?

NATE AND AMANDA arrived home about two. Eye to eye with Nate, I felt guilty about my cyber-sleuthing, and I knew I'd have to tell him. But not now.

"They want a doctor's note," Nate said, "but it was good to be back. I had a good time."

"He fixed some things for them," Amanda said. "A lawnmower, a restroom ... what else, Nate?"

He grinned. "The president's desk was broke. The drawer needed a screw is all. It took me two seconds."

"And it helped your case," I suggested.

"That too." He walked over, opened the front door, and stepped out on the porch. I followed him. "Ain't seen rain like this for years." He gestured toward the horses, grazing at the bottom of the hill. "We'd best bring them in afore nightfall. I don't want to be dealing with them in the dark."

"The creek looks high again."

"It is. I was afraid Amanda's Rogue weren't gonna make it." He shook his head. "Hay crop's so beat down I'm not sure it'll recover."

"Scott called."

Nate turned to me. "Yeah? What's the news?"

I updated him.

"Same kind of device?"

"It looks like it so far."

"I'm expecting them feds to come knocking on my door again."

My eyes widened. "Again?"

Nate's jaw shifted. "Yeah." He told her about Carmichael.

"You didn't tell me about that! Have you told Laura?"

He shrugged.

I frowned at him, which is as close to a rebuke as I could get. "Did you contact that lawyer?"

Nate stayed silent for a minute, then looked over his shoulder. The front door was standing wide open, but Amanda was nowhere in sight. "I ain't been working. Laura neither. I need to buy another vehicle. Payin' for a lawyer when I ain't done nothin' sticks in my craw."

"Nate, I'll loan you the money. If Scott says you should have a lawyer, you should do it. These feds ..." I let my thought trail off. I mean, Scott was a fed, but I'd seen too much for me to trust they were all as honest and fair as he was.

Nate's jaw was set.

"Have you prayed about this?" I asked. "Are you being proud by refusing my offer?"

He blew out a breath and shook his head in frustration. Then he looked at me and grinned. "Funny, I couldn't hear none of that," he said.

. . .

In late afternoon, the rain stopped. We called the horses into the barn. I took a picture of Ace and sent it to Scott. I'm sure he missed his horse, just like I would miss Luke.

The four of us, Nate, Laura, Amanda, and I had dinner and were playing a cutthroat board game called Wahoo while discussing the best way for Amanda to tell Scott about Ethan, her boyfriend. That conversation was as hilarious as the trash talking that's part of the game.

But when she told us she was going to move in with Ethan, we all got quiet.

"What?" she said. "You all don't need me here anymore. I love him. So what's the problem?"

Five years ago I would have said the same thing. That was before Nate, even before Luke, before my whole life got turned upside down by God.

"I think you should talk to your dad," I said quietly.

Amanda tossed her head. "Why? I know what I'm doing."

"He cares about you. He wants what's best for you. And he's developed some wisdom over the years."

She shrugged. "And he's conveniently never around." Although they were directed at Scott, her words stabbed me right in the gut. I realized then that Amanda, too, had holes in her heart.

"I'd like to meet this guy," Nate said, his voice surprisingly upbeat.

Amanda smiled. "Okay! I'll invite him out some time."

Yes, I thought. *Let Nate get involved in this.* He had a way of reaching people that didn't want to be reached. Like me.

About nine-thirty we were tiring of our game. I was anyway. I was ready to call it a day.

Then my phone buzzed. So did Nate's, so I knew without looking it was a callout. "A hiker missing up near Rapidan," Nate said.

"In a park?" Laura asked.

"A wildlife management area," I said. "Must be a couple thousand acres." I knew the place, sort of. I'd run a race through there. Lots of woods and a pretty stream running through it. "The roads are rough getting in there, but there are some pretty hiking paths. Are you in?" I asked Nate.

He started to say yes. I know he did. But then Laura put her hand on his. "Nate, honey, don't go. This rain ... it's started up again, and it'll be dangerous. And you with one leg, and your lungs aren't fully healed."

He glanced at me.

"She's right. Let this one go by. We can handle it," I said. "There's no reason for you to go out in this mess." I raised my chin, projecting confidence, but in my heart, I wished he would come. Nevertheless, I stood up to seal the deal.

"You sure?" Nate said, looking at me.

"Yes, we're fine. I'm texting Bill that Luke and I are coming."

Luke's head had popped up when I rose from the table. "You want to go?" I asked him. Of course he did.

I gathered my stuff—a rain jacket, an extra set of clothes, and my SAR pack. I decided to wear my old boots since it was so wet outside, but I put my new ones in the Jeep as a backup. Laura quickly gathered some food for me and filled a Thermos with coffee. When I was ready to leave, we all gathered and Nate put his hand on my back and prayed for me. His words enveloped me like incense, and I felt the warm rush of faith.

Minutes later, Luke and I were on the way, headed about an hour south and west toward the eastern slopes of the Blue Ridge mountains. At just after ten in the evening, traffic was light, and it was easy to see to drive. That was good. Water still stood on the roads and in some places washed over them. "Turn around, don't drown" remained the mantra of the radio stations. I'd seen enough in my years of living in the country to remind myself of that now.

One year when I was living in the basement apartment of a lawyer's house not too far from Nate's, the rains were heavy for three or four days. I drove home from a Battlefield meeting around ten that night and noticed the farm fields were flooded. Water spilled over the road and creeks rose out of their banks.

I heard the next day the firefighters (all volunteer by the way) were called out to do a water rescue around midnight. An older woman living in a little brick rambler got up to use the bathroom and decided to open her window to listen to the rain. She heard a faint cry for help and called 911. A man driving home to Culpeper in a small sedan had been swept off the road. His car floated into a field and lodged in a cluster of small trees. He climbed out of the car and onto the roof and was clinging to those scrawny trees when rescue workers found him.

Country roads in flooding rain are nothing to fool with.

I hoped that my friend Carol would respond to this search. Turns out the rains south of Nate's had been even worse than what we had, and she'd been called out for her job as a deputy sheriff.

"They need everybody," she told me when I checked to see if she was coming. "We have so many accidents and people off the road. We're working double shifts."

By the time I entered the conservation area the rain had begun again. After crawling for about a mile and a half on the rough access road, I pulled up to the search command center. I saw Bill's SUV, an ambulance, and two sheriff's cars. Were Luke and I the only K9 team responding?

17

I CHECKED my weather app before I got out of the car. Wind was projected for the next day, which would help dry things out, but overnight it would be dark and wet, rain dripping off trees and mud under my boots.

"Thanks for coming, Jess," Bill said as I walked up to him. "I thought you'd be too far away."

"I was at Nate's," I responded.

"He said he's not coming."

"No. Not this time." I heard some noise and turned to see two other SUVs approaching. *Ah, good,* I thought. *Joe and Emily.*

"Let's wait until they get here, and I'll brief you then," Bill said.

A few minutes later, four of us gathered. My friend Emily, who'd brought a walker with her, Joe, and myself. Bill was over talking to the deputies. He briefed us when he returned.

"We're looking for a fifty-six-year-old male, white, about five feet ten, two hundred twenty pounds, diabetic. He had an argument with his wife...left the house at about two this afternoon."

I immediately wondered why he wasn't at work, why he was home at that time.

"Deputies found his car," Bill said, continuing. He gestured toward a beat-up Jeep Wrangler beside the lane I'd driven up. "They've searched what they could. They're asking us to cover this area." He held up a topographic map and gestured toward an area that I guessed was around a hundred acres. "Tomorrow, they'll bring out drones and another search group if needed."

"Is he a suicide risk?" I asked.

"Not that we know, but he is diabetic. That's the concern about him being out overnight. His wife said he often came up here to hike. But he didn't take his meds with him, so we need to find him."

"He came up to hike with rain in the forecast?"

Bill shrugged. "Sometimes a guy's just got to get out."

I suspected he knew what he was talking about.

"Here are your assignments." He handed out topo maps. I was impressed he'd come prepared with plastic sheaths to keep them dry. "Jess, you take this area all the way to the creek. Deputy Danny Poland is going to be your walker."

I looked at the area marked on the map. You can tell how steep the terrain is by how close the elevation lines are on the map. My area was the least steep of the three we'd be searching, but it was also the largest, which was pretty smart since it would take more energy to work those steep areas.

"Okay, go when you're ready. And good luck."

I GOT Luke out of the car and let him sniff and water the bushes. Then I put on his new SAR vest—reflective material with LEDs in a cross pattern. It was a breakaway style. I sure didn't want him getting hung up in brush, but I thought it would be nice on a night search to be able to see him better.

The deputy came over, and I introduced him to Luke. "Have you done this before?" I asked Danny.

"No, ma'am, but I've hiked and had dogs my whole life."

I explained to Danny the basics of what I needed him to do. He knew how to work a GPS, thankfully, and a little about topo maps. The lane we were standing on branched off to the left, and that was the way we'd be going. The other two teams would follow the lane further into the conservation area, then branch off from there.

I like to play a little game with Luke sometimes to get him revved up (not that he needs much revving up!). With him facing me, I touch one front leg and then the other. He turns his head first one way, then the other, until we're in a little dance. I love that dog!

After that, I had him heel, pointed him down the path, and said, "Seek! Seek, Luke, seek!"

He shot off, his LED lights bouncing through the darkening woods. "He doesn't need a scent article?" Dan called out. He was behind me about ten feet.

"Nope!" I yelled. I'd explain later that Luke was an air-scent dog, trained to find any human in the search area, which I defined for him by directing him with hand signals and commands. We were a team. He was the nose, and I was, well, maybe the brain? Well, *part* of the brain.

Searching the woods at night is always dicey. Your flashlight casts shadows that move. You can't see your footing. It's not unusual to see animal eyes staring at you. And occasionally a bat will fly by way too close. Once we had an owl dive-bomb us like in a scene from *Harry Potter*.

We searched for an hour, then took a break. I poured water into Luke's collapsible bowl. Danny had brought a bottle for himself, and I was packing several. Humidity seemed to hang in the air like a gauze curtain. The ground was slippery under foot and periodically rain-soaked tree branches dumped a load of water on our heads. At least the temperature was moderate. We weren't cold, and we weren't sweltering.

Two hours in, we had searched the south route. Then we

turned east, paralleling the stream that formed the edge of our search area. The normally placid, bubbly mountain creek raged from all the rain. I could hear it, although heavy brush kept us from seeing it.

We reached an old fence line, the boundary of our search area, and turned north, heading back to where we'd started. Suddenly, Luke doubled back, catching a whiff of something. I turned and saw he'd taken an interest in a place just off the path. Was he smelling an animal?

I went back to him. He looked up at me. "Seek, Luke! Seek." He took off and headed toward the creek. I gestured toward Danny. "C'mon."

We followed him through the dense vegetation on what might have been a deer path. Branches lashed me, rocks slid beneath my boots, and brambles caught my ankles. Luke headed straight, his head lifted, his nose picking up whatever scent he had caught. He started running and disappeared ahead of us, his LED lights occasionally showing up between the trees. Then he disappeared altogether.

I quickened my pace. My SAR pack seemed to weigh a thousand pounds. I slipped, falling to one knee. Danny caught my elbow and helped me to my feet. "Thanks," I said, breathless.

I heard a bark. I expected Luke to come back and tug on the braided rope on my belt. That was his indication. That's what he always did.

Not this night.

Back on my feet, I suddenly got disoriented. Which way had Luke gone?

"That way!" Danny said, pointing.

I took him at his word. The roar of the creek grew louder. I fought through a thick patch of mountain laurel, the stiff branches ripping and tearing at my clothes. Then I heard something that terrified me. Dogs! Fighting!

I jerked away from the bushes and ran. When I emerged from

the woods, I saw a man lying on the ground next to the white, raging water of the creek, and Luke and another dog in mortal combat. They were rearing, mouthing each other, paws flying, teeth flashing, growls piercing the night. The other dog, twice Luke's size and a mountain of white, had his mouth around Luke's neck.

I yelled, grabbed a stick, and raced toward the dogs. Before I could get to them, I saw the white dog put Luke on the ground. Luke squirmed out from under him, and as he was getting up, the dog knocked him sideways. Horror raced through me as I saw my dog roll over and fall down an embankment and into the water. I heard a splash. I screamed "Luke! Luke!" But the roar of the creek carried my voice away as swiftly as the water carried him.

I panicked. "Take care of the man," I yelled to Danny. I dropped the stick and threw my radio his direction. "Call it in." My heart was in my throat.

I had to save my dog.

My chest felt tight as I took off running downstream, tripping over branches, sliding down the embankment, climbing back up again, fighting, fighting to catch up with Luke. And then I saw it! His lights. I saw his LED lights blinking up ahead.

"Oh, God, please, please ..." was all I could say. In the darkness I could barely make out the tree that had collapsed into the creek. The lights were caught on it. Luke was caught on it. But where was his head? Was he trapped underwater?

I raced toward that tree. I set my pack down and, my jaw clenched, I crawled out over the thick trunk, then worked my way through thinner limbs and branches hanging out over the water. Some broke under my weight, and I fell partway into the creek. I managed to climb back up. I gripped the tree tighter.

"I'm coming Luke, I'm coming," I called out. I continued crawling out, the branches growing thinner, the smell of fresh mud and crushed leaves filling my nose. And I made it to the lights, grabbed the vest, and pulled hard, thinking I'd pull up my eighty-pound shepherd. Instead, the breakaway vest emerged, alone, empty.

I panicked. Again. Had I freed him only to lose him again? I scrambled over to the downstream side of the fallen tree and saw nothing, nothing but white, frothing waters, mud, rocks, debris floating by in a mad parade. No dog.

I lost it. I screamed, "Luke!" *Luke! Where was Luke? Oh, God, where is my dog?*

Then I heard a terrible roar. I looked upstream and saw a black wall of water, trees, and debris racing toward me. I squeezed my eyes shut, ducked my head, and gripped the tree. The wall hit. I heard a loud *crack!* My tree broke loose, rotated, and pitched me into the water.

Instinctively, I fought my way to the surface, kicking with my heavy boots. Suspended in inky blackness, tangled in tree branches, I fought and fought until by some miracle my head broke free. I gasped for air. I choked. I sputtered. I went under again, and then, when I thought I could take no more, that raging stream slammed me into a mound of debris, debris that was stationary, and I grabbed onto it.

It was, I would later discover, a shed washed down from an old farm upstream. The roof had come off in one piece, and I pulled myself up on it and lay exhausted, gulping air, willing my shaking muscles to relax, thankful the roof was stable.

When another surge of water hit me, rocking the roof, I knew I needed to move. I could barely see in the dark. I reached for my phone with its flashlight in my back pocket. It would be better than nothing.

No phone. I'd left it in my pack.

Squeezing my eyes shut against tears, I took three deep breaths. The words, *You've been bought with a price,* rose up from somewhere deep in my soul. *I'm not my own. I'm not alone.* "Lord," I said, "please help me. Help me get to land. Help me find Luke. Please, please help me find Luke."

Setting my jaw, I worked my way across the rubble. I found the fallen tree the rubble was wedged against and the collection of large rocks holding it firm. "Help me, help me." Holding onto the tree I made my way over those rocks until my hand touched soil and leaves and with one more microburst of energy I scrambled onto land. Sweet land.

I lay there for a while gasping, gagging, recovering, and listening to the roar of that creek, then I rolled over and sat up to assess my injuries. As far as I could tell nothing was broken. I had pain in my left arm, but I could move everything. I was soaking wet and cold. My feet ached. Before I could stop myself, I tugged off those boots.

When the wall of water hit, I was on the tree and my SAR pack was on the side of the creek. Now, separated from it, I catalogued my losses: my compass, dry clothes, rain jacket, water, first-aid kit, food, emergency shelter, emergency whistle, mylar blanket, and everything for Luke. For a few minutes, that list overwhelmed me.

There's a mnemonic hikers use for situations like this: S.T.O.P.

1. Stop. Don't panic.
2. Think about your situation.
3. Observe. Gather information so you can figure out where you are.
4. Plan. Consider possible courses of action, then pick one.

I knew I was downstream from where I'd left Danny but probably hadn't gone as far as Luke. My pack was upstream. Luke was downstream. I was cold. I had no food or water. In addition to losing my phone, I'd lost my watch, so I had no idea what time it was. I was not the type of person to passively wait.

I decided the logical thing to do was walk back to my pack with its food, clothes, and raingear, and then reevaluate. The downside? Every step would take me further and further from my dog.

Right away, things went bad. My feet had swollen, and I could not get my boots back on. I made my first irrational decision. I'd walk in sock feet.

I felt the rain pelting me, just a little at first, then in great sheets pouring down like a waterfall. Within minutes, I was soaked to the skin again. My hair lay plastered to my head.

I walked and walked for I don't know how long. It seemed like hours. The pack I had expected to find just upstream was MIA. I lost track of where I was and how far I'd come. I tripped on an exposed root and fell flat. I was collecting stone bruises like souvenirs. And I was farther and farther from Luke with every step.

My dog. My search partner. My buddy.

I stopped in my tracks. I dropped my head and prayed. *Oh, God, please let me find him. Please.*

My lack of sleep, water, and food, plus the stress and exertion, finally overtook me. I made my second irrational decision. I turned around. I could not stop looking for my dog.

I don't know how long I walked downstream. My mind played tricks on me. Had I heard a dog bark? Was that my pack up ahead? Had I seen a light?

I walked and called, walked and called, until I literally fell asleep walking. I had no idea you could do that, but I was moving forward, my eyes closed, and I fell into a small feeder stream. The fall woke me up with a jerk. It was everything I could do to drag myself out of that little creek and collapse under a tree.

I jerked off my wet socks, curled into a fetal position, and slept, shivering, for the next several hours. Hypothermia and thirst set in. When I awoke, I knew I was in trouble.

18

Nate's call at 3:00 a.m. made Scott bolt out of bed in his hotel room. He began pulling on clothes as he listened.

"Alls we know," Nate said, "is she took off after that dog and nobody's found her yet." The emotion in Nate's voice made Scott move faster. "We got everybody searching, twelve people, and more on the way. We'll get a chopper up at dawn if the weather holds. I'm just hoping she didn't go in the water."

"The water?"

"The creek that dog fell in is more like a river now, draggin' trees and debris down the mountain. Mud. Took down some houses and barns on the way. Storm came in and just sat. Didn't move for like eight hours. We got bridges out, landslides, debris washing down. Things are a mess. Two confirmed dead already."

Scott tried to absorb that information. "She's not answering her cell phone?"

"No."

"Radio?"

"She left the radio behind."

Oh, Jess. "Send me your exact location. I'll be on the road in ten minutes."

"You drive careful, Scott." His voice had a catch in it.

SCOTT CALLED MIKE, waking him up from a sound sleep. "Unlock your door. I'll be there in five."

He finished packing, grabbed his laptop, and went next door to Mike's.

"What's going on, man?" Mike asked through a big yawn.

"I need to leave. Family emergency. I need you to take over these interviews. I'll be gone for a bit."

"Okay. Something wrong with your wife?"

"I told you she's involved in volunteer search and rescue. Now she's missing. I've got to go." There was no point explaining about Luke. A lost dog wouldn't be a reason to leave a task force operation.

"You don't think they'll find her when it gets light?" Mike yawned again.

"There are complications." *Jess will be devastated if we can't find Luke,* Scott thought. *I need to be there for her.* "Look, here," he said to Mike. "These are the interviews you need to cover for me. I'll call Hitchens and tell him I'm leaving. I'll be back ASAP."

"Okay, man, I'll pick up the slack. No worries. Go find your wife."

DRIVING his Bucar for personal business was not allowed. Scott couldn't risk such an obvious infraction. So he drove an hour and a quarter to Manassas, navigating those roads as fast as he could, his mind jumping with scenarios. He put the Bucar in the garage. On an impulse, he ran upstairs, found all the clean laundry Jess had done, dumped some in an overnight bag, and grabbed some clothing for Jess, just in case. Then he jumped in his new personal SUV, a black Toyota Sequoia, and headed for Greene County.

He didn't call Hitchens until 6:00 a.m. No sense waking a sleeping bear. By that time, he was within half an hour of the search location.

He'd been praying on and off all the way down. He couldn't imagine Jess losing Luke. He'd seen her handle a lot of hard things, but losing Luke? That was a bridge too far, and he had to be there to support her, even if it was hard to explain to the task force.

And if Jess herself were ...

He couldn't complete that sentence, not even in his own head. His throat grew tight at the thought of it. That would be too much for him. Way too much. *No, God. Please, no.*

The call with Hitchens went as he expected. Hitchens was irritated. Scott assured him Mike would cover for him. Hitchens fumed. Scott held the line.

He would be there for Jess, regardless.

Hitchens threatened to write him up. "Do what you have to do," Scott responded.

THE DAY HAD dawned sunny and bright. The storm had moved east, sucking all the clouds away. Water still stood on the roads, deep in some places. The hay in farm fields next to the road had been beaten down. Cornfields were flooded. Scott wondered how much of the crop would be lost.

Scott hadn't had a chance to study maps of the area where he was going, but he could imagine it. Acres and acres of woods in the foothills on the eastern slope of the Blue Ridge, a few trails running through. Hilly, rocky. Dense tree cover. Lots of deer, possums, racoons, birds, snakes, and other animals. On the radio he heard the rains had washed out some bridges. He hoped he wouldn't get caught up in any detours.

He didn't want to think about Jess in the creek. Not now. Not ever.

Oh, God, no. Not that. Please.

Scott turned on the radio to derail the obsessive fear wrapping around him like a snake. Unfortunately, all he got was news, first of the bombing, then the floods.

He turned it off, took a deep breath, gripped the wheel, and prayed.

19

THE SUN WOKE ME UP. I tried to check the time but didn't have a watch. Why? I thought I had one. Where ... ?

I groaned and sat up. My entire body hurt. Then reality hit me like a bolt of lightning. *Luke! Luke!* Luke was gone, and I hadn't found him, and why wasn't I looking for him? Fear shot down my spine. I needed to get going. I tried to find my boots, but I couldn't. Then I remembered taking them off in the night.

I couldn't just stay there. I had to move. I had to find Luke.

I pulled on my socks, still wet with rain, and got to my feet with the help of the tree. My head swam. I waited for it to clear. Dry heaves overcame me. When it was over, my tongue felt big as a cow's.

I'm thirsty. God, I'm thirsty.

I thirst.

I knew not to drink the stream water because of bacteria. Instead, I sucked rainwater out of my shirt and licked it off broad green leaves. When I had gotten what I could, I stumbled forward, sock-footed, aching. I had to find Luke.

I don't know how long I walked. My chest felt tight. I thought I saw Luke up ahead, lying next to the stream. I hobbled forward, rocks cutting my feet. When I got close, I realized I was hallucinating. No dog. No Luke. Just rocks and debris.

The stream was calmer than yesterday, still over its banks but calmer. (Was it just yesterday? How long had I been walking?) Luke was strong, I told myself. Active. A good swimmer.

If he saved himself, if he swam out of that creek, at least he'd be alive. And maybe somebody would find him and then find me. Or some family would adopt him, and he'd have kids to play with, something I couldn't give him.

I began to cry, then sat down on a broad flat rock to catch my breath. The sun had warmed that rock, and it felt so good. I lay down and soaked in the heat. I laid my cheek on it. It felt like ... like my dad's warm chest when I was little and sat on his lap. Soon my eyes closed. I saw a sunny meadow with Scott standing in the middle, a huge bottle of water in his hand. Scott. I reached for him. He disappeared. I opened my eyes. No Scott. No water.

I jerked awake. *No. You can't sleep. You have to find Luke.*

Luke, oh Luke. Please come back to me.

20

WHEN SCOTT PULLED up to the search command post at 0700, the first thing he saw was Jess's white Jeep, parked off to the side. Seeing it there, empty, made his throat close. He swallowed hard, put his SUV in park, and stepped out.

The chopper was already overhead. He could hear its rotors beating the air. But he knew that forest was dense, and Jess could be down there hidden from view. *Unless she builds a fire. But with wet wood? Unlikely.*

Nate stood in a cluster of sheriff's deputies and volunteers gesturing toward a map. Scott could instantly tell he'd taken control of the volunteers, probably the whole search. He walked over. Nate acknowledged him with a nod. "This here's Jess's husband. Scott Cooper, FBI."

The men nodded. A few of them shook his hand. But they were all business, and Scott was glad for that.

Nate had a topo map just for him. Scott studied it while he listened to what Nate was saying. The K-9 searchers on scene were about to rotate off. They'd been searching for five hours. Another group was getting set to take over. Nate gave them instructions. They were to start at 0800.

Listening to Nate's briefing gave Scott a chance to gather questions in his own head. As the others walked off, he was able to go one-on-one with Nate. "Help me understand the order of events," Scott said. "Jess came here to search for a man ..."

"We got the callout at 2200 last night. She responded, and I imagine she got here about 2300."

"So it was dark and raining," Scott said.

"Yes. So she began searching at 2330 with that deputy yonder, Danny Poland. There were three teams out. She and Luke ran their course, then he alerted on a side path, just a deer trail. Jess followed him. A few minutes later, Danny says they heard dogs fighting, and Jess, she takes off. The victim was on the ground but his dog, he and Luke was goin' at it. Jess throws her radio at Danny, picks up a stick and starts chargin' at the dogs. Before she gets to 'em, Luke, he falls in the river, stream, really, but it looked like a river last night. And Jess, she takes off after him."

"What time exactly was that?"

"Danny, he was occupied, lookin' at the victim and dealin' with his dog. He calls it in a few minutes later. The log has it at 0135."

"So that's the last time she was seen."

"Yes. This right here," Nate pointed to a place on the topo map, "this is her LKP."

Scott frowned.

"Last known position."

"So she's running at first, but it's along the riverside in flooded woods. She's not making much time."

"Right. I'm told at some points the river, it was running at about twenty miles per hour last night, the water racing down the mountain."

Scott shook his head. "So no way she's catching up to him."

"Right. But that won't keep her from trying."

"So the furthest she could have gotten by now is maybe, what, five miles?"

"She could have gone into the woods, or become disoriented, or be hurt," Nate suggested.

Or she could be in the water, Scott thought. He didn't want to say it. "We know she's headed downstream if she's following Luke. Has anyone walked that distance along the stream? Why haven't they found her?"

"We ain't got the whole way yet. They may have missed her. There's places the brush is so thick she could be hid. Plus we been doing it in the dark. And let's say she found Luke and is trying to make it through the woods back to the road. We haven't looked there yet."

"You're saying she could be anywhere in this area."

Nate nodded. "Right."

Scott took a deep breath, frustrated. "Hey, wait. Can I use Find My iPhone for her phone?" He looked on his phone to find the answer. "Yes! Let me try this." Nate stood by watching. Then Scott shook his head. "Not working. Either the phone is dead, or it has no signal. Wait. Let me try her watch."

That, too, proved fruitless. The snakes crawled in Scott's belly, fear and frustration combining in a writhing mass.

Ten minutes later, Nate's radio came alive again. "Found her pack!"

Nate asked, "Does it look like things are missing?"

The voice responded. "It's zipped up tight, but ... wait, her watch is in the outer pocket."

"She took it off," Scott said. "Why?" He rubbed the back of his neck.

"Look around," Nate said into his radio.

The silence that followed seemed to go on forever. *Why would she take off her watch?* Scott wondered.

"The pack is all muddy and scratched up," the man on the radio said, "like she's been through some heavy brush. Looks like to me it was intentionally set down by a tree up off the high side of the path."

Why would she put her pack down?

"On the creek side," the searcher said, "there's a place where it looks like a tree fell and got swept downstream."

"Take some pictures and send them to me," Nate said, glancing at Scott.

"What?" Scott said. "What are you thinking?"

Nate didn't answer. A couple of minutes later, he turned so Scott could see his phone. Together they looked at pictures of a spot along the bank from which a large tree had been torn out, leaving roots behind.

Scott blew out a breath and turned away. "You think she's in the river?" Fear sounded like anger in his voice.

"Could be. Could be she crawled out on a tree, and it broke loose."

Scott's fist tightened. "Why would she do that?"

"Only reason would be she thought she saw the dog."

Scott's heart sank. He fought to regroup. "So why don't I go downstream and start walking up?" Nate eyed him. Scott continued. "Look, if she was chasing Luke, I know her, she was moving as fast as she could. And, God forbid, if she's in the river, she's going a lot faster. So let's go downstream and work up."

Nate nodded. "You're right. If she ain't hurt, she could be further east than we think."

A car pulled up. Scott turned. His heart jumped. His daughter, Amanda, got out of her Nissan Rogue. "Daddy!" she said, running to her father. "I'm so sorry!"

Scott hugged her. Then he saw the young man who climbed out of the passenger seat. Tall, lanky, no tats that Scott could see, wearing jeans and boots and a T-shirt with a jean jacket over top. Long hair. Who was this kid?

Amanda let go of her dad and saw where Scott was looking. "Dad," she said, "this is Ethan Callahan. Ethan, my dad, Scott Cooper."

"Glad to meet you, Mr. Cooper," Ethan said, extending his hand. "Sorry we're meeting here. What can we do to help?"

Straightforward. Respectful. "I appreciate you coming," Scott said, nodding. He thought about suggesting he and Amanda begin at the bottom and search upstream, but they weren't trained searchers. Then he had a better idea. He turned to Nate. "Tell me if this is okay." He turned back to the young people. "When ..." He closed his eyes and opened them again. "*When* we find Jess, if Luke's not with her, it's going to take some convincing to get her off that trail. Why don't you go back to Nate's and start the lost-dog search. Here ..." he looked at his iPhone, found a picture of Luke, and sent it to Amanda. "Use that, make a bunch of posters, put them on Facebook and Instagram, hang them around the area, let people know we're looking for Luke. Call the shelters, the vets. That way, when we find her, we'll be several steps ahead. How's that sound?"

"Sounds good to me," Nate said.

"Us, too," Ethan responded. He shook Scott's hand again. "We'll see you soon."

Amanda hugged him again. He wanted to hold her forever. "Be safe, Daddy," she said.

They left, and Scott turned back to Nate. "What do you think about me starting at the bottom? I've been studying the map. Look, here's the five-mile mark. Right here, about four miles down, there's an old fire road. See it?"

"Yep."

"I'm wondering if we can move a search team or two in there up to the creek. I want to go with them."

"Hold on." Nate turned and walked toward the cluster of men standing nearby. Scott followed him. "You fellas, can you tell me about this here fire road? Can we get a light truck up there?"

The three men, dressed in boots, jeans, and T-shirts, bent over Nate's map. One guy said, "I hunt there every deer season.

Four-wheelers could make it. It's rough in spots, but if you know what you're doing you got it. But, uh, they ain't allowed."

Nate nodded. "I 'spect we can get permission."

"Permission ain't the problem," a bearded man said. "You can't carry two on a four-wheeler, not safely on that kind of road. Much less add a dog. Be better to try a four-wheel drive pickup. My wife's got an old Toyota that she loves. I'm betting that could do it."

"I'd like to move five people and two dogs up that way."

"Okay," the burly, bearded man said. "I'll ask her to bring it up. Only thing is, if it gets messed up it's on you. I want nothing to do with breaking her truck."

Nate nodded. "What's your name?"

"Buck. Wife's name is Brandi."

"We appreciate your help, we surely do. Y'all meet Scott and the two teams I send you right here, where this fire road cuts off."

TWENTY MINUTES LATER, Scott parked his car down by the fire road. While he waited for the truck, he sent Mike a message asking for an update. He got a text right back. It boiled down to "nothing new." *Same,* he replied.

It was now 0830. Jess had been missing for seven hours. Scott's gut tensed when he thought of it. Why in the world had she tried to find that dog on her own in the dark?

He knew the answer to that. Jess loved that dog, and she would do anything, anything, to save him. Even put her own life at risk.

"Ah, Jess!" he groaned, out loud.

Waiting was killing him. He wanted to run up the fire road, find the river or creek or whatever it was, and turn west. But he forced himself to do the smart thing and stay put. One impulsive decision had ended up with Jess lost. They didn't need another.

To distract himself, he pulled out the small backpack Nate

had given him. Inside he found four bottles of water, a mylar blanket, and a first-aid kit. Good stuff. *Thank you.*

Nate called him. "Searchers found her boots further downstream."

"Her boots?" The words exploded out of Scott's mouth. "Her boots? Why would she leave her boots?"

Nate's silence seemed to roar. Then he cleared his throat. "Wet feet cause a lot of problems. I'm guessin' she took 'em off and couldn't get 'em back on."

"So she kept going? Barefoot?"

"Be patient, Scott. She ain't thinkin' right."

That was an understatement. Scott clicked off his phone, frustration and fear mixing in his gut. "I've got to move," he said out loud. Then he heard engines—vehicles making their way toward him. *Let's do this!*

THE SEARCH TEAMS ARRIVED FIRST, a man and a woman, both with border collies and two deputies to act as walkers. Minutes later, Buck and his wife showed up. Brandi's truck was a beat-up old red Toyota, single cab. She got out, all blonde hair and energy. "Who's in charge?" she asked.

"Scott Cooper." He shook her hand. "It's my wife we're trying to find."

"Show me where you need to get."

Buck stood close as Scott showed her the map, tracing the fire road up to the river.

Buck pointed to a place. "See here? That's where I got that big buck last year. You got to watch the ruts. And mud. But go slow … you can do it."

The two searchers with their dogs and the two deputies squeezed into the back of the truck. Scott climbed in the passenger seat. Reflexively, he looked at the dashboard. The odometer read 253,001 miles.

"Y'all hang on!" Brandi yelled to the people in the back. Then she got in.

"Thanks for doing this," Scott said.

Brandi buckled her seat belt. "My man, he talks big, but he'd go crazy if I was lost in the woods." She glanced in the rearview mirror. "We got a lot of weight back there. We'll see how she handles it." She started the engine and began to move.

Scott's mind was running way ahead of the truck as it crawled up the hill. He was imagining scenarios, preparing for anything. Jess alone. Jess with Luke. Luke by himself. Jess hurt. Luke with her. Anything but death. He could handle anything short of that. *God, please ... please.*

The old truck lurched and groaned as they drove up the fire road. Twice Scott had to get out and move fallen tree limbs out of the way. Once the truck got stuck in a rut, and everyone had to help push it out.

Finally, they crested the last rise. Brandi stopped. "I'm not sure I'm gonna get back up this hill if I go down there. Can you make it on foot from here?"

"Yes," Scott said. "Thank you!"

Everyone piled out of the truck and started walking. Several times one of them slipped. *Smart of Brandi to stop where she did,* Scott thought.

Once they reached the river, they could see the mudline a good ten to fifteen feet up from where the edge of the water was now. Debris was everywhere. Branches, even full trees, and what looked like pieces of a shed had piled up. It was still running hard. Scott could imagine how it must have looked flooded and wondered if Luke could possibly have survived it.

"Okay," Scott said, gathering the group. "Nate said one team should search upriver until you meet up with the folks coming down. The other should go downstream, but no more than a mile. We're just guessing how far Jess could have gotten. Do you have any preferences who does what?"

The two handlers murmured they did not. Scott looked at the guy with the border collie. "Why don't you take the downstream leg. Meg, you go upstream." He hesitated. "I'll go with you." An instant decision. He wasn't sure why he chose that route.

The downstream team set off while Megan got her dog ready. The black-and-white border collie, Bolt, was wired. She could hardly keep him steady. Finally, she told him to search. Within seconds, he disappeared in the woods.

Scott fell in line behind Megan and the deputy. It was rough going, tromping over roots and rocks, slogging through mud. He kept trying to imagine Jess doing it barefoot. Barefoot! In a couple of places, they ran into a dense patch of mountain laurel. The woody branches, hard to push through, tore at their clothes. The second time, they went around them.

At least they were moving. Scott, focused on the task at hand, had to fight impatience. He wanted to be in the lead. He didn't want to be following a dog, going at what seemed like a snail's pace. But he had to trust the process.

After about an hour, the dog began following a scent that led them away from the creek. That, for Scott, was too much. He had to assume Jess was searching for Luke in or near the creek. She wouldn't just strike off into the woods. She would be near the creek, he told himself.

He was about to quit the group and go off on his own when the dog swung back to the creek. Scott heard noises up ahead. His heart quickened. They sped up. He tripped once over a root and nearly fell in the creek himself. Then he heard yelling. A woman screamed, "No, no!"

"Jess!" he cried out loud. "Jess!" He began running, jumping over fallen trees, crashing through underbrush, branches whipping his face. "Jess!" She was alive, alive!

Then he saw them, a small cluster of people and one excited black Lab down next to the water, right next to the water. And he half slid down the muddy bank, yelling, "Hold on! I'm her husband!"

She was sitting on a broad, flat rock, her back up against a fallen tree, her hair disheveled and her eyes wild, her arms outstretched as if she was warding off an enemy. The black Lab who had found her stood nearby, barking.

Scott knelt in front of her. "Jess, Jess," he said softly, "it's okay. It's going to be okay now."

21

Confusion fogged my brain. Why was this dog barking at me? Who were these people? *Leave me alone,* I wanted to scream, but I could not form the words.

And then I saw him, his familiar blue eyes brimming with love. I reached out to feel his skin, to make sure he was real. I felt the slight stubble of his beard, the strength of his jaw, the wetness of the tears on his face.

"I can't find him," I said, my voice strange in my own ears.

"I know, Jess." Scott stroked my cheek. He took my hand in his and kissed it—my dirty, bruised, cut hand—kissed it so tenderly you would have thought it was a baby's. "But we've found *you,* and we're not going to stop looking for Luke."

At the sound of my dog's name, I began to sob. I felt a pain in my chest as if an invisible hand squeezed my heart. "I prayed. I prayed all night."

"I know. Now it's time to get some rest," Scott said, his voice gentle.

"No, no, no."

"Come home with me. They'll keep looking. And when you've rested you can come back."

He pulled out a water bottle and held it to my lips. I drank some and immediately threw up. "Sip it. Just tiny sips," he said.

Someone, some man with a radio in his hand, leaned over and said to Scott, "There's a two-acre cleared field about half a mile away. They think they can put a chopper down there."

Scott nodded. "Let's get you some help, Jess. Will you come with me? Then we can look for Luke."

I hesitated at first, but then his love drew me. I started to stand up, but I had no strength at all. I was a dishrag, limp and wrung out, a dishrag with bloody, swollen feet.

So Scott gathered me in his arms and lifted me up, all one hundred and fifteen pounds of me. As he stood upright, someone steadied him, and Scott shifted my weight in his arms. I buried my face in his chest, and that man carried me, away from the river, through the muck and the brambles and the mountain laurel and the woods, until we reached that grassy meadow. I know people helped him, especially as we went through rough areas, but Scott carried me, and I believe Jesus carried him.

I saw cell phone pictures later and two things stood out—the determination in Scott's jaw and the glint of the tears in his eyes.

In those pictures, I was a mess.

Once we found the meadow, people helped Scott sit down with me still cradled in his arms. I remember hearing the helicopter, I remember them putting me on the rescue board, and I remember tears as they carried me away from Scott. There was no room for him in the chopper. And like a bird, I flew away.

THERE'S a place I go mentally when life gets too hard. It starts out like a cave, a safe cave, the type of cave where a wounded animal would go to recover. The cave offers privacy and protection, but the longer I stay there, the deeper it grows, deeper and darker until it becomes a pit, the Pit of Despair. Unlike the Pit of Despair in *The Princess Bride,* in my pit the anguish is mental, and I am my own torturer. And unlike Westley, I lose my will to escape. Even for true love.

That's where I found myself once I was away from Scott, in the chopper and in the emergency department being treated. I curled into a fetal position, eyes closed, and moved into my cave. I tried to pray, but the cave was too dark, so I moved in deeper and deeper.

They gave me fluids, IV antibiotics, and they cleaned and bandaged my feet. I cooperated as any dishrag would. I answered questions robotically. I didn't care when they stripped off my wet clothes, when they bathed me, when they pricked, prodded, and poked me. I didn't care.

Sometime later, much later, Scott showed up. Reality hit me again. Luke. Where was Luke? I searched Scott's face for hope. What I found was fatigue and sorrow.

I found out later he had walked upstream, retracing my steps, searching for Luke in case I'd missed him in the dark. He didn't find him either.

Scott pulled a chair beside my bed and sat down. He took my hand in his, and he kissed it. "Hey, honey, good news. They're going to let you go as soon as your fever comes down a little. They say you just need to rest and rehydrate and take some meds."

He paused, waiting for my response, but I didn't have one. "Nate is coordinating the search for Luke. Your friends from Battlefield and a bunch of other SAR groups are combing the riverside, all the way down, looking for him. And look ... look what Amanda did!"

Scott held up his cell phone, and I saw a lost-dog poster with Luke's picture and a five thousand dollar reward. Tears gathered in my eyes. "She's putting them all over the area, up and down the river. Everybody's trying to help, Jess. Everybody. Even the radio stations and the news media.

I curled up again, too sad for words.

I drifted in and out of sleep. Then I heard Scott quietly talking. A nurse said the doctor was signing my discharge instructions.

Scott took my hand and squeezed it. "Hey, kiddo, you ready to hit the road?" I opened my eyes. "I've got some clean clothes here for you, and I brought your slides. The doc says you can leave."

I didn't want to leave. I didn't want anything, just Luke.

But obediently, I sat up in bed, then swung my legs over the side, and Scott helped me get dressed. I could barely fit my swollen feet into my slides.

The nurse came in with the discharge papers. I signed them without reading them. Scott left to get the car, and a volunteer wheeled me out. Scott helped me get in, and soon we were on the road.

"Are we going home? To the townhouse?"

"Nate's," he said.

My stomach clenched. *Why? Nothing can heal this. Nothing. Not even the Tanner House of Healing.*

I dozed on and off during the drive, waking up when we started bouncing over Nate's driveway. The stream at the bottom was higher than normal, and it made me think of the churning river and my lost dog. "Could he have survived it?" I said out loud.

I wasn't expecting an answer, but Scott reached over and took my hand. "Nate always says, 'with God, all things are possible.'"

I hobbled into the house. Laura gave me a big hug, then Scott helped me take a shower and wash my hair. He carefully dried and re-bandaged my feet. The cuts were deep, but the swelling had already decreased.

Scott showered, and by the time he was finished, I was most of the way asleep. But I felt him slide in bed behind me and wrap his arm around me and it was a comfort to me.

. . .

When I woke up, Scott's side of the bed was empty. I needed to use the bathroom, so I got up. When I opened the bedroom door, I heard Scott say, "I've got to tell her, even though it's going to be hard."

What? I turned right instead of left and hobbled into the kitchen, where my husband, Nate, and Laura were sitting around the table. "Is he dead? Tell me." I practically screamed the words. My heart raced, my fists clenched.

"Hey, hey," Scott said, jumping up.

He tried to help me sit down in his empty seat, but I wouldn't move. "Tell me!" I demanded.

"It has nothing to do with Luke. We haven't found him yet." Scott gently guided me to the chair. "A lot of people are looking for him. A whole lot. But we haven't found him. Yet."

"Then what's hard? What do you have to tell me that's so hard?"

Scott pulled another chair close and took both my hands. "Jess, you remember the bombing case I'm on? Well, I've got to go back to work. I hate leaving you, Jess. I'm so sorry. Nate said—"

"Just take me to our home." I pushed my chair back and struggled to my feet. "I'll be okay." I pretended I didn't see the looks that passed between them.

"Jess, wait."

"I have to go to the bathroom."

Scott held onto my arm as I hobbled back to the bathroom. Neither of us said a word. When I was finished, he was still out in the hallway. "You ready for something to eat?" he asked.

"No." I hobbled back to my bedroom and crawled into bed. Scott followed me. He gently pulled the covers over me and then leaned over. He found my hand and squeezed it. "Jess, I have to leave."

"Now? Tonight?" I bolted straight up, suddenly wide awake. I swung my legs over the side. "I'll get dressed."

"No, Jess, you're not coming. You're staying here."

"No! I want to go home." I started to get up. The walls of this once friendly house practically screamed *'Your dog is gone. Your dog is gone!'* Luke was the reason I'd met Nate. Luke was the bond between us.

Scott put his hand on my shoulder. "You need to stay here, hon."

"Why?"

"Because the doctor said to watch for signs of increasing fever, pneumonia, and kidney failure. You were in rough shape, Jess, when we found you. You need to be with people."

"Take me home. I'll be fine."

"I won't do that."

"I'm not your prisoner!" I started to stand up, but in my haste, I stepped on my foot wrong, and a searing pain shot up through my whole body. I almost passed out. It was that bad. I sat down and began to cry.

Scott touched my face, stroking my cheek with his thumb. I could not resist his gentle touch. I turned my head and kissed his hand, tasting my own tears. "Jess," he said, his voice soft. "I need to know you're safe, and you will be safe here with Nate and Laura. They'll take care of you. Will you do this ... for me?"

I was too stubborn to say yes, or even nod. I just laid back down, turning my back toward him. He covered me up, leaned over, kissed me, and said, "I love you, Jess. I'll call you."

EXCEPT FOR USING THE BATHROOM, I stayed in my room for three days. Laura would come in to bring me water or soup. I ate very little, but I did drink. Even deep in my cave, kidney failure didn't sound like fun.

One morning when I woke up there was a rose on my night table, a beautiful, perfect red rose.

In a fit of anger, I grabbed it and crushed it in my fist. When I opened my hand, bruised petals fell all over my pillow, red like splotches of blood. Their fragrance, released by the crushing, filled my nose. I wept. That night, I slept unwillingly embraced by the scent of rose.

The next morning, there was another rose, beautiful, perfect, red.

On the third day, I woke up and saw Nate sitting in a chair by my bed, silent, impassive, that empty pipe stuck in his mouth. He didn't say a word, and he didn't look at me. I turned over and went back to sleep.

An hour later, he was still there. I got up and went to the bathroom, and when I was done, I walked past my bedroom door and into the living room. I curled up on the couch, covered myself with a blanket, and went back to sleep.

When I woke up sometime later, Nate was sitting in his chair next to the couch. Not reading. Not watching TV. Not playing his guitar. Not doing anything but staring, his pipe in his mouth.

I sat straight up. "I'm angry. My dog is lost. Nobody'll let me look for him. I'm stuck here."

I went further. "I prayed," I said, challenging him, "the whole time I was looking for him. I begged God to let me find him. I pleaded. I groveled. I made promises and offered to sacrifice anything I had." I looked straight at Nate, straight into those electric blue eyes. "I lay in the mud, freezing, shaking like a leaf, begging God. You know what I got for an answer? Nothing! What kind of father ignores his child like that?"

Nate remained silent.

"Why would he do that?" I braced myself for his defense of God.

Instead, he opened a Bible and took the pipe out of his mouth, and read this:

I cry to you for help and you do not answer me.
I stand and you only look at me.
You have turned cruel to me;

with the might of your hand, you persecute me.

The pipe returned to his mouth.

I sat stewing for a few minutes, then curiosity got the best of me. "Where's that from?" He raised his eyebrows. "That verse. Where'd you get it?"

Nate turned the Bible around and handed it to me. Job.

I gritted my teeth, but I could not resist reading that old book.

22

THE DAY after Scott got back, he called his boss, Gary Taylor, and told him he wanted off the task force. And he told him why. He was concerned about Jess.

Six hours later, Scott got a call from the assistant director. The AD said the director specifically wanted him on the case. He wouldn't say why. He just wanted Scott present. So if there was any way ...

Of course there was a way. There was always a way if the director wanted it.

So Scott stayed. He didn't want to, but he did.

Frustration ate at him. Hitch had him doing interviews of potential suspects and witnesses, but it was all third-rate stuff. Not challenging, and he believed not productive.

Mike had told him the bomb they'd found undetonated, like the one at Deer Park, was a pipe bomb, made of galvanized pipe, black powder, with a cellphone initiator. Both had been placed in black backpacks manufactured in China. Both were constructed the same way.

"Okay," Scott said, "so the guy wants to deliver a message. What's the message?"

Mike shrugged. “We don’t know. We’ve had a few yahoos claim responsibility, but we’ve checked them out. It was all bull.”

“Where are we on materials?” Scott asked.

“We have people checking hardware stores, home centers, and Walmart for purchases of three-penny bright steel nails. We know the backpack came from Walmart. We’re also checking black powder sales and hunting licenses for black powder season.”

“And online?”

“Yep. That, too. They’ve got analysts on it.”

“Okay, I’ll check in with you later. Hitch wants to see me,” Scott said.

HITCH HAD ASKED Scott to stop by the room in the local sheriff’s office that was now serving as the team’s headquarters. He could hear Hitch talking with another investigator.

Scott exhaled his frustration. Grief over Luke and concern for Jess weighed him down. Nothing about the bombings engaged him, nothing seemed so urgent, so critical, so complex that it needed his focus. He wanted to be with Jess. Why was he here?

Because the director wanted him to be.

Why did the director want *him*?

Scott heard a noise and looked up. An ATF agent he didn’t know emerged from the room. Hitch appeared in the doorway and motioned Scott in.

“How are you doing, Scott?” Hitch said as he sat down at the conference table. “Your wife okay now?”

Scott hesitated. He hadn’t expected a friendly exchange, plus he didn’t know how Hitch had found out his family emergency involved Jess. Was he getting paranoid? “She’s fine now, staying with friends.” *No way am I telling him more.*

“Good,” Hitch replied. He stared at his pen, then fixed his

gray eyes on Scott. "You work at BAU. You got any theories about our bomber?"

Scott shifted his weight. His hip was killing him. Ever since he'd carried Jess out of the woods it had felt like someone had shoved an ice pick into it. He hoped he hadn't messed up one of the screws and plates holding it together. Still, he'd do it again. For Jess.

"Sit down, sit down," Hitch said, gesturing toward a nearby chair.

Scott hesitated, then sat down. "I think," he explained, "that the bomber is trying to make a statement."

"What kind of statement?"

Scott thought carefully. "It may be just that he's mad at the world. He could also have a grudge against government, specifically the postal service."

"Because ..."

"Mailboxes, social security office, mail truck, post office."

"What else?"

"He's organized. His patterns are logical. This would contraindicate PTSD as a motivator. The mailbox bombs were a test run. He was perfecting his technique. Now he'll probably stick to that methodology. He plans his moves. We haven't caught him on a security camera or by witnesses. My question is, what was he doing before all this started, what, eight weeks ago? Was there a triggering event?"

Hitch nodded. He seemed to be absorbing Scott's thoughts. His jaw shifted. "You know the surviving victim of the Deer Park bombing."

How'd he know that? "That's right."

"What's his name?"

"Tanner. Nathan Tanner."

Hitch nodded. "He lost his hearing, right? And his memory?"

"Yes, both."

"Any improvement?"

"His hearing is coming back."

"And his memory?"

"No."

Hitch nodded, then continued. "Here's what I'd like you to do. Reinterview these five potential suspects." Hitch handed him a printout.

"What makes them suspects?"

"One lost a job with the post office, three are veterans, and the last guy, well, he is known around here for his black-powder rifle and general hell-raising."

"Why does being a veteran put you on a suspect list?"

Hitch grimaced. "They all dealt with or were injured by bombs."

"Who interviewed them before?"

Hitch waved his hand. "I'm just not satisfied they should be cleared."

"I'd like to see the interviews."

"They're in the database. Mike can help you with that. He's around here somewhere." Hitch slapped Scott on the shoulder. "Glad you're back." Then he walked out of the room.

Scott watched him go, then stared at the paper in his hand. *Busy work. That's all it was.* He pushed his chair back. *I just need to do my job.*

23

In my dreams I could still hear that dogfight. Still see in my mind Luke's head bobbing in the rapids of that river. Still feel the panic as I chased after him.

Anxious thoughts possessed me. What if there were an overhead dam downstream? Would Luke be perpetually caught in the whirlpool in the bottom? I shivered when I thought of that. Even if he was dead, I wouldn't want that. His body going up and down, up and down forever.

I squeezed my eyes to force that image out of my head.

What if someone had found him and decided to keep him, despite the reward? Should we double it?

What if ... what if ... what if?

Anxiety became my food and drink, sorrow the air I breathed.

I was getting reports from Emily every day on the search for Luke. I peppered her with questions, with ideas, with strategies. The reports diminished to every few days, then now and then.

Carol called to check on me. I saw who it was on caller ID and didn't answer. I don't know why. Maybe I didn't want to hear about her new puppy.

On those occasions when I ventured from my room, I either

avoided Nate or badgered him about taking me to the search area. Finally, he agreed to once the swelling in my feet had gone down enough to get my boots on. I kept checking, but they still were too swollen, despite icing and elevating them.

When Scott called, which he did twice a day, I kept my answers short. I knew he'd try to talk me into not going to the search site. I didn't want the conflict, so I kept that to myself.

I also didn't express the depth of my anger or frustration to him. Or my despair. I figured he had problems of his own, problems he was not sharing with me either. So our relationship became polite, shallow. We didn't dare venture into deep waters. Neither of us had the time or emotional energy to pull the other one to safety.

I hid from him the panic attacks I was having at night. Amplified by losing Luke, other losses populated my nightmares. I dreamed of my father kissing me goodbye early in the morning of 9/11 and, in my mind's eye, saw the videos of the towers falling over and over. I saw my Fairfax PD partner, dead in the car next to me. I was jolted awake, crying, night after night, and there was no dog and no Scott there to comfort me.

One day, after a particularly bad night, I sat on my bed and took the point of a knife and pressed it into my hand, hoping that pain would eclipse the sadness I felt. It didn't. So I traced the blade across my wrist, imagining what it would be like to see my skin separate and blood pour out.

My love for Scott was the only reason I put that knife down.

Why would God do this to me? He could have saved my dog. He could have brought him home. He could have at least let me find Luke's body.

Five days went by. I was in my bedroom, reading, when I heard Nate, along with a child's voice. I peeked out and saw the foster child, Harper, playing with him, and I felt a pang of jealousy, longing for my old comfortable times with Nate, yet clinging hard to my hurt. I saw Harper hiding behind Nate's chair, then reaching around to touch his arm. When he swung around fast to see who was touching him, no one was there. Just disembodied giggles.

The two of them were having fun.

He would be a wonderful father.

Sometime later, I heard a tap on my door. I decided to feign sleep. It didn't work.

"Hey," Nate said, coming in.

I pushed myself up to a sitting position as if he'd woken me up. He sat down on the side of my bed.

There's no hiding from Nate. Why do I even try?

"How are you doing?"

"Okay."

"Grievin's hard."

I didn't answer him.

"Anger's easier. It just ain't productive." He stuck his pipe in his mouth.

"I have a right to be angry."

Nate didn't respond at first. Then he said, "Yeah, I used to think that too."

He did? When ...

Then I remembered his service in the war, the dog he lost, the buddies killed, the scars he accumulated, the emotional wounds. And I remembered those wounds still came back on him now and then.

I took a deep breath.

"The thing about grievin' is it brings you face to face with your weakness, your lack of control. That feels bad, but it puts you on the path."

The path to what?

"I get it, Jess. You love that dog. Losin' him is like cutting out your heart." Nate reached over. I thought he was going to take my hand, but instead, he wrapped his fingers around my wrist, the one I'd cut with a knife. "If somethin' happened to you, I'd never get over it. I'd go on, but I'd never get over it."

He'd seen my attempt at cutting. At first, I burned with shame. Then something collapsed inside me—a hardness, a fortress. I began crying. Nate turned toward me, and we clung to each other like Titanic survivors. I shed every tear my body could make. I felt his beard against my face and the strength of his arms around me and the wetness of his own tears. I whispered, "I don't know what to do, how to get through this."

He squeezed me. "When you're weak, Jesus comes near. He don't necessarily fix it, but he comes close and walks through it with you. He hates your suffering."

"Then why doesn't he stop it?"

"One day he will. All the pain and sorrow will be gone. But right now, he's working out a bigger story, one with threads and patterns we cain't see. In the end, though, we'll know he worked it out for the best."

"I miss Luke so much!"

"I know."

"I don't know who I am without him!" Immediately, the phrase taken from the old Heidelberg Catechism popped into my head. *I belong body and soul to my faithful savior, Jesus Christ.* My throat caught.

Then I said, "I can't walk away from God. I just can't. I know he's real. I know Jesus saved me."

He squeezed me again. "And you know he is good, whatever your circumstances look like."

I sat back and blew my nose, then I spoke up. "I want to go back to the conservation area." I waited for Nate's objection. It didn't come. "I need to see it."

His jaw shifted. "Your boots fit?"

I couldn't lie. "No, but my running shoes do."

He nodded. "That's good enough."

I grabbed him. "Thank you!"

Did I expect to find Luke? Frankly, no. The area had been well-canvassed by my SAR friends. The lost-dog finder I had hired had recently been over the place again and had found no trace of him.

So call it a pilgrimage. Or a grief-walk. Call it whatever you want. I needed to go back to the last place I'd seen my dog.

Laura packed some lunch for us, plus bottles of water and coffee in a Thermos, and Nate and I took off in my Jeep. He drove and I sat in the passenger seat, staring straight ahead, thinking, and silently praying.

"You want my pipe?" Nate asked, glancing over with a grin.

I smiled for the first time in weeks.

THE CONSERVATION AREA looked so different in the daytime. The bright sun beat down on fields full of bachelor buttons and Queen Anne's lace, orchard grass, and field daises. As we entered the wooded area, shafts of sunlight pierced through the canopy like swords.

Nate said, "This here was the command post." He parked the Jeep, and we got out. After the air-conditioned ride, the heat and humidity slapped me in the face. Nate opened the back gate and pulled out two sturdy walking sticks, each about five feet long. "These might come in handy," he said, handing one to me and leaning the other against the car. He pulled a map and a compass out of the backpack, then swung it on his back.

"I can carry that," I said.

"No. I got it." He picked up his stick, closed the back, and gestured uphill. "We'll start this way."

I followed him up the path, single file, just like we would if we were searching. We remained silent, both to conserve our breath and absorb the emotions of the moment. I needed to feel everything I needed to feel—sorrow, grief, anger, fear, despair. The whole gamut. Luke was gone. This was the last path we'd taken together.

It took us about twenty-five minutes to reach the spot where my dog had left the trail. My walker had marked it on the GPS, and someone had put a stake in the ground. We pushed our way through the woody mountain laurel patch and memories flooded back. I remember working my way through that mess, then hearing the dogfight and racing forward. In my mind's eye, I could see Luke and another dog, a bigger, white dog, wrestling, hear their snarls, feel the alarm in my chest.

"I picked up a stick," I said out loud. "I was going to hit that other dog. I was screaming at them when I saw Luke tumble into the river."

The "river" today was back to being a creek. The rolling, whitewater rapids that Luke fell into were now a gentle mountain stream, less than half as wide as when I saw it before. I shook my head. All that rain had made it a death trap. "The man we were looking for was on the ground over there," I said, pointing. "I kept wondering why he didn't call off his dog."

"He was passed out," Nate said, quietly, "from diabetes." He looked at me, his eyes soft. "You saved his life, Jess. You and Luke."

"What do you mean?"

"He'd gone too long without food. Blood sugar dropped. He got disoriented and collapsed right there. Your walker recognized the problem. His little brother has diabetes. So he called for help, then found a can of apple juice in his pack and gave him sips 'til the medics could get there. He saved his life, but it was all because you and Luke found him."

"I just wish I'd known he had an aggressive dog with him!"

Nate took a deep breath. "I met that dog. She's a Great Pyrenees, beautiful dog. She ain't aggressive, Jess. She was defending her best friend, lying helpless on the ground, just like Luke would've."

I stood stunned. Tears came to my eyes. I wanted so much to hate that dog, be angry at that man, now ... how could I?

Nate moved next to me and gave me a side hug. "It's so sad. But I don't think it's by chance that you and Luke found him and that your walker knew what to do." His eyes were full of compassion.

We walked downstream a little ways, but with the stream so different, I wasn't sure of the exact path I'd taken. So after about twenty minutes, with a heavy heart I told Nate I'd had enough. "Let's go back," I said.

And so we did. We trudged back to the Jeep, opened the back, sat down, and ate our lunch. While we ate, we talked, and we cried, and we told stories about Luke, and it was like a funeral—good memories, funny moments, loss, tears, laughter, sorrow, and joy. "I was privileged to have him," I said, "and I don't know what I'm going to do without him."

"You know," Nate said after a time, "when I was lying crushed under that building, all I had was Jesus. Not Laura, not you, not Sprite, not anybody. I didn't want to die, but somehow, I knew that having Jesus was enough, whether I lived or died."

For me to live is Christ and die is gain.

"I'm not there yet," I said.

Nate hugged me.

A FEW DAYS after we went to the search site, the man we helped save, Barry Hopkins, called Nate and asked if he could meet me to express his thanks. I said I didn't want to, but Nate insisted. We drove to a café near Charlottesville that had an outdoor eating space. And there I met Barry and his dog, Belle.

I didn't want to like her or him. My heart was hard, my jaw was set, but within minutes, I broke down. Barry was truly grateful Luke and I had found him. And when Belle offered me her big white paw, when I stroked her coat and looked into those liquid brown eyes, all I could see was a good dog, a noble dog. A dog who would protect her best friend with her life.

Luke getting thrown into that river was just ... unfortunate. Dogs being dogs on my darkest night.

I let go of my anger toward them, and a tiny section of my heart healed.

24

In the pre-dawn hours of what would be a hot July day, Scott stood listening to the instructions for the raid about to go down. The phone call with Jess the night before had energized him. She sounded so much better. And as far of a reach as this raid was, he was hoping against hope that it would be productive, and he could finally go home.

"Perez, I want you and Cooper to take the outbuildings," Hitchens said, pointing to a shed and a smokehouse drawn roughly on a sketch pad. "I'll be on the front assault team, and Brody will take the back."

After weeks of interviews and evidence gathering, and under pressure from Washington for progress, Hitchens had obtained a search warrant for a small house outside of Winchester—home of Ronald Burris, a truck driver, bar fighter, and general roughneck. The warrant was based on information from a source, a local unemployed roofer who had called the tip line claiming he knew Burris had been experimenting with explosives. His anti-government opinions were well-known, plus he was in Washington on January 6.

In Scott's opinion, that was pretty thin evidence for a raid of the scale they were executing. But then, he was not the one who'd issued the warrant.

Twenty agents stood in a school parking lot working out the plan. Two explosives-sniffing dogs were on the way. Hitch wanted to hit the home before people woke up. "He's got a woman living with him," Hitch said, "so I expect there to be two people in the house."

"No kids?" an agent asked.

"No. Just Burriss and the woman."

"They have a dog?"

"I don't know," Hitch said, "but if there is and he threatens you, take him out." He looked around at the group. Then he began pointing to people. "You, you, and you go with Perez and Cooper. You and you, and let's see, two more, you and you hang with Brody. The rest of you come with me."

"Should we wait for the dogs?" Scott asked. Having bomb sniffers would help, especially with the outbuildings.

"They'll catch up with us," Hitch said.

The five agents assigned to the outbuildings all piled into Scott's Suburban and started working out their game plan. Mike took the lead, which was fine with Scott.

As he drove, Scott realized his stomach was tight. Was it normal pre-raid anxiety or something else? He listened as Mike outlined a plan of attack.

"Right after they breach the house, we'll hit the outbuildings. Three of you take the barn, and Scott and I will take the shed and the smokehouse. You're looking for black powder, galvanized pipe, burner phones, other bomb-related material, instruction books, or anti-government pamphlets." He paused. "The evidence response team will come in behind us and process anything you find."

"I think it would be smart to wait for the bomb dogs," Scott said. "If what we're looking for is evidence, it's not going to run away."

"Good point," Mike responded. "we'll do that."

Scott pulled off the road, following the three cars in front of him. The plan was they'd park there and creep up the driveway in the dark.

Hitch led the way. When they got to the house, he motioned the outbuilding team and the rear breach team around to the back of the house. As they did, a yellow Lab emerged from under the smokehouse, barking. An agent took aim. Scott touched her arm. "Don't," he whispered. "She's friendly. Look." He held out his hand and the dog dissolved into wags.

A minute later, the *go* command came over their radios. Scott listened from behind the cover of the shed as the team breached the house. His hand on the Lab's collar, he heard a man yelling, a woman screaming, and then kids crying.

Scott looked at Mike. There weren't supposed to be any kids in the house.

Mike shrugged.

The dog, agitated, squirmed out of Scott's grasp and raced toward the house. "Don't shoot her!" Scott yelled.

The sky began to grow light as dawn approached. The yells of alarm in the house had died down, but Scott could still hear the kids crying. He began to wonder just how long it would take for the bomb dogs to arrive. Looking around he noticed something unusual—what looked like a dog house built under the shed's porch. He wondered why the dog hadn't been sleeping there instead of under the smokehouse.

Maybe a raccoon had taken it over. Or a possum. Or a skunk.

Ten minutes after the breach, Hitch came out of the house, agitated. "What are you guys waiting for?" he yelled. "Do your job!"

Scott and Mike looked at each other. "What about the bomb dogs?" Mike said.

Hitch cursed. "Who needs dogs? Just do it!"

Scott took a deep breath. The three other agents moved

toward the barn. "You want the shed or the smokehouse?" Scott asked.

"I'll take this." Mike nodded toward the shed.

"Okay."

Scott had taken five steps toward the smokehouse when something registered in his brain. He turned. "Mike, wait!"

Mike's hand was on the latch. He turned to look at Scott, now running toward him. "Stop!" Scott yelled.

But Mike's hand and his body were already set on opening the door. His thumb pressed the latch just as Scott jerked him away.

The two men tumbled into the yard. The shed exploded with a roar. Scott covered Mike's body as wood and nails and tools flew at them. He could feel the heat of the flames on his back, feel burning debris as it hit his body.

They had to get further away. Scott rolled off Mike, got to his feet, and pulled Mike up. "Come on!"

Dazed, Mike stumbled after Scott. They turned to see the shed fully involved. "You hurt?" Scott asked.

Mike shook his head. He looked at Scott. "Thanks, man. Wow."

Scott brushed himself off. Embers dotted his pants, his jacket, his vest. He touched his neck and felt pain, a burned spot.

It could have been worse. So much worse. Still, Scott's heart pounded. *Man, that was close!*

Hitch strode toward them, cursing. "What happened?"

Scott said, "The door was rigged. As soon as Mike released the latch it blew."

Hitch cursed again.

"This is why we wanted to wait for the dogs!" Scott said, his heart drumming.

"Burris said he had black powder. He didn't say it was rigged to go off! This is attempted murder of two federal officers, that's what this is!" Hitch's face was red.

Something else exploded with a POP! inside the shed. "Move back," Hitch yelled. "Back up."

Scott wanted to say more, so much more. Instead, he turned to Mike. "You need to be looked at. I've got a burn on my neck. You may have burns too. Let's go." As they walked toward the front yard, he turned back to Hitch. "I'm taking Mike to the ER. That smokehouse needs to be checked still. If I were you, I'd wait for the dogs." Too angry to wait for a response, he turned and kept walking toward his car.

·

FOUR HOURS LATER, he and Mike were released from the ER. Scott had a few minor burns on his body. Mike had more, plus the explosion had impacted his balance, a condition which the doctor said should improve in a few days. Scott drove them back to the motel where they'd been staying, and after showering and changing his clothes, he grabbed his laptop so he could hang out in Mike's room just to keep an eye on him. By the time he got there, Mike had stripped off his outer clothes and was in bed asleep and snoring.

Mike's room had a couch and kitchenette on the other side of a divider. Scott moved away from his slumbering friend and called Jess. He needed to talk. He needed to process the anger and frustration raging in his gut. He needed a game plan going forward. He needed Jess.

Before Jess, he would have gone to a bar, had a few, maybe gotten into a fight, at least driven home half-drunk. Or he would have spent several sleepless nights by himself ruminating over the jerk in charge of the mission. Or he would have gone running until exhaustion had expelled the anger.

Now he had someone to call.

So he thumbed her number. When she picked up, she sounded good, more like his Jess. His spirits lifted.

He told her about the case, and the raid, and the explosion.

She was angry Scott had been put at risk that way. She sounded protective. She cared, and that felt good to Scott. They talked about his options and possible outcomes. She told him what her plans were, now that she was starting to feel better. They dreamed a little, about when they could see each other again, about the house they might potentially buy, about places they could go.

By the time he hung up half an hour later, Scott knew that whatever happened with this case, or with his career even, he had a future to look forward to because he had Jess.

Now after talking to Jess, he had a plan.

WHEN MIKE WOKE up late in the day, he said he felt better. Scott went out and got them both dinner, big barbeque burgers with sweet potato fries. They talked about what had happened and then Scott hung around while Mike took a shower.

"You okay if I go out?" Scott asked while Mike crawled back into bed.

"All I'm gonna do is lie here and watch the game," Mike responded, nodding toward the baseball game on TV.

"Your head still spinning?"

"It's better."

"Okay, I'm taking one of your keys. I'll check on you later."

SCOTT CLOSED the door quietly as he left Mike's room. He put his laptop back in his own room, just down the hall, checked to make sure he had his wallet, and then took the elevator back down to the first floor.

Scott knew Mike had gone out after hours with Hitch the week before, and he'd casually asked him where they'd gone and what they'd done. The team was still based in that same motel, and Scott took a chance and drove to the same bar. Sure enough, the parking lot was full of black SUVs.

Putting on a relaxed, happy face, Scott entered the bar. Right away, the smell of sweat and beer hit him hard. He'd spent many nights in bars like this, usually for the wrong reasons. Loneliness. Frustration. Anger. Depression. The four horsemen of his own personal apocalypse. He breathed a silent prayer that this night would be productive, not destructive.

He spotted Hitch right away, sitting at the end of the bar, his back to the wall, talking to three guys near him. Hitch saw him, too, his eyes flicking away quickly when he recognized Scott.

Scott walked up to the bar and ordered a beer. Turning and finding an empty chair, he sat down with three other agents. One of them was part of the crew that went into the barn. "Hey, man," the agent said, "how are you? And how's Mike?"

Scott filled them in and then started asking questions. The barn and the smokehouse were both clear, the agents told him. Only the shed had been loaded with explosives.

"I'll tell you, you saved Mike's life," one of the other agents said. He'd been near the house when the shed exploded and had a clear view of the whole event. "If you hadn't stopped him and pulled him away, he'd have taken the full force of that blast." He took a long drag on his beer. "What made you do that?"

Scott shook his head. "I don't know."

They continued to talk for another half hour. Scott nursed his beer to make it last, casually keeping an eye on Hitch at the same time. Finally, two of the guys decided to leave. Scott took that opportunity to join Hitch, who was now alone, at the end of the bar.

"You're not much of a drinker," Hitch said, firing the first volley as he nodded toward Scott's half-empty glass.

"I have to watch my girlish figure," Scott retorted with a grin. He slid into the empty chair next to Hitch. *Keep it light.* "Sorry I got a little hot back there." He studied his beer. "That shed blowing up shocked me."

"You have a reputation for being a loose cannon."

Scott shrugged. "I prefer to say I think outside the box."

"I heard you assaulted a prisoner during an interview."

Scott's jaw shifted. "Tried to. A good friend stopped me."

"I'm surprised you kept your job."

"Me, too!" Scott turned toward Hitch. The man was probing for a trigger point. Scott wasn't going to let him find one. "Who knew the bureau has a heart?"

"So they buried you at BAU. Couldn't risk having you on the street."

"Yep. It sure worked out for me. Nice, cushy office. Easy job." Scott tried to turn a corner. "So where'd you work before? You got assigned to BAU what, eight months ago?"

"Twelve. I was at headquarters before."

"How long are they going to keep you at BAU?"

"I'm trying to get out now."

Scott took a sip of beer. "Don't like it?"

"Boring. Not enough action for me."

"You still live up near DC?"

Hitch shifted on his barstool. "Fairfax."

"That's a long commute."

"I get a room at the Jefferson when I need to." The Jefferson Dorm at the FBI Academy often had empty rooms agents could use.

Scott nodded. It was time to up the game. "You got a family?"

The skin around Hitch's eyes tightened. Why would that question cause a reaction?

Hitch finished his beer before he responded. "A wife. Kid is grown." He turned toward Scott. "How's Mike?"

"He'll be okay in a day or two. He was watching a ball game when I left."

Hitch nodded. "What made you stop him from opening that shed door?"

Scott shook his head. "I wish I knew. Something about the dog sleeping under the smokehouse, not in the doghouse under the shed. It just triggered something in me." He frowned. "Why'd the guy do that? Why'd he rig his own shed like that?"

"Who knows. He's an idiot."

"But the way it was set up, wouldn't it have blown if he tried opening it himself?"

"Who can figure these guys out? All I know is he's gonna get charged with attempted murder. He says he didn't do it, but who else would have?" Hitch looked at Scott. "What I want to know is did someone leak information about our raid? Did he know we were coming?"

"The way he was yelling made it sound like we surprised him," Scott said. "And with the woman and kids in the house ... seems like he might have sent them away if he knew we were on the way."

"What, you think he's a knight in shining armor?"

Keep it light. Scott chuckled, then looked straight into Hitch's eyes. "I don't know, but I'd want to protect my family. What if those kids had tried opening that door? Or the woman? They'd have been blown up."

Hitch held his gaze for a few seconds, then looked away. Scott saw his jaw flexing, his hands tighten around his empty glass, his neck grow red. Why?

"I got to go," Hitch said suddenly.

"Hey, one more thing before you leave. I'd like to interview Burris."

Hitch raised his eyebrows. "Burris?"

Scott cocked his head, keeping his expression relaxed, friendly. "That's why I'm on the task force, right? Because I'm good at interviewing?"

"Not much to quiz him on. The man had a shed full of explosives. Could 'a killed somebody."

"But did he plant the other bombs?" Scott let that question hang in the air. "I'd really like to talk to him."

Hitch scowled. "I'll see what I can do."

25

AFTER SCOTT TOLD me about the raid, I was angry. Why had he been put in such a dangerous position?

And why did Scott stop his friend from opening that shed door. What made him do that? What about Hitchens' reaction? Scott said it seemed odd.

I lay in bed, curled up under the covers while we talked. After we talked about his job, I told him about going to the conservation area with Nate, about the grief-walk, and talking with Nate afterward, and even about meeting the dog Luke fought with and her owner and letting go of my anger.

Scott was very quiet after all that spilled out, especially when I cried a little. Finally, he said, "I should have been there."

"No, Scott ..."

He interrupted me. "I'm your husband. I should have been there for you."

"I know," I whispered through unbidden tears. I did wish he was there. Desperately. I love Nate, but honestly, I wanted my husband.

"I never told you this," he said, "but I called Gary Taylor and asked to get off the task force."

"You did? When?"

"Right after ... right after I got back from coming to find you."

"What'd he say?"

"He totally got it, and said he'd send it up the chain, but later that day, I got a call from the assistant director asking me to stay on. I asked him why. He wouldn't tell me. He just said the director specifically wanted me on the team." Scott paused. "Jess, the AD advocated for me last year, strongly, when I was in all that trouble. I felt like I owed him. So I stayed. I'm sorry, Jess. I can't do both."

I swallowed the lump in my throat. "I understand, Scott. You stay in the game. They need you." *And so do I.*

No way was I going to be able to sleep after that conversation with Scott. Not for a while. My adrenaline was pumping.

After everyone else went to bed that evening, I made myself a cup of herbal lemon tea and sat down at the kitchen table with my laptop.

My plan was to work on my PI business, but my mind was still spinning with the news from Scott. So instead, I began cyber-sleuthing James C. Hitchens, ATF.

Yes, I knew Scott wouldn't be happy with me. But I wanted to be part of his world. And I was only using the information available to the public ... if the public knew where to look. As I said, I am a curious person.

I ignored social media. Most law enforcement agents aren't going to out themselves on Facebook or Instagram or whatever. If they're there, they're using an assumed name.

Instead, I went straight to five different search engines and collected and sorted through all the "James C. Hitchens" listings. I figured Scott's team leader was maybe fifty. That was a guess, but one based on Scott's comments and on the senior position he held. Then I looked at associated addresses of the four, and when

I found one who had lived in Brunswick, Georgia, Austin, Boston, and was currently in the DC area, I pounced on it. Sounded like an ATF career to me.

I found James Hitchens's current address, two speeding tickets, his marriage license from twenty-nine years ago, his divorce papers dated fourteen years ago, and records of three houses he'd bought and sold.

Then I got a surprise. I pressed deep into the judicial databases, thinking I'd find cases he'd testified on or his record as the arresting agent. No. Instead, up popped convictions for drug possession and distribution. *Not possible,* I thought. Any drug conviction would get a federal agent dismissed immediately. *I must have the wrong guy.*

Confused, I got up from the computer to refresh my tea, my mind working through that problem.

Tea in hand, I turned back to my work. I looked more closely at the drug convictions. I finally found a date of birth and did a quick calculation. This James Hitchens was younger. He would be twenty-eight years old now. His convictions began at age eighteen and repeated every two or three years. It's possible there were juvenile convictions too.

Then I found a middle name: Corbin. James Corbin Hitchens. No "Jr." But what was my original guy's middle name?

I went back to square one, dug deeper, and found Mr. ATF Agent's full name was James Curtis Hitchens. There it was, right there on a court transcript.

So the names didn't match. But wait—could they be related? I needed James Corbin's birth certificate.

That should have been easy. I had the date of birth. But where was he born? I checked the three jurisdictions in the DC area, then worked backward, based on James Curtis Hitchens's prior addresses. Nothing.

By this time, I was hours into my search. It was after 1:00 a.m. I wasn't tired yet. I got up to make more tea.

Sitting down again, I focused on my computer. I knew I could go into the databases I use for my PI work, but if it ever came up, I wanted to be able to say to Scott that I only did what anyone could do. So I kept looking, searching state after state after state. I started with the ones in proximity to Hitchens's known addresses. Then I worked outward.

Hours later, I finally found what I thought was the right record—in California of all places. I didn't see California anywhere on Agent Hitchens's background, but there his name was along with the name of his wife, which I'd found on their marriage record.

So it looked like Hitchens had a son, born in California, who was into drugs. Or is into drugs. Could that explain Hitchens's irritability? His disorganized search methods? Was he dealing with a difficult personal situation, which was distracting him?

I had no way of knowing.

THE LOSS of my dog and Scott's absence felt like a weight, a burden I carried. Other times it felt like an emptiness inside, like my core was hollowed out. Either way, it hurt.

I was well enough now to do a lot of the searching on my own. I'd made a list of vets downstream from the area I'd last seen Luke. I knew I was duplicating my friends' efforts, but I wanted to be sure the list was thorough. I'd also made a list of animal shelters and rescue organizations. I redesigned the lost-dog flyer, adding two more pictures of Luke and my phone number and increasing the reward. Then I spent two days delivering those flyers to vets, pet stores, gas stations, grocery stores, coffee shops, grooming salons, and libraries in my target area.

I rested the next day. Not a single call came in.

Discouraged, I decided to drive to our townhouse in Manassas to pick up the mail and a few other things.

It took me an hour at the post office to retrieve what was

mostly junk mail. After that, I went to the townhouse. The first thing I noticed when I went upstairs was Luke's water bowl and food dish. My chest tightened.

I washed the bowls and started to put them away, but then I stopped myself. That seemed so ... final. I would not admit defeat. I put them back on the floor in their usual place. Then I went through the house. I grabbed some fresh clothes and stared at our empty bed for several minutes, trying to process the wave of loneliness washing over me.

When I was chest-deep in the ocean as a little kid, before I learned to swim, sometimes a swell would lift me off my feet. Even holding my dad's hand, I'd feel unsettled until it passed by and my feet were on the bottom again. That's how these waves of grief felt. And I wondered if I'd ever learn to trust I'd eventually find my footing again.

After a few minutes I went downstairs to the kitchen. I combed through the refrigerator and collected all the outdated food. After looking around once more, I gathered up the clothes and the trash bag and left.

I missed them both, Luke and Scott. On the drive back to Nate's, I fought off my sadness with music and prayer. "I trust you," I said out loud to God. "I'm sad but I trust you. I miss my husband, but I trust you. I miss my dog, but I trust you. Help me trust you, Lord. Help me."

My mother would have thought I'd lost my mind.

I WAS glad to see Nate's old truck when I drove up his long driveway. I wouldn't be alone. When I walked in the house, he was standing in the kitchen with a letter in his hand. I thought it was his medical clearance. I was wrong.

"Look," he said, and he handed me a letter from a lawyer.

Worried, I began reading. Then I saw the words, *RE: The estate of Helen Satterfield Thorpe.*

What? I glanced up. Nate was shaking his head. I read on to find that Helen, who had no children, had left the bulk of her estate to the college. But she'd left Nate $50,000 out of gratitude for his help over the years.

I looked up at Nate.

"I didn't do nothing," he said, "'cept be a friend."

"How many friends do you think old people have?" I thought back to Miss Lottie, a client-turned-friend from a couple years back, who'd left me an inheritance. "You can replace your Tahoe!"

"Nope. This is for a lawyer."

"Good. Scott said that—"

Nate shook his head. "No. Not for that. In case we find out we can adopt Harper." He smiled, his eyes full of light.

They were serious. Okay then.

"How much can you find out about her background," I asked, "before you commit?"

"I don't know. And it don't matter," said Nate. "If she needs a home, she's got one here. Don't matter what her family were like."

That's fierce, steadfast love.

26

FOUR DAYS LATER, Scott still hadn't interviewed Burris. He started looking for ways to make it happen. When Mike let it slip that Hitch would be gone for twenty-four hours, Scott decided to make his move.

He found out where Burris was being held, charged with attempted murder. He knew investigators had found remnants of a bomb similar to what was used at Deer Park at the scene. So Scott worked up a plausible reason to question him. By lunchtime, he was in an interview room seated across the table from Ronald Burris. So there would be no question about what he found out or his demeanor, he brought another agent, Brody Harrison, with him.

Burris looked rough, like he hadn't slept. His eyes were red and puffy. Unshaven, he slouched in his chair listlessly, barely looking up when Scott walked in.

"Take his cuffs off," Scott asked the corrections officer. Burris sat up, rubbing his wrists.

"Mr. Burris," Scott began, "I'm Special Agent Scott Cooper, FBI. I was at your house—"

"I know," Burris interrupted.

"I have some questions about that night, but before we begin, I want to be clear you have a right to have an attorney present."

Burris waved his hand dismissively.

"So you are waving your right to an attorney?"

"I'll talk to you. You're the one saved my dog."

"She was friendly."

Burris nodded. "That's right. And I'm innocent, but that didn't stop them from trashing my house and locking me up. Scaring my family half to death."

"Yes, sir. Let's see if we can clear up some things. Mr. Burris, did you rig your shed with explosives designed to detonate when someone pressed on the latch?"

Burris straightened his shoulders. "No sir, I did not. I wouldn't destroy my own shed. And I wouldn't risk blowin' up those kids."

"Your kids?"

"No. My girlfriend's. They live with us."

"Did you keep explosives in that shed?"

"Yes, sir. Some black powder."

"How much?"

"I had two cans. Been there for a couple of years."

"Why do you keep black powder?"

"I used to hunt with a black-powder rifle. And I played a little with reloading."

Scott nodded. "What else did you use it for?"

Burris shook his head. "Nothin'." Then he frowned. "Oh, I did light up a little in the yard last Fourth of July. Just for the kids."

"A small amount?"

"A tablespoon maybe. Just to show them."

"Did you get word of the search warrant we were executing?"

"No." Burris shook his head emphatically. "It were a shock, you all busting in like that."

"So you didn't know we were coming."

"No, sir. Else I woulda got my girlfriend and her kids outta there."

"On the day we served the warrant, I saw your dog come out from under the smokehouse. But it looks to me like there's a doghouse built under the shed porch. She doesn't sleep in there?"

"Hadn't the last couple of nights. Seemed odd to me too. But I got more to think about than where Daisy sleeps."

Scott nodded. "Mr. Burris, have you ever been to the Deer Park Office Park?"

"No idea. Where is it?"

"In White Springs."

"I been to White Springs. There's a taxidermist near there. But I ain't been to no office park. Not that I know of. 'Less I got lost."

It was time for show and tell. Scott opened the briefcase that was with him and pulled out replica components of the pipe bombs their unknown subject had been using. "Do you know what this is?"

"Looks like the makings of a pipe bomb."

"Ever seen one before?"

"No, sir. Is this what blew up my shed?"

"Maybe."

"Can I touch it without somebody accusing me because my fingerprints are on it?"

"Yes."

Burris took the pieces and started trying to put the bomb together, like it was a puzzle. But as he did, Scott noticed something—he barely used his right hand. "Are you left-handed?" Scott asked as he watched Burris awkwardly twist wire.

Burris looked up. "No, sir. Right-handed." He held up his hand. "I broke it workin' on my truck last year. Had three surgeries s'posed to fix it. My thumb don't work. I got no strength in my fingers, no grip." He demonstrated his inability to bend his thumb or flex his fingers well. "Drivin' me crazy."

Scott's heart thumped hard. "When did this happen?"

"'Bout nine months ago."

"You had surgery?"

"Three surgeries!"

"Then you were in a cast?"

"Cast. Sling. Had to drive my truck mostly with my left hand. Still have to."

"Do you remember the dates of your surgeries?"

"I could tell you if they hadn't taken my daggone phone!" Burris shook his head. "I can say this, the last one was in April."

Scott glanced at Brody, sitting off to the side. The Deer Park bombing was April 19. "How long were you in a cast?"

"Two weeks. Got it off on my birthday, April 21."

There was no way he could have rigged the bombs with one hand in a cast. They were too neat, too professional. Scott cleared his throat. "Mr. Burris, anybody got a grudge against you?"

The man shrugged. "Some."

"Like who?"

"My wife's brother. He ain't too happy."

"Wife? Or girlfriend," Scott asked.

"Wife. We ain't divorced. Sam don't take kindly to me living with Sandy." Burris shrugged. "I tole him if he wanted to pay for the lawyer, I'd cut ties with Mary Ann legal-like."

"Okay, so Mary Ann is your legal wife and Sandy's the lady you live with."

"Right."

"Let me get some last names here." Scott went on identifying the various personalities populating Burris's world. Then he asked, "Are you a member of any political group? Patriot organization?" Scott knew that analysts were already working on that background, but he wanted to hear what Burris said.

Burris averted his eyes. It looked like he wanted to spit. Then he leveled with Scott. "Me and some boys, we talk a lot. That election was stole!" He gestured for emphasis. "Makes us mad as all get out. So when we heard about the rally in DC on January 6, we went. Three of us. Did we go into the Capitol? No. None of us did.

Did we tear into anything? Hurt anybody? Nope. We just yelled, that's all. Peacefully demonstrated. And if that's a crime, well, this country ain't worth savin'."

Scott began packing up his replica bomb components. "Mr. Burris, you hang in there for a little longer. I'm going to see if I can get you out of here."

Burris's eyes widened.

"Just to make things quicker," Scott said, writing on a pad of paper, "you sign this, releasing the information about your injury from your doctor, and I'll take it to the prosecutor."

Burris nodded and signed the paper. "I 'preciate it. Being cooped up here's about driving me crazy." He pushed the paper back toward Scott. "Find out who rigged my shed."

Scott nodded. "You bet."

"I'd like to bust his head."

Scott started to leave, then thought of something. "By the way, Mr. Burris. Who do you haul things for?"

"The postal service. I haul mail to Dulles."

"As a contractor?"

Burris nodded.

"You have a normal route you take?"

"Yep."

"Describe it." Scott listened, and by the time Burris was finished, six things had fallen into place.

27

SCOTT WAS SO PUMPED when he called me and told me about Burris.

"That's why the director wanted you on the case. You're a good investigator! You go after the truth," I said. I was so proud of him.

"What did you do with the information?" I asked Scott.

"I messaged Hitch," he told me, "but then I took the transcript to Caldwell who told me to take it to the AUSA."

The assistant US attorney would be the prosecutor. "What did he say?"

"She ordered him released. He'll be out by dinnertime."

"That's awesome, Scott! You did it."

"I followed a hunch. Now I'm braced for blowback." He laughed.

Sure enough, when Scott called me that night, he told me Hitch was ticked off. He tried to minimize it, but I kept asking questions. Turns out, Hitch was furious.

"I think he's trying to earn points by being the lead on this case," Scott said, "and I messed that up."

"He should be glad you figured this out before it went further," I said, not bothering to disguise my anger.

"Jess, you know how these things go. By going to the AUSA, I undermined him in his eyes. Embarrassed him. It'll blow over."

I was well aware of the damage bruised egos could do. "Watch your back, Scott," I said. "Watch your back."

EARLY THE NEXT MORNING, I got a call from a lawyer I'd worked with before. He had an urgent "cheatin' heart" case he wanted me to take. "Cynthia thinks her husband's been having another affair. If that's the case, she's going to divorce him, but that could have financial implications for her." He paused. "Here's the thing. She's stayed home raising the kids for the last twelve years. The youngest is five. She'll need money to support her until she can establish herself in the workforce and pay college tuition for the kids. She'll get that if he's having an affair. But we need proof."

"Where is this?" I was expecting to hear *Northern Virginia*.

"Cynthia and the children live in Berryville. Her husband commutes to Frederick, Maryland."

"Why would anyone do that?"

The lawyer laughed. "It's about sixty miles. With no traffic it's not bad, but then, there's never no traffic." He paused. "She has family in the Winchester/Berryville area, and he has a good government job. So they made the decision to buy in that area. The husband, Gary Gibbs, sometimes has to stay in Frederick to fix problems. He gets a hotel room, or an Airbnb, depending on how long he thinks he's going to be there. One time, she found out he was having an affair."

"How'd she find out?"

"Found a note in his pocket from the woman. Confronted him and he admitted it. They went to counseling, tried to get past it. Now she thinks he's at it again."

"How long ago was this?"

"Three years."

"What does he do for a living?"

"He's an IT guy for the VA."

"How'd you get involved? Your office is still in Fairfax, isn't it?"

I heard the lawyer sigh. "She's the daughter of a good friend of mine. He died about six months ago. We're in the process of settling the estate. She's a beneficiary. Of course, I told her not to comingle the money, to keep it in a separate account. But in a divorce, having a hunk of change like that could affect the rest of the settlement." He took a breath. "You did such good work for us before, when she asked for help I thought of you."

The whole time I was talking to him, I was deciding whether to take this case. Truth is, it would help take my mind off Luke and get me out of the house. Nate was going back to work, and Laura had a job. Plus, it didn't seem like Scott was going to be finished with his bombing case any time soon. So why not?

"All right," I said. "I'll give it a shot. Send me all the information you can, and I'll get started on it."

"Thanks, Jessica. You're the best."

I DOUBTED I was the best, but I knew I was pretty good. I was glad to have a job to do, a purpose for my life, especially one that could help a woman being wronged.

I began where I always begin, on the Internet. I checked out Gary Gibbs social media, his official online records, and any news reports about the Frederick VA office. I read where they had revamped their computer systems three years ago. I could see where that would cause a lot of overtime and justify him staying in Frederick away from his family. The affair was him being a jerk.

It took me four hours to feel like I'd picked those bones clean. Gary's social media presence was pretty sparse. I found him on Instagram and searched deeply into Facebook, but there was no mention of him on other women's pages, no hint of recent wrongdoing. I couldn't find him on Twitter or any of the others at all. I did notice some photos of an IT conference he'd been to.

Then I turned to Cynthia. If I was going to push into Gary Gibbs's life, I wanted to give equal time to his wife. After all, women can get paranoid or scared and misrepresent things. They can act out too.

Cynthia was all over Facebook and Instagram with pictures of her kids, her friends, her lunch dates, her church activities, her sisters and their families. I noticed a dark-haired guy smiling and laughing in many of the pictures, and I wondered if he was a relative or just a good friend. I downloaded some photos, sent copies of some others to an Evernote file, and basically created a book on this family.

The couple had three kids, boys who were ten and seven, and a little girl, five. The boys were tall and thin, brown-haired, and the oldest wore glasses. The girl was a blonde cutie. I could tell she was full of energy.

I had asked the lawyer to have Cynthia call me at a time when she could talk. I had a bunch of questions to ask her. We spoke for over half an hour. She seemed confident and assertive. "You know, we've been through this once, and I thought we'd put our marriage back together. I'm not willing to put up with it a second time."

Perfectly reasonable, I thought. I asked her what made her suspect her husband was cheating again.

"Two words," she responded. "Liz Deveraux."

"And she is ..."

"His supervisor. She's a blonde bombshell. Former Miss North Carolina runner-up and a computer whiz. She calls him all the time, at all hours of the day and night. He always leaves the room to take the call and comes back energized, upbeat, like he really loved talking to her. And, of course, there have been a lot of late nights and overnights working together as they're upgrading their computer systems."

"I thought they just did that."

"So did I," she said drolly.

"Is she married?"

"Married twice. I don't think she and the second husband are still together."

I assured her I'd check into it. "I'm pretty good at discovering when a spouse is cheating."

"That's what my lawyer said."

MY GOOD CAMERA with the long lens and most of my clothes were in Manassas. Before I left, I called every one of the places I'd left a lost-dog flyer. Then I wrote a note for Nate and Laura telling them what I was doing and that I'd be gone at least one night but would text them. Nate had taken Sprite to work with him, so I had no dog to pet goodbye, no waggy tail sending me on my way.

Sad.

But it was a little easier going into the Manassas townhouse this time. I grabbed my camera gear first, then packed a variety of clothes in my suitcase. A little summery dress, jeans, shorts, strappy sandals—plenty of costume changes to maintain anonymity as I surveilled my subject.

I decided to drive to Frederick, Maryland by way of Berryville. Although I hadn't mentioned this to Cynthia, I wanted to get a picture of the family home and then drive the route Gary would take to work. I found the neat two-story colonial on a cul-de-sac in a new subdivision. There was a silver minivan in the driveway, and behind it, a black Hyundai Sonata. I expected to see kids playing in the yard. It was summer after all. But everything was quiet, and I wondered if video games were keeping them inside.

I took a few pictures with my cell phone, and then a few with my good camera. The house next door was for sale, so I positioned myself as if that were my real target and casually swung around and shot the Gibbs's house.

Then I drove on to Frederick, following the route Gibbs normally took, according to his wife. Frederick is about sixty miles northwest of DC, snuggled up next to the Catoctin Mountains. For a long time it was a quiet little city, but in recent years it had grown into a busy, exurb of Washington and gained some high-end businesses and good jobs within its own area. It took me about an hour to drive the distance, swinging past Charles Town and Harper's Ferry, then over the Potomac River and into Maryland.

My plan was simple. I knew where Gibbs was working, the car he was driving, and where he was staying—at least, where he'd told his wife he was staying. I figured the easiest way to connect with him was find his car in the VA parking lot, wait for him to leave work, and follow him.

But it was only three o'clock when I arrived, so first I checked into my motel which was, not coincidentally, the same one where Gibbs was staying. Scott and the rest of the team were in Quantico for meetings for several days. I texted him and told him what I was doing and where I was staying. *Don't worry if I don't respond at ten. I may be in a bar, watching him.*

That stimulated an immediate response. *Are you carrying?*

I'm in Maryland.

I could almost hear him sigh.

I MADE the rounds of vets, pet supply stores, and grooming salons in Frederick, leaving lost-dog flyers. Then I spent the rest of that day and the next two watching Gary Gibbs. It's true, his supervisor was stunningly beautiful. But I never saw the two of them alone. There was always at least one other person with them. They didn't eat with each other, travel together, or hang out in bars as a twosome. They weren't even staying at the same motel.

Once I thought they were having lunch together and I managed to wrangle a seat in the café next to them. They were all business. Yes, Gary was animated. Apparently, they were breaking new ground in terms of VA computer systems. They had come up with an innovative idea to track patient prescriptions and had been given permission to install it at the Frederick clinic as a test. Both were excited.

And then two more people joined them, and it was clear, this was not a date at all.

I tried all my tricks. I followed Gary, took notes on his actions, grabbed some pictures, even stalked him in the VA building. At night, I'd sneak out and put a little chalk mark on his tire, then, the next morning, I'd see if it had moved.

It never did. On the last night, I changed things up. Concerned that my Jeep was too obvious, I'd slipped out during the day and rented a white Kia Forte. Then I followed Liz Devereaux as she left the jobsite.

She wound through Frederick, doubling back once so that I almost lost her, and ended up in a motel eleven miles out of town on the road to Gettysburg. I parked and watched as she went inside. About twenty minutes later, I saw a man I thought I recognized exit a car carrying flowers and what looked like a liquor bottle. I snapped pictures. He started walking toward the motel. As luck would have it, he forgot something, and came back to his car, so I got a good shot of his face. Then, he went inside.

Sure enough, when I compared those photos with ones I'd shot earlier, I was able to identify the man as a coworker of Gibbs. If something hinky was going on, my guess is it wasn't with Gibbs.

I mean, it's possible that man's wife had come along with him and was waiting inside for him. Possible. All I know is that it wasn't Gibbs.

I sat in my rental car in that dark parking lot until midnight. Sitting there alone, my mind went to another dark night and

Luke, disappearing down a swollen creek. I fought those images. I tried listening to music, sermon podcasts, and true crime stories. Nothing worked. Loneliness tugged at me like a tide.

Then Scott called early at nine-thirty. He missed me. He told me about their meetings, relayed some funny things Mike had said, and the sound of his voice cheered me up. While he was talking, I silently thanked God. I never worried about Scott being in a motel on business with his attractive coworkers. We were a bonded pair.

Plus he knew I'd kill him.

Scott asked me what I was doing. He was not happy with me sitting unarmed in a dark motel parking lot. "I've got my pepper spray and I'm being careful," I assured him.

"You're not going to stay there all night, are you?"

"Just until midnight, unless I see something."

"Okay, text me when you leave and when you get back to your place."

"I don't want to wake you up!" I protested.

"If I roll over at one o'clock and there's no text from you, I can guarantee I'll be awake the rest of the night."

His protectiveness felt good.

"Hey, I've got something I want you to think about," he said.

"What's that?"

"Don't say no right away."

"What?"

"I was talking to Gary Taylor today. Had lunch with him. A guy in BAU was just diagnosed with Stage 4 cancer. Serious stuff. This guy has a young female shepherd ..."

"No." My heart drummed a protest.

"He's got a young female shepherd ..."

"No."

"... and he's looking for someone to take her for about five months while he goes through chemo and radiation. It's just temporary ..."

Wait, five months?

"... until he gets through the worst of the treatments and can exercise her again. Think about it, would you Jess? Please?" He paused. "I've seen pictures of her. She's a beautiful dog. All black."

All black? My heart opened just a little.

"I haven't given up on finding Luke, but this guy needs help."

"It's just temporary," I said, to confirm.

"Right. About five months."

"I'll think about it."

"Great. Thanks, Jess. He's getting desperate. He starts chemo soon."

WARMED BY SCOTT'S CALL, I mulled over the idea of dog sitting for the next couple of hours. Having another dog around would feel like cheating on Luke. Giving up on him too soon. But dog sitting for a few months? To help someone out? Maybe.

28

I GOT UP EARLY the next morning and went through all my notes and photos. I felt comfortable saying that Gibbs wasn't cheating, not on this trip anyway. I tallied up my hours and expenses. I didn't want to spend any more of Cynthia Gibbs's money on what I saw was a dead end.

So I checked out, returned the rental car, and started to head home.

Then I got a text from Scott. "Mike and I returning to Winchester. Credible lead. Will be there several days."

Hmmm. First, I felt sad, then, a couple miles down the road, I had an idea. It was a little crazy, and to do it, I'd need to kill some time. But why was I hurrying back home anyway?

I'd seen the Gibbs's home, but I could swing by there again. It was right on the way. I could go to a coffee shop and write up my report—that would take several hours. Eat lunch, make some calls to shelters, vets, and rescue groups just beyond the area where Luke had been lost. Yes, I decided. I could do it. I could kill a few hours.

And something like excitement swept over me for the first time in three weeks.

. . .

We were going through a hot, dry spell, and as I drove, the sun challenged my Jeep's air-conditioning to a duel. The Jeep won, of course, but the sun showed off, sparkling on the farm ponds I drove past and bathing fields of waist-high corn with light. I tried listening to music as I drove, but my mind shifted to a review of my life. Taking this job had helped me take a step back into life, but the empty crate, bolted to the space behind me, was a reminder of my loss, a loss which, if it were permanent, I knew I'd never fully get over.

My childhood dog, Finn, was ten when he died of cancer while I was at college. That's a more "normal" scenario. I knew that loss was coming. Luke was a robust four when he disappeared down that raging creek. That was traumatic.

I wound my way through the development in Berryville, past houses under construction and others that were occupied. Work trucks and pickups cluttered the streets, and I steered carefully around them. When I got to the Gibbs's home, again I wondered, where were the kids? I was surprised to see that black Sonata in the driveway again, parked behind the minivan. Call me suspicious, but either they had a third car I didn't know about, or she had a good friend that visited a lot, or something else was going on. That's when I noticed the small "clergyman" sticker on the Sonata's back bumper.

I quickly shot a couple of pictures with my cell phone. I'd noticed that the street behind the Gibbs's was full of houses still being built, so I circled back there. The workers were occupied in another section, so I parked and slipped up to the house behind and uphill from the Gibbs's. Lifting my camera and zooming in, I saw Cynthia Gibbs sitting at a round, black iron table on the patio behind the house. Across from her was the dark-haired man featured in so many of her Facebook posts. A couple of drinks sat in front of them. The last time I'd seen glasses like that they held margaritas.

Maybe he was counseling her. Helping her with her marriage.

Maybe ...

When they stood up, embraced, and walked into the house hand in hand, my "maybes" lost all credibility.

I DROVE ON TO WINCHESTER, my head buzzing. I found a sweet café, and over coffee and avocado toast, I wrote up my report. I'd been hired to investigate Gary Gibbs, and that's what I reported on. Then I attached an addendum. Oh, and my bill. I emailed that, created a DropBox file full of photos, and sent that link. Then I called the lawyer. The least I could do was forewarn him that his client might be projecting her own behavior onto her husband.

People never cease to amaze me.

I SENT my files off at 2:03 p.m. After making my phone calls, that would give me about five hours to do whatever. The "whatever" I chose was, well ... let's just say if I were a client, I would amaze me and not in a good way.

Harper Lee's father, Charles Lee, lived about forty minutes away from Winchester where I was. I had five hours to kill. And I am a curious person.

I just wanted to see what his house looked like. Is that so wrong?

I left Winchester, following my GPS out into the country. Memories flooded back. The first case I'd ever worked with Scott had taken us up to the mountains near here. We were searching for a missing college student. We found a serial killer. Oh, and saved the girl.

That's when Nate lost his leg, and Scott and I started a relationship, which after several hairpin turns and switchbacks, had led to our eventual marriage. I never thought I'd love a man like I love Scott.

I knew from Google that Charles Lee's house sat on a two-lane road out in the middle of nowhere. I followed that road, spotted what I thought was his house, and confirmed it with a look at his mailbox. And just like that, I sailed past it.

There wasn't any traffic on this two-lane road, and I had to be careful not to drive by too often, but I wanted to see it better. I didn't see any place to park and watch the house. So I continued down the road until I came to a small white church. I pulled in to the little gravel parking lot, turned around, and checked my map. No way around it. I needed to go back up that same road.

This time, Charles Lee's house would be on my left. As I approached it, I glimpsed a "for sale" sign on the wooded property across the road and a gravel pull off big enough for my Jeep. I quickly pulled in and parked. If anyone asked, my husband and I were looking for property to buy. Which was true, but not here.

I grabbed my camera and long lens, exited the car, and walked uphill into the woods. Stopping behind some dense undergrowth, mostly hidden by a thick tree, I aimed my camera at Lee's house. I knew from Google that his closest neighbor was easily a football field away, up across the field behind him. No other houses were visible.

Lee's house looked like it was built in the 1950s, with asphalt shingle siding and no garage. Built into a hill, the back door was at ground level, the front was up about twelve steps. Two trees stood on either side of the steps—thin, gangly trees that looked like they were fighting the rocks to live. An old blue pickup sat parked in the gravel driveway that extended from the road up to the right side of the house. The house had a basement or cellar with an outside entrance. I could see the door near the driveway. I also saw five-gallon mud buckets, a small bike, an oil tank, and a propane tank. Plus a couple of sheds in the back and about four cords of stacked firewood. My camera whirred as I documented his home.

Then (glory!) a man—I assumed it was Charles—stepped out

of the house. He was short and wiry, full beard, and he had on the country uniform—jeans, boots, and a plaid shirt. When I looked at those pictures later, I about fell over. He could have been Nate's younger brother. Same full, brown beard, same shape head, same frame. No wonder Harper had instantly bonded with Nate!

Charles climbed into his truck, and I watched as he pulled out. If I tried to follow him there was a pretty good chance he'd spot me on that empty two-lane road, so I contented myself with taking pictures.

"What are you doing?"

The gruff voice behind me made my adrenaline shoot up. I whirled around to see a scruffy guy glaring at me from about eight feet away. He had a full beard, shaggy hair, and a nasty looking knife on his belt. His thick eyebrows accentuated his frown, and the whites of his eyes were showing. He looked like a walking nightmare.

Heart pounding, I said, "My name is Ann. I'm looking at the property for sale. Who are you?"

"Git!" His hand was on his knife. I kept my eyes on it. A knife at close range will kill you quicker than you can draw and shoot.

Especially if your gun is in the car. Locked up.

Fear flooded me. I felt helpless. No dog, no husband, no backup, no gun. "I'm leaving," I said, trying to back down the hill. "I'm sorry. Is this your land?"

His eyes were crazy. Light blue and flashing with anger. I prepared to use my camera as a club if he came toward me. I kept talking, hoping to make him see me as a person. I slipped on leaves, stumbled over a branch and backed into a tree. But by God's grace, I made it down to my Jeep.

"You leave him alone, you hear?" the man yelled as I jerked open the Jeep and slid in. As I slammed the door, he raced forward and pounded on my hood. "Git! Git!"

I got. Fast.

. . .

IT TOOK me an hour to stop shaking. Then I wondered if I should —could—continue with my plan to surprise Scott. But here I was in Winchester near him. I couldn't just drive off. Plus, I could use a big hug right now.

I needed to calm down. That meant being around people, safe people. So I walked around inside the mall for an hour, letting the exercise, the bright lights, the silly teens, moms pushing strollers, and hand-holding couples diffuse my emotions. Still, despite the "No Guns" sign on the door to the mall, I was back in Virginia and carrying.

By seven o'clock, I felt ready to proceed with my plan. I got in my car and pulled into a big gas station/convenience store. I filled the tank, then found a parking place on the side. Getting into the back of the Jeep, I ruffled through the clothes I'd brought and found my summery little dress and strappy sandals. Putting the dress over my arm, I slipped into the bathroom and changed clothes. I pulled my hair out of the low ponytail it had been in all day and fluffed it up. Then I gathered up my other clothes and left.

On the way out, I spotted a rack in the store with ridiculously large, dark-lensed sunglasses, and I bought a pair.

The tricky part was getting to the right hotel before Scott, but not so soon I looked suspicious sitting in the lobby. I had chosen 7:45 as my target time. Don't ask me why.

At 7:43 I pulled up to the four-story Hilton Garden Inn and parked behind some bushes near the dumpster. My gut knotted. Slipping on my ridiculous sunglasses and a floppy hat, I walked in and found a seat with a good view of the front door, but partially obscured by a pillar. Then I waited. And waited. And waited.

Just when I was about to think they'd gone somewhere else, I saw Scott walk in with a guy who had a hundred-dollar haircut. A really, good-looking guy with dark hair and a fit body. The two of them made quite an eyeful.

Casually I stood up from my seat. The men waited for the elevator, engaged in conversation. Baseball, I realized, as I came up behind them. The elevator doors opened. An older couple joined us. By this time, my heart beat so hard I was sure they could hear it. The men walked in. I followed, then the older couple filled in the spaces on the side.

The two agents turned around.

I couldn't fool Scott. He cried out in surprise, grabbed me, and kissed me hard on the mouth. My hat flew off and my heart about hit the ceiling! His grip was so strong. I clung to him like he was saving me from drowning, which in a way, he was. I heard the elevator doors shut. He kept his lips planted on mine. When he finally came up for air, he cried out to Mike, "This woman is stalking me! Do something."

Everybody laughed. The elevator doors opened. Out of the corner of my eye, I saw the gray hairs walk out. Mike had his hand on the door, keeping it from closing. His grin was Cheshire-cat wide.

"Come on, Cooper. You're hogging the lift," he said. He was holding my hat in one hand. He flopped it on his head.

"Have you ever seen anyone this beautiful?" Scott said. We started walking down the hall, Scott hugging me so closely I could feel the warmth of his body.

"Too bad we need to go over our notes tonight. We're still doing that, right?" Mike said. "Scott? Uh ... Scott?"

Scott only had eyes for me. I leaned on him. He pulled out his room key, opened the lock, and we walked in. Mike tried to follow. Scott shoved him hard back into the hall and slammed the door.

"Hey, we have a meeting at seven!" Mike yelled from the hallway.

"Take notes," Scott yelled, and he took me in arms and kissed me.

"You want her hat?"

Scott didn't bother to answer.

Alone with my husband. Finally!

Scott threw the deadbolt. I could barely breathe. Then tears began to flow. Of course, I was happy to see him, but it was like I had a hidden reservoir of sorrow and fear saved just for him, and it spilled out. He took off his suit coat, draped it over a chair, and set his gun on the table. Then he guided me to the bed. We sat on the edge, and he held me while I sobbed. I felt the warmth of his cheek and smelled his familiar aftershave as the waves of grief and fear nearly overwhelmed me.

Scott was so good. He didn't press me to talk, he just held me. He whispered his love in my ear, stroked my back, and steadied me while the sea inside raged. Then he kissed me gently and told me how proud he was of me, and how much he'd missed me.

"I didn't expect to cry," I said, my voice weak.

"You needed to."

I started talking about Luke. I reminded him of how Luke came to me at a low point in my life, how his crazy energy forced me to find him a job, and that led me to search and rescue, which led me to Nate, who led me to Christ. "And then I met you," I said, "and now, I don't know what I'd do without you."

I expected him to say something similar, but he didn't. Instead, he kept the ball in my court. "I'm so sorry about Luke. I keep thinking we'll find him somehow."

"Me too."

He asked me questions. What about Luke made him a good SAR dog? Why did we make such a good team? What was the most satisfying thing about SAR? What was the hardest thing about training Luke? Was there anything he refused to do?

On and on Scott talked, question after question, gently drawing words out of me like a surgeon lancing an abscess.

Then I told him about going to see Charles Lee's house. I had to remind him who that was. When I got to the part about the man in the woods, I felt him stiffen. "Oh, babe," he said, his questions muted by his own fear. He held me, kissing my face and head. "Thank God, you're safe. *Thank God!*" He stood up quickly, stress driving him to his feet. "You had your gun?"

"It was in my car. Locked up."

He rolled his eyes. "Because of Maryland." He sat down again and drew me close. "Don't do that again. Please."

We held each other for a long time. When finally we both calmed down, he said, "You know? I used to think I was independent, tough. Didn't need anybody, especially a woman. Then you came along," Scott touched my jaw, "and it's like you cracked open my shell. Exposed my heart. Loved me despite what you saw. You brought me back to life. I'm feeling things now I don't even have names for. I don't know what I'd do without you. And I never want to let you go."

I turned toward him, cradled his face in my hands, and kissed his lips, so thankful we were together again.

29

TEARING ourselves away from each other the next morning left ragged edges on both of our hearts. But we had jobs to do. He had a bomber to find, and I had more PI cases to develop. To ease the pain of separation, Scott and I vowed to meet every other week until we could be together again. "I don't want to go these long stretches without seeing you," he said.

I agreed.

I told Scott I thought I'd move back up to our townhouse to be closer to Quantico and Winchester, but he suggested I stay at Nate's. "It's not good to be alone too much," he said. "It does funny things to your mind."

Plus, I knew that incident in the woods had scared him.

He walked me to my car. As I was getting in, I turned to him. "Tell Gary Taylor's friend that I'd like to meet his dog. And if we get along, I'll keep her for him. Temporarily. Just temporarily." I sat down in the driver's seat and buckled up. "I haven't given up on Luke."

Scott smiled. "Of course not."

"But I can take on another dog, temporarily."

. . .

With tears in my eyes, I left him and headed back down to Nate's, taking back roads straight south to avoid battling the trucks on Interstate 81.

No one was home when I got there. The house felt empty, really empty. Even Sprite was gone. Loneliness washed over me and settled inside like a cold pond.

I had to cope. First, I prayed and told God exactly how I felt. That's what Nate had told me to do. The good and the bad, just lay it out there, he'd said.

Then I decided I'd take a run. A jog actually. My feet had healed. I felt okay. It was time to start exercising again.

For what? That thought ran through my mind. I wasn't going to be searching anymore. Not without Luke.

But long before SAR, fitness had been a thing with me. It started with my father, continued after his death when I was doing agility with Finn, then became essential when I joined the Fairfax County Police Department. I ran 10Ks, half-marathons, and mountain-trail races and worked out in the gym to maintain my strength. I liked feeling fit. So I decided to run.

I checked my watch. 1:00 p.m. Thunderstorms were predicted for the late afternoon. Typical Virginia weather. The heat and humidity would build until you thought your head would pop, and then the storms would come over the mountains and bring some relief. If I was going to run, I needed to get going.

I had just changed into my shorts and laced on my running shoes when I heard Scott's horse, Ace, raising a fit in the pasture. I looked out of my window. He was half-rearing, running in small circles, kicking up his heels. What in the world was going on?

I figured some stray dog or maybe a fox or a deer was down in the woods near the bottom of the pasture. Or maybe he saw a snake. Still, I'd never seen Ace acting like that. I hoped he hadn't gotten into some poisonous weed.

I stepped out onto the front porch into the heat. The sun

shone brightly overhead, and I had to shade my eyes. Ace was focused on something near the woods, running back and forth along the fence line, bobbing his head and whinnying. I started that way, jogging down the hill. My eyes caught movement. I squinted, straining to see what it was. I wished I'd brought a stick or a gun, something in case it was a rabid animal. But I didn't want to turn back now. What had Ace going crazy?

I jogged toward the field. My heart was pounding, my eyes watering from the bright sunlight. I moved faster. I heard a vehicle on the driveway, turned, and saw Nate's truck. He must have seen what I saw, because he turned up into the field next to the garden and drove toward me across the grass.

I looked back at Ace. I saw whatever was bothering him slip under the fence near him. When I saw that familiar movement, a shock of adrenaline, like a zillion watts of electricity, shot through me. "Luke!" I screamed. "Luke! Luke!"

Then I turned and yelled, "Nate!"

I thought my heart would burst. I rolled under the pasture fence and raced toward my dog, my crazy, lost, I-thought-he-was-dead-but-didn't-want-to-admit-it dog, lying in the grass in front of Ace.

He tried to get up, tried and fell. "I'm coming, I'm coming," I said. I crossed the last ten yards like Usain Bolt, and I threw myself down and swept that dog of mine into my arms. "Luke, Luke," I said, sobbing. Slurpy kisses have never felt so good.

Sprite jumped out of Nate's truck and raced up, whining and crying for joy. Nate hobbled fast in our direction. "Luke," I said, sobbing as I looked into those deep brown eyes, "where have you been? Where in the world have you been? Luke, Luke!"

My tears flowed freely as I stroked his muzzle. He was muddy, full of briars, thin, and his pads were worn down. But he was home, and my universe exploded with joy. *Thank you God, thank you, thank you!*

"I cain't believe it!" Nate said, bending down beside me. Tears slid down his cheeks. His hands went all over Luke. "He's lost weight."

Meanwhile, Ace towered over us, stomping his foot and whinnying. I looked up at him. "You missed your buddy, didn't you?"

Nate glanced up at the horse. "We'd best get out from under his feet. Hold on." To my surprise, he awkwardly got to his feet, pulled his phone out, and took a picture of me and Luke. "Can Luke get up?" he asked when he was done.

I got to my feet and called Luke. "Come on, boy." He responded, limping, and we guided him out of the pasture.

We put him in the bed of the pickup, and I climbed up with him. Nate drove us to the house, and I called the vet, who said bring him in and not to worry about washing him. On the way, I turned to Nate. "Where has he been?"

"I wish I knew! He looks okay though. Thin, but okay."

"How in the world did he find his way back?"

"I don't know. But it's the answer to a lot of prayers!"

Then I heard Scott's ringtone. "Nate sent me the picture!"

"Can you believe it?" I said.

"It's a miracle," he said. "I'm so happy for you. I'm happy for *us*. Thank God!"

"I know!"

"How is he?"

"Exhausted. I'm taking him to the vet."

"I was in a meeting when I got it. I walked out with a big grin on my face, shaking my head. Unbelievable!"

"I know, it's crazy! Look, I gotta go. I'll call you later."

"For sure. I want to hear all about it."

WE THOUGHT we might need to carry Luke into the vet, but that amazing dog walked in on his own, wagging his tail, and the staff treated him like royalty.

Except for being undernourished (he'd lost twelve pounds!) and dehydrated, Luke was fine, the vet said. He had a few superficial wounds, his pads were cut, and it looked like he'd been in a fight or two. "His gut is probably a mess from the crazy stuff he's been eating," the vet said. "I'll give him some meds. Feed him lightly at first, give him plenty of water, let him rest, and I think he'll be fine." She looked at me. "He's an incredible dog. I wish he could tell us his story!"

I had my dog back. A miracle! I could hardly believe it.

THE NEWS of Luke's return spread quickly throughout the SAR community. I got calls, emails, texts ... some people even sent gifts to Luke. New tennis balls, chew toys. Even the news media came out. A Richmond TV station sent a reporter and a video crew. We were famous.

One of the Battlefield officers said, "Come back as soon as you can. We've missed you."

I was vague in my response, but in my mind I was thinking, *No. Not now, not ever.*

Just the thought of sending Luke into the woods on a search off-leash chilled me. I didn't see how I could ever risk that again. In fact, I kept him on leash any time we were out of the house, even here at Nate's. There was no way I was going to lose him again.

Nate quickly picked up on my obsessive behavior. I mean, it was totally odd to walk out of his house with my dog on a leash. Luke and Sprite were so well-trained, so bonded with us, they wouldn't think of running away. Yet, after he was back, the first time Luke went into the woods to poop, I panicked. After that, my boy was on leash.

Crazy, I know.

"You realize, you cain't keep this up," Nate said, eyeing me as I walked Luke around the yard. "That dog'll go bonkers if you don't let him run. And I'll go bonkers watching you."

"He can run with me."

"He needs a job. He's made for searching. He ain't a lap dog."

I raised my chin. "I know what I'm doing."

Nate made a clicking sound with his mouth, a note of disapproval. He started to walk toward the house, then turned back, his neck red. "I learned a thing or two about trauma over the years," he said, pointing his finger. "You've had a traumatic incident. Now you can get rigid, or you can move toward healing. It's your call."

Yes it was my call. My dog was back. I'd keep him safe, whatever it took.

DESPITE THAT KERFUFFLE, I had to talk to Nate and Laura about Ember. So I brought it up at dinner. "I just wasn't sure you'd want a third dog around," I said. "I need to make sure she's okay with Luke, but if she is, I'd really like to help this guy out." I took another bite of the Mongolian beef I'd made. "I mean, I can move back up to Manassas if y'all don't want her around."

I saw Nate give Laura a pointed look. She smiled at me. "Let us talk it over, okay? We'll give you an answer later tonight."

I found out months later that Nate had told her he thought it would be good for me, that having two dogs on leash all the time would prove cumbersome, ridiculous, and would push me toward trusting God and healing. Plus, Scott had asked Nate to let me stay there a while longer.

All I knew at the time was that Laura came to me and said, "How about if you take Nate to see this dog, and if he's okay with it, I will be too."

That made sense. Nate's the dog man. He had some time the next day. We put Luke in the Jeep and drove up to Stafford. We stayed out in neutral territory on the sidewalk, and Alex brought Ember out to meet us. It was love at first sight, not only with the two dogs, but with Nate.

Who knew at the time the impact that Ember would eventually have on all of us?

30

Two weeks later, Emmy, as we called her, had settled in beautifully. Nate was already working with her, doing basic obedience and nose work, the beginning of SAR. "No sense her just lyin' around," he'd said.

I loved watching them. Sprite was already well trained when I met Nate, and Luke was half-trained, so this was the first time I'd seen him lay the foundation with a young dog.

"He's in his zone, isn't he?" Laura said to me as we watched them one evening. "He was afraid that his artificial leg wouldn't let him maneuver smoothly enough to work a new dog. But look at that!" She gestured toward her husband who was taking Emmy through a figure eight. "I guess he had to move into his fears to find they weren't real."

That hit me right in the solar plexus, but I chose to ignore it. What did Laura know of my fears? I was still waking up several times a night to assure myself that Luke was with me in the bedroom. I still saw images of him going down that river in my dreams, dreams that jerked me awake, gasping. There was no way I was going allow that scenario to repeat in real life.

Meanwhile, the whole time Nate and Emmy were working,

Luke paced, his big ears twitching, his nose shoving my hand. It was like he was saying, *Why are they having all the fun? Let's go!* Clearly, he didn't understand my fears either.

Harper was still coming over at least twice a week. She'd progressed to riding alone. Laura walked next to the horse, Harper guiding it with her reins and legs. Harper still wasn't talking, although every once in a while I'd see her whisper something to Nate. That was enough to keep Crissy, her foster mother, bringing her back. Plus, the little girl clearly loved being at Nate's. She'd taken to Emmy right away and vice-versa, which was a big relief to everyone.

One Friday, however, Harper didn't show up. When I asked why, Laura told me her caseworker had approved a long weekend visit with her father, Charles Lee. It was the first step in restoring custody to him. He had cleaned up his gig. He was going to AA, seeing a counselor, and the caseworker wanted to give him a chance to regain custody.

I studied Laura. She was bent over the sink, washing dishes, but I could see her eyes shining with tears. "How do you feel about that?" I asked, in my best amateur-counselor voice.

She sighed and blew out a big breath. "I'm trying to want what's best for Harper, but my own feelings keep getting in the way. I love her. I want her to live here with us." She stopped, grabbed a dish towel, and wiped her hands, turning toward me. "We are praying the Lord will allow us to adopt her. Of course, Nate always adds, 'nevertheless, your will, not ours be done' at the end of every prayer."

I smiled. "He is so annoying."

Laura shook her head. "I'm not there, I'm just not. I want her to join our family! Why would God give me a desire this strong if it wasn't his will?"

I remembered something Nate told me long ago. "Nate always says that he prays that God would either give him his desire or take the desire away."

Laura groaned. "I know. But I don't want God to take away my desire. I want Harper."

I hugged her.

TWO NIGHTS LATER, Luke woke me up at about four in the morning. He needed to go out. That was unusual, but I dutifully put my robe on and leashed him up. As we passed the laundry room where Emmy slept in her crate, she gave a low bark greeting. Concerned she'd wake up Nate and Laura, I opened her crate and leashed her up, too, then we all went outside.

The air was soft and warm, thick with humidity. Bugs swirled around the light I'd switched on. The higher the humidity, the more bugs swarmed, in Virginia anyway. Also, there was some formula about the number of cricket chirps equating to something. Humidity? Temperature? Nate told me about it, but I could never remember it.

"Go poop!" I told my dog, who was playing with Emmy rather than doing what we'd come out for. I ended up walking them down the tree line, one leash in each hand, clumping along in Nate's boots, which he'd conveniently left by the back door.

Fifteen minutes later, I thought it was safe to go back in, and I made my way up to the back door. I walked in, dogs swirling around me, got their leashes off, and kicked off Nate's boots. That's when I noticed he was up, standing at the kitchen counter on one leg, looking through the cabinets.

"Nate! What are you doing up? What do you need?" I said, moving toward him.

"Coffee."

"Let me get that. Sit." I helped him as he dropped back down in his wheelchair. "You know, this isn't going to help you get back to sleep," I said, spooning grounds into the coffee maker.

"Don't want to."

I let that thought hang in the air. I pushed start on the coffee maker. "What's that rule about crickets and ... what? Temperature? Humidity?"

"Count the number of chirps in fourteen seconds. Add forty. That's about the outside temperature."

I smiled. "Thanks. I couldn't remember. They were chirping like crazy outside." I opened a cabinet door. "You want something to eat?"

There was a pause, then he said, "I could really use some bacon and eggs."

"Sure, why not?"

I got busy and made breakfast for both of us. At one point, I glanced over at the table, and he was sitting there, staring off to the side. Had they gotten bad news about the adoption? What was he thinking about?

I slid a plate of bacon and eggs in front of him and a mug of black coffee. Then I put my food and coffee down at my place opposite him. "Want to say grace?"

"You go ahead."

Okay, that was super weird. But I said grace and let him eat in silence before I finally said, "Okay, Nate, what's up? Why can't you sleep? Is it the adoption?"

He put his fork down and wiped his mouth, then looked at me. "You remember that dream or vision or whatever it was that I had when ... when I was under the pile?"

"The black cloud approaching you?"

"Right. I been having it again. Over and over."

Now it was my turn to frown. "The same dream?"

"Right. Four times. Twice tonight."

"Which is why you didn't want to go to back to sleep."

He nodded.

"Wonder why you're having it now?"

"I been startin' to remember that day."

"The day of the bombing?"

"Right."

"What do you remember?"

He shook his head, like he didn't want to remember anything. "A young man. Kinda thin. Beard." He stroked his own beard. His eyes focused far away on some spot across the room. "His eyes, that's what got me. When he looked full on me," Nate paused, "a chill ran through me."

I tried to stay logical. "What was he doing?"

"Coming up the stairs."

"What were you doing? Where were you?"

"I had just taken Helen to the ladies' room upstairs in that building, and I was standin' in the hallway waitin' for her."

"So he comes up the stairs and then what?"

Nate shook his head. "That part ain't in focus yet."

"Maybe you saw him doing something and that's why you pulled the fire alarm."

"Maybe. I just don't know." He sighed. "I keep thinkin' he had something in his hand, but I don't know what."

Giving myself time to process all that, I picked up our empty plates, rinsed them off, and put them in the dishwasher. "So maybe the fact you're starting to remember that day has brought back the black cloud dream. One is associated with the other."

Nate nodded. "True enough. But I cain't help feelin' it's a warning."

"A warning? Of what?"

"I don't know."

I shivered. My heart had sped up, and I felt a tightness in my chest. "You need to tell Scott."

Nate looked up, and I saw in his eyes that he didn't want to.

"You need to tell him about remembering. Not the dream. What you remembered."

He looked down and away.

"Call your lawyer and ..." I saw Nate's mouth twist. "You never called a lawyer."

He didn't need to respond. His look said it all.

I took a deep breath. "Call Scott anyway. You need to. As soon as you can." I added a postscript. "This morning."

I WENT BACK to my bedroom, but I couldn't fall asleep. I had too much what we call "dirty knowledge" running around in my head. I knew things about Harper Lee's family that Nate didn't know. I had background on Hitch that I'll bet Scott wasn't aware of. And now, I knew that Nate was remembering things about the bombing and hadn't told Scott.

I couldn't let that one ride. Withholding that information was obstruction. I had to make sure Nate did the right thing, although he wasn't any easier to push than I was.

I laid in bed worrying until the sun dawned through the window. Then I got up and dressed for a run. That got Luke excited, but even I could see his mood lower when I clipped on his leash.

Nate had already gone, I presume to work, when I emerged. I released Emmy from her crate, leashed her up, and the three of us went outside.

Breathing in the muggy air was like inhaling through a wet paper towel. Ugh. The heat today would be oppressive. I could tell just from the way it felt that early. But what did I expect for August in Virginia?

We set out jogging past the barn and onto the trail through the woods. I admit it, running with the two of them leashed was a pain. The trail, the same one we rode the horses on over to the meadow, was not that wide. If I kept both on my left, they kept pushing me to the edge or even over into the trees. If I kept one on each side, giving myself the middle ground, Emmy kept trying to move in front of me. She wanted to be next to Luke. A couple of times I had to stop and regroup.

By the time we reached the house half an hour later, I was frustrated and tired and the two dogs were panting like crazy.

They flopped down on the cool tile floor in the kitchen. I made sure they had water and went to take a shower.

I was getting redressed when Carol called me. A little pang of guilt shot through me. I had ignored her calls the whole time Luke was missing. I hadn't talked to her in over a month. I stabbed the green answer button on my phone. "Hey, Carol." I expected her to ask how Luke was, to talk about him going missing, and ask if I was ready to do SAR again. Then tell me all about her puppy.

But no.

"I'm calling to ask for a favor."

Surprised, I said, "Okay."

"We've had a four-year-old boy missing up here for almost three days. We've searched, we've had the K-9 groups search, and no luck."

I remembered the call out. It's one I ignored. "Luke's not fully recovered," I said, pre-empting her.

"It's not Luke we want, it's you."

I pressed the phone to my ear.

She continued. "I've told the sheriff about you. He'd like to hire you as a consultant, to come up here, review what we've done, and tell us what we're missing."

I sat down on my bed. "Why me?"

"Both Nathan Tanner and the Virginia Department of Emergency Management recommended you. We need to find that boy. His mother is hysterical." Then she added, "You don't have to bring Luke. Just come and help us."

"Where is this?" She told me. I asked a few more questions, then said, "Okay. Send me the exact location. Get me copies of the topographic maps, and I'll be there within," I checked my watch, "an hour and fifteen."

Thankfully, my SAR pack was already in the car. There's no way I would have gotten out of the house without Luke if I was carrying that. I put Emmy in her crate and told Luke I'd be back. He didn't seem to notice the hiking boots in my hand.

Nate called me on the drive up. "You goin'?" he asked.

"On my way." I paused as I made a turn, then told him what Carol had told me. "Do you know anything more?"

"No."

"I don't understand. Why did you recommend me? I don't see what I can do."

"You know search and rescue. You know law enforcement. And you got faith. Pray your way through it. I think you can help them."

"Are you sure you're not just trying to pressure me back into searching?"

"It's a little boy! He needs help. I'm not asking you to do SAR again. Just help them."

I didn't know what to say, so I parried with guilt-thrust. "Did you call Scott about what you're remembering?"

I could almost hear him counting to ten. "Go do your thing, Jess. This is what you were made for. And God bless you."

31

NATE HAD JUST MADE his last turn around the pond at the community college when the phone in his pocket vibrated. Reaching for it with his left hand, he turned the big mower off with his right. "Time for a break, girl," he said to Sprite. He helped her down from the mower—the old girl was hurting in her joints—as he answered the call. "Tanner."

"Hey, it's Scott. What's up? Is Jess okay?"

The sky overhead was a beautiful, clear blue, dotted with white clouds. Not a dark cloud in the bunch, but Nate could feel it coming, feel it as surely as he felt the grass under his feet. "Jess is fine," he responded. "It ain't about Jess, it's about me."

"What's going on?"

"I'm remembrin' that's what. Remembering stuff about the bombing, and I need to tell y'all."

"What's the quick version?"

So Nate told him about the guy he'd seen coming up the stairs. "All right, that's great," Scott responded. "We'll need to get a statement from you. I can send someone to the house—"

"I just gave you a statement!"

"It'll have to be official, and it can't be with me, because we're friends."

"Then not at the house. I don't want nobody coming on my property." Anger combined with fear twisted Nate's gut. He touched his belly, willing it to calm down. Ahead he saw Sprite rolling in the freshly cut grass, her four legs twisting upward as she rubbed her back.

"Okay, then, here are some options. You can go into Charlottesville or come up to Quantico. You choose and make arrangements with your lawyer—"

"I don't need no lawyer. I ain't done nothing wrong."

"Nate ..."

"No. I ain't payin' for no lawyer when I haven't done nothing!"

There was a long pause. Then Scott said, "Okay, come up to Quantico. I'll find someone to take the statement, but I'll sit in on it. That sound okay?"

Nate breathed a sigh of relief. "Yes."

"When? It needs to be soon."

"Harper's comin' today. How about tomorrow, first thing?"

"Okay. I'll set it up and give you the where and when." Scott hesitated. "Something going on at your house that you don't want someone out there?"

Nate stiffened. He shifted his jaw. "Just don't want to. That's all."

"Okay, buddy," Scott said. "I'll call you when I've got a plan."

Nate hung up the phone and sagged back against his tractor. "Lord, I'm sorry. Scott's a friend, and I'm lettin' fear take hold of me, turnin' me stubborn. More stubborn than usual," he corrected himself. "God, help me remember you're my protector and my provider. And whatever's comin' on that dark cloud, let me stay focused on you. Help me be wise. Help me seek truth. Help me stay strong. I pray this in Jesus' name."

Sprite had come over while he was praying, nestling herself

next to his feet. He reached down, and she turned over on her back so he could rub her belly. "I saw what you were doin'. You think it's St. Patrick's Day or something? You gotta wear green?" He gave her another pat. "Come on. We got work to do."

32

WHEN I ARRIVED at the search location, I quickly spotted the players. The county sheriff, with his uniform and badge; the SAR teams, two of them, off to the side resting in the shade; the hysterical mother, clinging to a man I presumed was her husband; and my friend Carol, who greeted me at my car.

"Thanks for coming, Jess," she said. "We need help."

"Let's get the sheriff and go someplace private so we can talk," I said, glancing toward the hysterical mother. Honestly, I didn't want her emotions getting into my head. Of course, it's panic time when you lose a kid, but if she got to me, I'd have a harder time staying logical. And logical was what I needed to be.

Carol gestured toward the sheriff, and he and one of his deputies, who gathered up an armful of papers, walked with us over to a picnic table far away from the others. Carol introduced me to Sheriff Bobby Ross and Deputy Allen Ricks. I guessed Sheriff Ross to be about fifty, with short gray hair and a build like a wrestler. Ricks was as fresh-faced as they come.

We were in a five-hundred-acre park on the edge of the Shenandoah National Forest, a mountainous, heavily wooded area alive with foxes, deer, bears, and other wildlife, including mountain rattlesnakes. Soaring trees surrounded the meadow-like picnic area, pointing upward to a crystalline blue sky with not a cloud in sight.

The men spread papers and maps out on the picnic table and ran through the facts for me. Four-year-old Jackson Morrison had come to this park with his mother, Shelly Donato, a thirty-five-year-old, part-time, gas-station employee.

"Different last name?" I asked.

"Right. The kid's from a prior relationship."

I nodded. "Go on."

"The mom says she went back to her car to get a Frisbee. She couldn't find it, so she was rummaging around. When she looked up again, her boy was gone. She figured he'd just wandered into the woods, so she called and looked by herself for about half an hour. Then she left to call us."

"Wait, why did she leave?"

"She said she had no signal."

I pulled out my phone. Three bars. Maybe she had a different carrier. I filed that away for now. "Nobody else was here?"

"She said it was just her and Jackson."

"Okay."

"We got the call at 1340 hours and dispatched a deputy."

"Me," Ricks said.

"You tell her," the sheriff said.

"I arrived at 1400. I immediately did a hasty search of the area."

Wow, he knows the lingo, I thought.

"... and when I didn't locate the boy, I called for a K-9 unit."

"We don't have one," the sheriff said, interrupting. "It's been in the budget for years, but we haven't been able to move on it."

"So it took an hour to get the closest K-9 unit from Louisa County. In the meantime, we initiated with VDEM and asked that the volunteer K-9 SAR groups be activated." Ricks took a minute to regroup. "I was hoping we'd find Jackson before they got here, but that wasn't the case."

For a young guy, Ricks was thorough and professional. "What time did the Louisa K-9 arrive and what area did he search?" I asked. I knew that K-9 team, Dan something, and a Malinois named Ryker.

He consulted his notes. "The Louisa K-9 team arrived at 1532. I briefed him, and he began searching at 1545."

"He worked this area." Ricks gestured with his pen at a five-acre arc around the picnic area. "The volunteers began arriving at 1700 and searched until 2000, when we called it for darkness. They've looked here, here, and here." He indicated areas on the map, including the steep terrain across the road.

"They searched again all day yesterday," Sheriff Ross said. "Basically, two different groups been here, working dawn to dusk.

"All right. Victimology. Tell me what you know about the boy and his family."

Sheriff Ross took over. "Shelly, she grew up here. I went to high school with her daddy. I played football with him. She went away for a while, then came back with him." He nodded toward the couple. "They been living here about two years, rentin' a house about five mile down the road. The boy doesn't go to preschool or anything. The neighbors say they're a quiet family, that they see the boy playing in the yard a lot by himself. He has no siblings. Mom works at the Exxon in town, part time, and her husband or boyfriend—"

"Which is it?" I asked. "Husband or boyfriend?"

All three cops looked at each other. The sheriff shook his head. "Not sure. We'll find out."

"That's okay," I said. "I want to interview them anyway. Continue. Where does the man work?"

"His name is Skeeter Dickinson. That's what they call him anyway. Skeeter. Owns a dump truck and hauls gravel. Makes pretty good money at it, I heard," the sheriff commented.

"What does your friend, Shelly's dad, think of him?"

"Casey? I hadn't seen him in years until yesterday when he showed up here. So I don't know." He looked up as a big Ford truck pulled into the parking lot. "That's him now. Casey Donato and his wife, Glenna."

"Shelly's mom?"

The sheriff shook his head. "Second wife."

"Okay," I said, regrouping. "Where was Dickinson when the boy disappeared?"

"Hauling a load over to the highway work site. We have him logging out of the quarry at 1200 hour, and at the work site at 1245, back at the quarry at 1345. He'd been working there all day."

"How about the boy's biological father?"

"In prison down at Keen Mountain."

"You checked the house?" I asked.

"There didn't seem no reason to, but we did look around. House and outbuildings. All clear."

"If the boy found the road, he might walk home," I suggested.

"Five miles is a long way for a little boy."

I honestly didn't know how far a kid could walk. I slid my small black notebook into my back pocket and gathered up my copy of the topographic map. "Let me go talk to the mom and stepfather."

The sheriff decided he would be the one to introduce me, so we walked over together. The sun was now high in the sky, and I glanced up to see a vulture soaring overhead. A few puffy white clouds had appeared, but it was hot. Sweat trickled down my neck.

"Shelly, this is Jessica Cooper. She's a search expert we've brought in to help," the sheriff said. He gestured toward the couple. "This is Shelly, Skeeter, and Shelly's dad, Casey."

Shelly's father looked the part of a fifty-year-old former football player who'd spent too much time on the couch recently.

I shook hands all around, then said to Shelly, "I'm so sorry.

You must be terrified. Why don't we sit down at a picnic table so we can talk?"

"It's past time for talking," Casey said, anger driving him. "We need some action!"

I stayed cool. "Mr. Donato, teams have been searching for two days. We need to try a different approach. That's why I'm here." He muttered something and turned away.

I looked at Shelly and Skeeter. "Let's go over there." I indicated a table away from the searchers and deputies.

Skeeter took Shelly's hand and began walking, and I followed them. Skeeter was tall and lanky, with long arms and legs, short-cropped hair, and a thin face. I could see where he got his nickname. Shelly, on the other hand, was short and plump. Her blonde hair had a streak of blue running through it. Tattoos covered her arms. As I sat down across from them, I could see her face, swollen and red, was streaked with tears, her eyes puffy and sad. It took me back to when Luke went missing. I never knew I could cry so much.

We sat down at an empty picnic table. I pulled my little notebook out of my back pocket, turned to a new page, and looked at the couple. "I want to hear your story. Tell me what happened, right from the beginning." I kept my voice soft, sympathetic, kind. "Shelly, you start."

Through tears the mom told me what I already knew, that she'd brought Jackson here to play, that at some point she'd gone back to the car to get a Frisbee, and when she looked up he was gone. I took notes as if I hadn't heard all this. Then I asked questions: Had he been here before? Did you see anybody else while you were here? Did any cars go by? Was he used to exploring woods on his own?

I asked Skeeter what his legal name was (Steven) and if they were married. "She's my fiancée," he said. I asked where they met and when they were going to get married. Then I asked where he was when the boy disappeared and got the same answers they'd given the sheriff.

Then I moved into more subjective territory. "Tell me about Jackson. What's he like?"

Skeeter pulled out his phone and showed me pictures of a little towheaded boy. Adorable. Sometimes muddy. Always smiling.

"Does he like trucks, firemen, animals? What?"

"He loves my truck," Skeeter said with tears in his eyes. "If he gets to crying, all I have to do is put him up in that truck. That boy loves to pretend he's a truck driver."

I nodded. "Do you like to play catch with him, Shelly?" I asked, thinking of the Frisbee and trying to draw her into the conversation.

She sobbed in response.

"Shelly, she's with him most of the time," Skeeter said.

"What's a typical weekday like?"

"What does this have to do with anything?" Shelly said through tears.

"Shh, shh." Skeeter put his arm around her and hugged her close. "Let her do her job."

I gave her time to regroup, then went on, asking about Jackson's favorite TV shows, his favorite food, cartoon characters he liked—keeping my voice calm and soothing while firing one question after another at them so they had little time to think.

It's one of my favorite techniques. And before long, I thought I had my answer.

"Okay, thank you. This has helped a lot. Why don't you two wait here and let me run some ideas past the sheriff?"

Law enforcement is part training, part experience, and part art. The "art" is being able to see beyond what's in front of you, to be able to interpret data and evidence in light of human behavior, to develop and trust your good instincts.

Before a search, Nate always prays that the Holy Spirit will help us. Shaped by his habit, I'd prayed on the way up that I'd be able to help them find the child. Now, I silently prayed that the truth would be revealed.

I left them and walked back to where Sheriff Ross and Deputy Ricks stood talking. With my back to the couple at the table, I said, "Let's talk."

We walked over to another picnic table. I turned so that if the couple looked at us they would see we were discussing the map. "I'm going to point at the map, like we're making a new search strategy, but you can ignore that. Just listen to what I'm going to say."

The men nodded, and I bent over the map and gestured. "I don't know if you noticed, but your friend, Shelly's dad, is carrying." Out of the corner of my eye, I saw the sheriff stiffen. "He's got a handgun in the small of his back." I heard a low curse. "I'm going to recommend two things—one, that you ask him to let you secure the weapon so your deputies don't get hinky. But be prepared if he doesn't cooperate. Secondly, you should start a flurry of search activity here, keeping Shelly and Skeeter's attention, while you send a cadaver dog to their house."

Both cursed that time. "You think he did it?"

"I think she did. While I was questioning her, I saw signs of deception, some verbal, some non-verbal. He seems genuinely broken up. I think her tears are an act."

"I can't believe it!" the sheriff said. "Shelly?"

"It's hard when it's someone you know, even tangentially."

"How sure are you?"

"Sure enough to send a human remains detection dog over there. Did they give you permission to search the property?"

The sheriff nodded.

"Then I'd go with that. I gestured broadly at the map, then seemed to point to a specific place. "Rustle up some new activity here, tell them I had a new idea, send some teams out, and then get going at their house."

The sheriff looked at Carol and gestured her over. "Do we have a cadaver dog?" he asked in a low voice.

"No. These are all live find dogs. Why? Do you think ..." She didn't finish her question. She saw the answer in our eyes.

"Carol, why don't you and I work on that," I said, "while the sheriff and Deputy Ricks get this other part of the plan together?"

We agreed and Carol and I walked toward my car. She asked, "Who else in Battlefield has an HRD dog? Who could we call?"

I had already pulled out my phone to calculate how far away Nate was, because I only had two answers to that question, Sprite and Luke. Yes, I wished I had Luke with me. I could trust my dog to find human remains. But Sprite was good too. My phone said Nate was forty-five minutes away, assuming he was at the college. And I knew Sprite was with him as usual.

I called him. He agreed to come out. And he didn't say a word about me leaving Luke at home. Bless him.

I explained the plan to Carol. "Go ask the couple if they would like something to eat or drink, and then you and I will go get it. Except you will drop me at their house, where I will meet Nate."

Smooth as silk.

An hour later, Nate arrived at Shelly Donato's house. I'd caught him just as he was planning to leave work. It was perfect timing for me, but not for him. He was leaving early because Harper was supposed to come over that day. "We'll see. I may get home in time," he said, disappointment coloring his voice.

Deputy Ricks showed up at the house, a small, gray house with a basement ringed by scrubby shrubs and kids' toys. I introduced him to Nate. We went over my findings and concerns. Then Sprite went to work.

The nice thing about springer spaniels is that they don't look like police dogs, with all those implications. They look like sporting dogs going after game. And their size makes them convenient. I'd even seen Nate rappel off a cliff with Sprite hanging down below him as they searched for the source of the smell of human remains. Sprite weighs about thirty-five pounds, compared to Luke's eighty.

Sprite was old but she was still eager. Her little stub tail looked like she was about to wag it off as she started searching. Nose to the ground, she carefully went around the house, through the back yard, and around the shed in the back. Nate followed, leaving her off leash.

After an hour, I was beginning to think my hunches were off base. Then I saw Nate walk Sprite downhill into the woods. Following at a discreet distance, my heart quickened. And then I saw what I didn't want to see at all—a piece of blanket, lime spilled all around it, partially buried in a ditch about a hundred yards back from the house.

As soon as I got within fifty feet, I knew what was in that blanket.

33

THE ARREST of Shelly Donato and Skeeter Dickinson quickly turned dramatic. Shelly started screaming. Her father Casey tried to interfere. Sheriff Ross had to muscle him away as a deputy cuffed her. Everybody was glad we'd secured Casey's weapon.

Skeeter stood stunned, breaking down in tears and expressing total disbelief as he was being handcuffed. When the sheriff told him about the blanket and the body in the woods, Skeeter threw up. Shocked, he refused to ride in the squad car with Shelly. "I don't think he knew anything about it," the sheriff said.

Nate and I went to the sheriff's office to make official statements. I let Nate go first, so he could go home. He and Sprite were a hit with the deputies and secretaries.

Then it was my turn, and I pulled out my little notebook and gave a complete report of all I'd seen and the basis on which my suggestions were made.

The sheriff asked me to invoice him, but I said no, that justice was reward enough. Still, he insisted. "A paid consultant sounds more weighty than a volunteer," he said.

Fine. I went along with it and told him I'd send him an invoice.

As I drove home, Nate's words echoed back to me. *This is what you were made for. Searching. Saving. Justice. Truth.* Even seeing those words in my mind stirred my soul. So what was holding me back from doing search and rescue? Fear. My old nemesis.

I GOT HOME a little before eight, leashed up the dogs, and took them out for a walk. Then I came back in and took a shower. When I emerged, Laura was waiting for me in the kitchen. She told me Nate had already gone to bed. "He says he has an early meeting," she said, "plus, I think he was sad because he missed seeing Harper."

"How did your visit go?" It was the first since Harper's long weekend with her father. I tried to picture the little girl in that house.

Laura shook her head. "Harper's not in a good place. Crissy and the caseworker don't know if something happened when she was with her dad, or if she just misses him."

"How is she acting?"

Laura turned her head away and when she turned back, I thought I saw tears in her eyes. "She was uncooperative. Crying at everything. Wouldn't look at Crissy. Didn't want to go see the horses. When she found out Nate wasn't here, she had a meltdown."

"Oh, sad."

"I tried everything I knew—reading books, singing. I tried getting her to draw. Nothing worked. Eventually, the dogs came over because she was upset, and that's when she finally calmed down. I told the dogs to lie down. She sat petting them over and over and then she snuggled up to Emmy and fell asleep."

"And Emmy let her?"

"It was amazing. But overall, a very sad visit." Laura's dark hair was pulled back in a low ponytail. Wisps caressed the sides of her face. She was one of those women who looked attractive at any age.

"I'm sorry," I said. "A rough day all around. Did Nate tell you about our case?"

"Not much. He said you found the little boy."

"Is that all he said?"

"He was exhausted. He said he'd tell me all about it tomorrow."

So I told her. Or at least, I started to. As soon as I began, the tears I'd been suppressing for the last six hours broke through my denial and spilled over my cheeks. Laura hugged me. "Let's talk in the living room."

I preceded her there, settling in the leather couch. She came out with two glasses of white wine and sat down in her chair. I told her about Jackson and wept as I did. She told me about Harper and cried as well.

We went on to talk about child abuse and death and sadness and suffering and where God was in all of this. We used up about half a box of tissues and settled nothing, but in the end, I felt closer to Laura.

I was tempted—oh, so tempted!—to share what I knew from cyber-sleuthing Charles Lee and scouting out his house. But I decided not to. I didn't want what I knew about his old drug use to give Laura false hope. I knew that Social Services' strong preference was to keep families together. It would take a lot to have Charles Lee's parental rights revoked even if he had used drugs in the past.

Had I known what was coming, I might have done differently.

I TOOK it easy the next day, letting my body and emotions rest from the case I'd worked the day before. I had purposely decided not to stay to see the medical examiner's assistants remove the body. I've seen plenty of dead people, even children, but I saw no need to expose my mind and emotions to what I'm sure was a very sad scene.

With both Nate and Laura at work, I decided to busy myself around the place. In the morning, when it was relatively cool, I worked in the barn, mucking stalls and cleaning grain bins and water buckets. The horses were down in the lower field, so the dogs (including Sprite who Nate had left at home for some reason) and I walked down to see them. I kept Emmy on leash. I wasn't sure how she was around the horses, but I let Luke and Sprite run free within the fence. It still made me nervous.

When we'd petted the horses, the dogs and I went back up to the house. They flopped down on the floor, and I started cleaning the kitchen. While I was scrubbing the sink, Deputy Ricks called with an update. Even before an autopsy, the medical examiner found clear evidence of abuse on Jackson's body. Whoever killed him did an amateurish job of trying to cover up the crime.

Despite what we see on TV, quicklime will not dissolve a body quickly enough to be effective. In fact, when combined with water, as it might be in the woods, quicklime will form calcium hydroxide (the chemical name for common lime) that can actually help preserve a body. So Jackson's body was intact, and they'd already pulled prints off him.

There was more that I found out later. Skeeter had only been living with Shelly for about nine months. He said he'd never seen her abuse her son, although he did notice bruises now and then. When investigators checked her computer and phone, they found messages between Shelly and another man. She was about to kick Skeeter to the curb, but the new guy wasn't interested in having Jackson around.

The depravity of humans sometimes takes my breath away.

. . .

I'D MISSED Scott's call the night before when I was in the middle of talking with Laura. I texted, asking if I could call him back. He'd responded with *Going to bed. Will call tomorrow.*

He must have been tired. So when Scott called at noon the next day, we had a lot to catch up on. He told me Nate had come in to give a statement. He'd arranged to use an interview room at the sheriff's office close to Quantico. "I thought he'd be more comfortable," he said, "but he was still on edge. Cooperative, but man, he didn't say one word more than he had to. And when it was finished, he buzzed out of there before I had a chance to talk to him."

"He probably had to get to work," I said, frowning. "I'm glad he came in though." I wondered for a moment if I should tell Scott about Nate's recurring dream. In the end, I opted not to. Instead, I told him about the case I'd consulted on.

"Girl, you've got good instincts!" my husband said. I could tell he was proud of me. Then he said he had to go interview a guy claiming credit for the bombings. "It's the fourth one," he told me. "The crazies are coming out."

"Are you working on anything solid?"

"We had one lead. A postal worker found a black backpack similar to the one the bomber used outside a post office. They called in the bomb squad, and some task force people went up there. No bomb, but inside was a screed complaining about the government. The BAU psycholinguist has it now, analyzing it. We'll see what that produces. I don't think it's going to lead to anything, but Hitch seemed upset about it."

"Why would he be upset? Seems like it would be good evidence, so he'd be glad."

Scott didn't answer right away. "I don't know him well enough to answer that. He's on edge most of the time. He walks around angry. Maybe that's just his default."

I thought about telling Scott what I knew about Hitch, but instead I kept it to myself.

After we hung up, I continued cleaning the kitchen and when I was finished straightened up the living room. On one of the end tables, I found a stack of childish drawings. I wasn't sure whether to throw them out or not. I leafed through them. The third one down made me stop short. It was a man with shaggy hair, a beard, and crazy looking eyes.

My heart thumped. It looked like the man in the woods, and I wondered if Harper had seen him too. I kept the drawings, placing them on a stack of coloring books on the bottom shelf of Nate's bookshelves.

I finished cleaning and spent the rest of the day puttering—reading and listening to podcasts. I tried to stay away from true crime. I had enough of that in real life. But the ones on processing trauma are very interesting to me. I had no idea how persistently our bodies hold on to trauma and how that affects the way we process future events.

So much to learn.

I rummaged through the fridge and found things for dinner. I made a chicken salad, adding nuts and dried cranberries, and sliced up some cantaloupe. I also made buttermilk biscuits from scratch, Nate's favorite.

Laura walked in around six, and that's when I found out Nate was working late to make up for the time he'd spent giving his statement. Fortunately, everything I made would hold. We went ahead and ate. I was so tempted to ask her about the drawing I'd found, but then I'd have to tell her about scoping out Charles Lee's place and I just didn't want to do that. It seemed so nosy.

Nate walked in about eight, looking hot and sweaty and tired. He looked at me and said, "Scott's got his hands full."

I thought he was talking about the investigation in general, so I said, "Yes, he does."

He cocked his head. "Did you hear?"

I frowned. "No. What?"

"Another bombing up near Winchester."

34

THE EXPLOSION OCCURRED at 1818 hours, completely destroying the small rural house. At first, authorities thought the source was a propane leak. But when they found the pipes, tracings of black powder, bits of wire, and nails, they called in the FBI.

By 1910, Hitch was on the way to the site with the task force. Scott and Mike drove straight to the hospital in Winchester to interview the survivors, a man and a woman, both badly injured.

"Funny how often these dudes blow themselves up," Mike said.

Scott shifted his position in the driver's seat of his bureau SUV. "Intentionally or not."

"Right. The Austin bomber lit the fuse on himself as cops closed in." Mike shook his head. "Another guy I heard about was delivering the bomb to his girlfriend's house, carrying it on his lap. It blew up and pieces of that guy were all over the place. These dudes are crazy."

"They're crazy, or they have an agenda, or they hate somebody an awful lot."

"Or all of the above," Mike said. He tapped his knuckle on the passenger side doorframe. "How do you want to handle this?"

"We'll split up. I'll take one and you get the other. If somebody's dying, we'll want to see if we can get something out of them."

"Okay, man. You call it."

Scott pulled up to the emergency room door at 1950. He parked halfway up on the sidewalk and walked in, showing his badge and creds to the security officer as he strode through the door. The officer, a young black woman, walked them up to the receptionist who opened the door to the exam room area.

Scott and Mike walked back and were met by a PA. "The rescue squad brought in a white man in his mid-thirties with a head injury, broken shoulder, broken ribs, and internal injuries. Oh, and burns. The doctors are working on him now."

"Did he have identification on him?"

"No, no wallet. He was able to give rescue workers his first name. Our patient advocate will work backward from that, trying to match the name with the address of the incident."

"And your other victim?"

"A woman, African-American, approximately fifty. No ID."

"Injuries?"

"Again, a severe head injury, broken pelvis, burns, and internal injuries. Doctors don't expect her to survive."

"Were either of them trapped?"

"Rescue workers said it looked like they may have been standing next to the house in the driveway when the explosion occurred. They were hit with the concussive wave and debris but were not trapped."

Scott nodded. "Are either of them conscious?"

"He may be. She has been out the whole time."

Scott looked at Mike. "You sit with the woman in case she wakes up. I'll talk to the man."

Mike's phone buzzed. He looked at the text and raised his eyebrows. "There are two vehicles in the driveway. One's an old truck. The other's a county car."

Scott nodded. *So one of them worked for the county.* He said to the PA, "Will you take us back?"

She gestured toward another security officer. "Will you take them? Rooms 3 and 11."

The guard guided Mike to Room 3, where the female victim was being treated, then walked Scott back to Room 11.

The minute Scott walked into the room he thought, *This guy isn't going to make it.* Blood seeped through the bandage on the man's head wound, and his breathing was irregular. "Can I talk to him?" he asked the doctor. "It's important."

She nodded. "We're about to take him back."

Whether "back" meant the operating room or to radiology for scans, Scott didn't know. "His name's Charlie?"

"Yes." She moved out of his way so he could get right next to the patient's head.

"Hey Charlie? Charlie?" Scott said. He touched the victim's shoulder. "Can you hear me? I'm with the FBI."

Slowly, the man turned his head toward Scott.

"We just need to know what happened. Do you remember, Charlie? How'd you get hurt?"

"House blew up."

"Charlie, we found bomb fragments. You been playing with bombs?"

Charlie's eyes widened. "No. No!"

Scott's heart thumped. "Who, then? Who would put a bomb at your house?"

The patient closed his eyes and for a minute, Scott thought he'd lost him. "Charlie, man, do you know somebody who makes bombs?" Scott jostled him. "Charlie?"

"My daughter," Charlie said. "Help my daughter."

"Was she in the house? Charlie was she there?"

The man didn't respond.

"Sir, they're here for him now."

Scott stepped back and let the imaging techs navigate the

gurney out of the room. Then he and the nurse looked at each other. "He doesn't look good."

"No," she said, agreeing.

Mike appeared in the doorway. "She's gone." He nodded his head back toward Room 3.

Scott nodded. "Let's talk."

They walked down the hallway and into an open storage area. Scott checked his watch—almost eight thirty. "You get anything out of her?"

Mike shook his head. "No."

"Hear anything from the scene?" Again, Mike said no. Scott told him what Charlie had said, that he didn't mess with bombs. "But he asked for his daughter. I don't know if she was there or what."

As he was talking, Scott tried to remember what Jess had told him about search-and-rescue protocols for bombings and fires. Did the fire marshal call for SAR? How long would it take a pile to cool down enough to search? Jess would know these things. Should he call her? It could potentially save a life. Scott reached for his phone.

35

NATE AND LAURA and I talked while he ate, then they went to bed. I teased them about that. It wasn't even nine o'clock yet. But as Nate said, "tired is tired" and it was a blessing to be able to sleep when you needed it.

Abandoned by my friends, I sat on the couch, reading *The Body Keeps the Score.* The sound of my cell phone made my heart jump. "Scott? Are you okay?"

"I'm fine. Hey, look, what's the protocol for searching a collapsed building after an explosion?"

I sat up straight, putting my book down on the end table. Luke looked up from where he was lying on the floor. I knew he was hoping for a callout. "What kind of building are we talking about? Where was this?"

"It's a house, a pretty small house from what I can gather, out in the country southwest of Winchester."

"Is anyone trapped?"

"We don't think so, but one of the injured victims asked about his daughter. I'm wondering if she could have been in the house." He explained that the victims were found in the driveway outside.

"So this was a single-family home?" I asked. When he

responded affirmatively, I outlined what kind of safety clearances we would expect before we searched a scene like that and how the responders on the scene could request help from us. "Where was this exactly?"

"Hold on." He yelled, "Hey, Mike, what's the address?" Then he came back and gave it to me.

My head spun. "What's the victim's name?"

"The female has not been identified. The male's name is Charlie."

"Scott, that could be Harper's father."

"Who?"

"Harper, the little girl that Nate and Laura want to adopt. That's her father's address. I was there, remember? What does he look like?"

"He's all bandaged up, but he's got brown hair, full beard, about Nate's height and weight."

"I'll bet that's him!"

"What's her father's full name?"

"Charles Edward Lee."

"He may be our bomber. Or he may be a victim of the bomber. Either way, it sure was his house blew up tonight. Wow."

"Is he alive?"

"He's critical. Look, I need to run. Hold off on telling anybody, okay?"

"Okay. I love you! Be safe." I clicked off my phone, my mind spinning. *Charles Lee is the bomber? How could that be"*

No, I decided. Charles Lee was not the bomber. Because why would he do that while he was trying to regain custody of Harper?

Luke paced, sure that the phone call would send me racing for my SAR pack. He was anxious to move. Emmy stood nearby, trying to figure out what Luke was doing. I could tell she was about to bark.

The house was dead quiet. I didn't want these dogs waking up

Nate and Laura. I checked my weather app; the temp was 72 degrees. I grabbed a flashlight and leashed up Luke and Emmy. We went outside and began walking down the driveway.

Thick humidity made the night air soft The locusts buzzed loudly in the trees. Overhead, the stars looked dim, muted by the August haze. I heard a noise up ahead and stopped. Luke growled. In the beam of my flashlight stood a beautiful buck, stock-still, staring at us from about fifty feet away. "Stay," I said to the dogs.

Emmy tried to obey, but temptation overwhelmed her, and she charged, barking. "No!" I said, my arm jerking as she hit the end of the leash. "No. Settle." The buck took off, crashing through the underbrush.

We started walking again, my mind working hard. If Charles truly was the bomber, Harper would be removed from his custody permanently, and Nate and Laura would have a good chance of adopting her. If he was a victim of the bomber, then why? He didn't work for the post office. Why him?

Again, if he was a victim—for whatever reason—and died, Nate and Laura would have a chance. If he lived, well, who knew? Maybe they would and maybe they wouldn't.

I looked up at the stars. How long has mankind been able to track the movements of the heavenly bodies, to observe the mathematical precision of the universe, I wondered. More than two thousand years. And yet life at ground level seems so chaotic to me. Could I believe it was ordered, too, and that there was purpose in everything we were going through?

I mulled these weighty thoughts while the dogs sniffed. By the time I got back to the house, I was ready for sleep. I was crawling into bed when I thought of one more problem. Nate had told me Harper was coming tomorrow afternoon. He hoped there wouldn't be a repeat of that last disastrous visit. He was determined to be home early.

Shouldn't he know about her father in advance?

I texted Scott, told him the situation, and asked if I could tell Nate and Laura, and I told him why. His answer came back hours later just as I was dozing off to sleep.

I'D SET my alarm for 5:00 a.m. once I'd gotten Scott's okay to tell Nate and Laura. I knew if Nate wanted to be home by three when Harper usually arrived, he'd go into work early, and I wanted to catch him before he left. What's more, I wanted to tell him and Laura together.

So I woke up at five, slipped into my clothes, and took the dogs out. When I heard Nate in the shower, I tapped on their bedroom door and woke up Laura. "I need to talk to you, both of you, before Nate leaves," I told her.

I know that alarmed her, but what could I do?

I made coffee for them while I was waiting. And eggs. I even found some cinnamon rolls in the fridge and had them ready when they came out.

"What's going on?" Nate said, his voice gruff.

"Sit down. Let me serve you and I'll tell you."

I put food in front of them and then sat down myself, coffee in hand, and I told them about Scott's call and the explosion at Charles Lee's house. I could see the shock of it fill their faces. They looked at each other, and I knew they were working out the implications in their heads as I had last night. They started talking about that, mostly with each other, while I sat and listened.

"I'm sorry to wake you up," I said to Laura, "but I wanted to tell you both together. I didn't want you to hear it on the news first."

"Thank you," Nate said. "Is it for sure his house?"

"I think so."

"Do they think he's the bomber?"

"They don't know."

"Is it linked to the other cases?"

"Not sure. The lab has to do an analysis."

Nate nodded.

Laura spoke up. "Thank God Harper wasn't there. Was her father the only one hurt?"

"There was another victim, a county employee. She died."

"A county employee? Could it have been Harper's caseworker?" Nate said.

"Could be. Scott said from their injuries it looked like the two victims may have been standing next to the house when it exploded, maybe talking in the driveway."

"I wish I could picture it."

I felt a tremor run through my gut. It was time to confess. "I have to tell you something," I said, my mouth suddenly dry. I told them how I'd stumbled on Charles Lee's address, how I'd looked him up online, and how, when I had time to kill in Winchester, I'd driven by his house. "So I have pictures."

"You went to his house?" Laura said, incredulous.

"I'm sorry. I am a curious person."

"Curious or nosy?"

That stung. I fought back shame.

"Well, let's see 'em," said Nate.

I looked up.

"The pictures."

I rose, got my computer, and we all got on one side of the table so we could view them together. We went through the pictures of the house, the yard, and then we got to the one of Charles Lee emerging from his house.

"Oh my gosh, Nate, he looks like you! No wonder Harper's taken to you," Laura said, leaning forward. "You could be his brother."

"True enough," Nate said. "Zoom in."

I did that and as we looked at Charles Lee, I said, "There's one thing I don't get. He's asked to get custody of Harper back, right?

Why would he be bombing things? That would undermine his argument."

Nate shook his head. "It don't make sense, for sure." He checked his watch. "I gotta run to work. Send me that picture." He gestured toward the one of Charles Lee. Then he looked at Laura. "We got a lot to pray about."

"Yes, we do."

"First off, that Harper's father will live."

Laura and I exchanged glances. "Yes," she said, turning to her husband and smiling.

I watched Nate kiss Laura goodbye. He touched my shoulder as he went past. "C'mon, Sprite," I heard him say. When I heard his truck start up, I said to Laura, "I apologize for snooping."

She gave me a wry smile. "I imagine, considering your job, it's pretty hard to resist." She picked up her plate and carried it to the sink.

"I was trying to protect you and Nate."

"I know."

"In case there was something ... you know ... something that might rise up to bite you later."

"I get it." She dried off her hands. "I forgive you." For good measure, she gave me a hug.

LAURA WENT IN TO WORK, saying she'd be home about two. I busied myself around the place, cleaning up the kitchen and putting in a load of laundry. Then I went out to the barn, where I courageously let Luke off leash, and he promptly enjoyed himself, wrestling with Emmy and lying around chewing sticks no more than twenty feet away from me. I was so brave.

Scott called around 10:00 a.m. I told him about my conversation with Nate and Laura, and how Nate was praying that Charles would live.

"So far, so good," Scott responded. "I haven't been able to talk to him again. They had to go in and stop some internal bleeding. He's in ICU, unconscious."

"What about the investigation?" I flopped down on the couch, tired from lack of sleep.

"They are proceeding as if he is the bomber. I don't think he is, but that's the premise they're operating under. All we know is that something exploded in his house, and we've found fragments of the materials used in the other bombs."

"That sounds pretty convincing. What makes you think he's not the bomber?"

"My gut."

I wondered how that would sound to Hitch and the others.

Scott went on. "Charles Lee told me he didn't do it, that whatever exploded in the house wasn't his. When I saw him in the ER, he was hurt bad. Close to dying. I thought so, and so did he. There's nothing like teetering on the brink of death to make a man honest. He gave me a statement, practically a dying declaration. 'I don't know nothing about bombs,' he said. And when I asked him about the other bombs, he said, 'I didn't blow up nothing.' And I believe him."

"There's one more thing," Scott said. "This morning when it got light, one of the investigators found a black backpack on Lee's property. No bomb, but inside was a long, typewritten letter railing against government intrusion. Whoever wrote it thinks the government has placed listening devices and scanners on mail trucks and in mailboxes so government agents can spy on us."

"Which explains why he targeted the postal service."

"Right. Where we found it would be a ridiculous place for Charles Lee to leave it. It's much more likely the bomber lives nearby, saw all the activity, and left it there as a message."

"Is it signed?"

"No, but it makes me wonder what's next."

"Is anyone else thinking about that?"

"No, they're all running down the 'we got him,' Charles Lee's trail."

"A stampede," I suggested. "Nobody's thinking."

"Right." Scott sighed.

"You must be exhausted." My own eyes had closed while I was listening to him.

"So is everybody."

"Did they send the document to BAU for linguistic analysis?" I yawned.

"Yes, they did. The stress must be getting to Hitch. Mike said he read the document several times, got red-faced, and left abruptly. Came back a few minutes later, then got a phone call and excused himself from a meeting. Said it was his wife."

I sat up, my heart quickening. "Wait. He doesn't have a wife."

"What?"

I got up quickly and walked to my laptop, which was still sitting on the kitchen table. "Hitch doesn't have a wife. He was divorced," I checked the date "fourteen years ago."

"How do you know this?" Scott's words were sharp.

"I ... I looked him up." I took a deep breath and began my second confession of the day. "After he gave you a hard time, I was curious so ... so I checked out some sources." Then I told Scott what I'd found.

"Jess," Scott said, exasperation streaming from his voice, "you better hope you never get investigated by the FBI. You're going to have a lot of 'splainin' to do."

36

SCOTT CLICKED OFF HIS PHONE, not sure whether he was irritated at Jess or proud of her resourcefulness. He was sure of this one thing ... he missed her. Missed her hair, missed her smile, missed the feeling of her lying next to him at night.

He inhaled sharply from the pain of missing her.

He stood on the hill across from Charles Lee's place ... what remained of it anyway. What used to be a house was now a pile of lumber and siding and glass and burned material on the ground. The fire was out. The volunteer fire department had left one piece of equipment, a brush truck, on the scene in case embers reignited.

Bucars and other law enforcement vehicles clogged the two-lane road, which was closed to traffic. The evidence response team van was parked in the yard, and Scott could see agents and other investigators working, probing the rubble, doing a grid search of the field behind the house, taking photographs, and collecting evidence. He saw a woman wearing an ATF raid jacket pull something—a scorched doll maybe?—out of the rubble, shake it off, and set it next to a scrawny tree near the front steps.

Off to the right, the team had erected a couple of ten-by-ten canopies, one of them with sides, so they could work out of the sun and wind. Scott checked the weather on his phone. High of 90 today, with 80 percent humidity and a 60 percent chance of thunderstorms in the late afternoon. His shirt already stuck to his back.

Scott slid his phone into his back pocket and walked down the hill and across the road. He prayed silently as he walked, for wisdom and strength to get through the day. Fatigue felt like syrup in his muscles, sapping his strength. He saw Hitch talking to Mike over by the canopies, and he walked that way. He could see the tension in Hitch's body language—in his jerky movements and hunched shoulders. Then he saw Hitch walk toward investigators looking at the rubble pile.

"What's up with him?" he asked Mike.

"Oh, you know Hitch. He always has a burr under his saddle." Mike stretched and yawned. "Something going on at home."

"With his wife?"

"Apparently."

Scott took a drink of water. "Somebody told me he was divorced." He recapped the bottle.

"Who isn't? Oh, that's right—you aren't." Mike grinned. "I'll bet you're glad we're wrapping this up."

"I don't think we are."

"You don't think we got the guy? Look over there." Mike pointed toward the open canopy where a table held a pile of six-inch lengths of pipe and pieces of black backpacks. "What more do you want?"

"Cooper!"

Scott turned toward Hitch.

"Why aren't you at the hospital?"

"The victim—"

"Suspect," Hitch countered.

Scott began again. "Charles Lee had surgery. He's unconscious in recovery. The officer monitoring him will call me when he starts to come out of it. If he doesn't call by noon, I'll call him back."

Hitch glared at him, his hands on his hips. "Is it normal for you to ignore all the evidence?"

Scott shrugged. "I don't think he did it."

"What proof do you have?"

Patience. "He denied bombing anything."

"And you believe that?"

"Yes, sir, I do. He was trying to get custody of his daughter back. Why would he jeopardize that?"

Hitch shrugged.

"Look. How about if I go up to the county and talk to the people in CPS who worked with the female victim? See if she ever mentioned Charles Lee having animosity toward her, the government, or the postal service."

Hitch blew out a breath. "Suit yourself. But I want you back at the hospital when he wakes up."

"Okay, no problem," Scott said. He watched Hitch walk away. "Whew," he said in a low voice, turning his back toward Hitch. "That man is working on a heart attack."

"And it'll be your fault if he has one," Mike said, laughing.

"Want to go for a ride?"

"Sure, why not?"

The two men got in Scott's SUV and headed toward the county seat. Within five minutes, Mike had rocked his seat back and was snoring. Scott looked over at him and shook his head. "Okay, I'm officially jealous," he muttered.

When they arrived at CPS, Scott parked in the shade and rolled the windows down. Mike opened one eye. "Are we there?"

"I got it," Scott said. "You sleep. You can drive back."

Inside, Scott showed his badge and credentials and met with

the supervisor of caseworker Vanessa Washington's unit plus two social workers who were close to her. They all agreed. As far as they knew, Charles Lee wanted his daughter back and didn't express animosity toward the government or the postal service.

"She wasn't afraid to go there," one of her friends told Scott. Her boss confirmed that.

Scott collected copies of the reports Ms. Washington had filed. Scanning them confirmed the information Jess had given him about Ciara Lee, drug use, and Harper's silence.

"We still don't know why Harper stopped talking," Vanessa Washington's boss said. "We can't confirm any abuse on the part of Charles Lee, and in fact, we've gotten good reports about him from his AA sponsor, his therapist, and Harper's doctor. Our default is to keep families together, which is why we've been inclined to return Harper to the home. Now, of course, there is no home."

"So she'll stay with the foster parents," Scott said.

"For now."

Scott walked out convinced he was right about Charles Lee. Now, how could he get Hitch and the investigation back on track?

He was so fixated on the answer to that question he didn't bother waking up Mike to drive. On the way back, he had an idea.

Scott reached over and jostled Mike to wake him up. "Hey!"

"What? Are we there?"

"Almost back to the scene."

"The scene of what? I thought we were going ..." Mike shook his head. "Oh, wait, you did that, didn't you?"

"By myself. While you slept, you lazy dog!"

Mike smiled and nestled back down in his seat. "Felt good."

"Listen. Tell me again. Where did they find that backpack with the long document in it?"

Mike sat up. "In the field, way in the back."

"Why would Charles Lee leave that document back in that

field in the weather? Why wouldn't he deliver it to his recipients, or leave it in the house or in his truck?"

"I don't know."

"He wouldn't have! I mean, who goes back there?"

"Then why would anybody leave it there?"

"Because it's a message to the feds. We were crawling all over that place. The bomber left it there. I think he lives nearby, saw all the activity, and dropped the backpack there."

"Nobody lives back there."

"What makes you say that?"

"Did you see any houses?"

Scott hadn't but he didn't want to admit it. "Call it up on Google Earth."

Mike pulled his phone out of his pocket. "Not enough signal. I think you need Wi-fi."

Scott picked up his phone and called Jess. "Do me a favor, hon."

"Hi, *hon,*" Mike yelled.

"Ignore him. No, that's not the favor. Look up Charles Lee's house on Google and tell me if there are any houses behind it that we can't see." He paused. "Uh-huh. Okay." Scott turned toward Mike. "She says there's what looks like a driveway cutting up into the woods behind the field."

"Wait. How does she know where Charles Lee lives?"

Scott didn't want to explain that, not right now anyway. "Okay," he said into the phone. "Thanks, hon. I love you."

"Me, too, hon!" Mike yelled.

Scott clicked off the phone and glanced toward Mike as he pulled into the crime scene. "She says there's a driveway leading to a clearing near the power line easement. There may be a trailer back there, northwest of here."

"Well, I'll be."

"Let's go find out." Scott opened his door. "We need to tell Hitch and get some reinforcements."

Hitch was nowhere to be found, but since he was so prone to being oppositional, Scott felt he needed to cover his bases. He called Caldwell and left a voicemail outlining his thinking and describing his plan.

He wasn't going to wait for approval. Instead, he fell back on the old agent maxim, *I'd rather beg for forgiveness than ask permission.* Gathering up four more agents, including two from ATF, he led a caravan of SUVs up through the back field to where the driveway disappeared into the woods. "Okay, listen," Scott said, "if the bomber lives here, he's paranoid. That makes him dangerous. Don't walk on the driveway. Don't get into the clear. And don't talk. Silence your radios. We'll use hand signals."

"Wow, fun!" Mike said.

"That's your last joke," Scott retorted, "until we're back here." He fastened on his ballistic vest. "If there is a trailer up there, when we get within sight, we'll spread out and circle it. If we see anybody, or anything related to bombs, we'll stop and call in the bomb squad. Got it?"

Everyone nodded. "Okay, let's go!" Scott said.

The group split up into two teams, traveling up either side of the driveway. Scott took the lead on the left side, the most vulnerable. The agents moved quietly and stayed ten to fifteen feet apart from each other. The "driveway" was barely a driveway at all. Rutted, filled with loose rocks, it even had tall weeds growing in it at places. Clearly, it was not used often.

A hundred yards in, Scott held up his hand. Ahead was a rusted, broken-down trailer. He motioned for people to get down and move slowly forward. The trailer sat in a clearing about twenty feet wide on the three sides Scott could see. He also saw twenty-gallon water jugs, gasoline cans, and old tires. When they still had about thirty feet between them and the clearing, Scott motioned the others to go around. He wanted eyes on all sides.

Within ten minutes, two things were clear. Someone lived there, but they weren't home. Mike, who was on the other side of the trailer, radioed Scott. "There's a second driveway running up from the back side of the trailer," he said in a low voice.

Made sense for someone who's paranoid. "It's his escape route," Scott said.

"There's also a nice collection of pipe here in the back, and boxes and boxes of nails. Wow. The local hardware store is happy to see this guy coming."

"That should be enough for a search warrant," Scott said. "I'll get someone going on that. You come back here, Mike. I have a plan."

While most of the agents held their positions, Scott met with Mike and one other agent. "We have to assume this thing is booby trapped, or at least, could randomly explode. I'm calling in the bomb squad. In the meantime, I want a scout on each driveway, watching in case this guy comes back. Everybody else should hang tight. Stay back from the trailer."

"Want me to go look in it?" Mike asked, gesturing toward it.

Images of Nate's buried driveway alarm flashed through Scott's head. "Nope. Don't go near it 'til it's cleared. I'll get a warrant. With any luck, we'll have it in hand when the bomb squad's done."

TIME SEEMED TO CRAWL, standing out there in the woods, with bugs biting and sweat dripping down Scott's neck. He dictated the justification for the search warrant to a first-office agent in the Winchester office, and that agent took it to a judge. An hour and a half later, Scott had the warrant in hand, and the explosives team was on-site, carefully preparing to enter the trailer.

As Scott watched, Mike came up to him, his face flushed. "Hey, man, look at this." Mike showed him a picture on his phone of an army-green ammo bag. On the front, someone had hand-lettered the name, "Corey."

Scott felt his heart quicken. "Where did you find it?"

"A little uphill from the trailer, on the ground, like somebody dropped it in the woods."

"Tag as evidence," Scott said, "and make sure the bomb squad collects it."

ONCE THE EXPLOSIVES team cleared the trailer, Scott went in. He wanted to see it before the evidence team started working. "No bombs, but there are components," the explosives team leader said.

Despite the clutter outside the trailer, the inside was surprisingly neat. Scott saw a small kitchen, a bed, and a bathroom, and in the back was a work area, sort of a drop-down desk. On built-in shelves above it, Scott saw shoeboxes labeled "CELL PHONES," "WIRE," "NAILS," "GLUE," "CORD," and "WIRE CUTTERS." The surface of the desk held a six-inch piece of pipe, end caps, and some wire. He saw a dusting of black powder on the floor.

Hanging on the wall were sections of Virginia, West Virginia, and Maryland maps, taped together to show the parts of each state just west of Washington, DC. Small circles studded the map, some of them x-ed out. When Scott looked closely, he realized the x-s marked the locations where the bombs had detonated.

"What's going on?"

Hitch's voice almost made Scott jump. He turned to see the man, red-faced, coming into the trailer. "We found the bomber's home," Scott said, gesturing toward the map, "but we don't know who he is yet."

Hitch leaned forward to look closely at the map. His breathing was hard, like he had walked fast up the hill.

"You saw what was outside—lengths of pipe, nails, and so on. Here's the map of where he's set off bombs. And we also found this." Scott showed Hitch the picture of the army-green bag. He saw Hitch's face grow white. Then the man cursed, turned quickly, and left the trailer.

What? Where was he going? By the time Scott emerged from the trailer, Hitch was well down the hill toward Charles Lee's, his shoulders hunched, his head down. That's when Scott put the facts together. Adrenaline flashed through him. He ran after Hitch.

37

NATE WAS glad to see Crissy's car still in the driveway. He was late, almost an hour late, but he'd still have time to play with Harper. The mower had picked a terrible day to break down.

As he walked up the ramp to the back door, he glanced to the west. The hill rose sharply in that direction, blocking his view of approaching summer storms. He never knew what was coming until chaos crashed down on him.

Sprite trotted right next to him. As Nate put his hand on the doorknob, he saw her pull back sharply, but he ignored it. All he could think about was Harper—seeing her, playing with her, helping her process whatever trauma had seized her body, soul, and spirit. So he pushed open the door.

What he saw next sent cold fear running through him, icicles in his veins followed by fire in his belly, fire so hot it made his hands tingle. And he knew the dark cloud that had been chasing him for months had finally caught up to him.

The man stood in his kitchen, a .44 aimed at Nate's chest. He had brown, shaggy hair, a beard, and wild, crazy eyes. Beyond him Nate could see Laura, his beloved, bound and gagged, tied to a chair in the living room, her eyes full of fear. Harper crouched on the floor behind her.

Nate thought fast and prayed even faster. *Help, help.* He pulled the door shut behind him, keeping Sprite outside. "Who are you? What do you want?"

The man gestured with his head, telling Nate to move toward the living room.

Nate stayed still. "No. You tell me what you want."

The man made a sound like an animal's growl, anger flashing in his eyes. He stood taller than Nate, although he was thin. He raised the gun.

Nate's heart hammered hard in his chest, but he kept his voice calm. *No weapon formed against you will prevail.* "Hold on, man." He raised his hands. "Why are you here? What do you want?"

"The girl."

"What girl?"

"Charlie's girl! She took her. He wants her back."

The man's eyes settled on Nate's name, embroidered on his shirt. "You're a cop? A cop!" he suddenly screamed, raising his gun.

"No, man. No!" Nate forced himself to grin, hoping to diffuse the tension. "I'm a maintenance man. I cut grass." He held his hands out so the man could see the grass stains and grease on them. The gun lowered ... just a little. "My name's Nate. I'm Harper's uncle." The wild man's head tilted. "Her daddy, Charlie, he's my little brother. Let me show you."

Nate eased his phone out of his pocket. He scrolled to the photos. He found the picture of Charles Lee that Jess had sent him just that morning and turned it around so the man could see it. "See? It's Charles Lee, my brother."

"Ah," the man said, looking confused. He muttered something, then he nodded toward the table and said, "Put it down."

Nate did not want to give up that phone. But what could he

do? "How do you know Charlie?" he asked, capturing the man's attention while he placed it on the table. "What's your name?"

Then the man gestured toward the great room. "Git."

Nate walked through the door, keeping his hands visible. He locked eyes with Laura, love pouring through him. He willed her to feel it, to take strength from it. *God help us.* To her left, Crissy, Harper's foster mom, sat tied in a chair, crying.

Nate looked at Harper, hiding behind Laura. "Hey, Harper. Come to Uncle Nate."

Bless her, that girl came right out and jumped into Nate's arms. She buried her face in his shoulder. "It's okay, honey. It'll be all right," he whispered. He wondered if she could hear his heart pounding. He turned toward the man. "Why do you want her?" he asked.

The man mumbled some unintelligible words. Was he a paranoid-schizophrenic? Delusional? Psychotic? Nate's mind raced. *Help me, Lord. Help me.* "What's your name?"

The man glared at him, his eyes wide.

"What do you need? How can I help you?"

"They're taking her. She's taking her!" The man kicked the chair Crissy was in. It fell over sideways. Crissy screamed behind the gag.

Nate ignored her. He had to. He had to keep the man engaged with him. He put together what he knew—about the bombings, about Charles Lee, about the explosion at his house—and he took a wild guess. "Government's gettin' into everything," he said, shaking his head. "Charlie, he's been missin' his daughter. Are you his friend?"

The man looked toward him, studying his features, thinking. "Corey," the man said.

"Corey's your name?"

"I'm taking her to him." The man suddenly moved toward Nate and when his hand touched Harper, she panicked and screamed.

"Wait! Hold on," Nate said, moving back. "She's scared." He rubbed her back. "Shh, shh, now." He looked at the man. "What do you say I go with you? We'll take her to Charlie together."

Corey tilted his head.

"I know you're trying to help my brother. Taking his daughter back to him. I got that. But you cain't drive and watch her too. Let me go with you. We'll do it together."

The man frowned and began pacing. Nate wondered if he could drop Harper and make a move on him. But at the point he decided to try, the man stopped and stared at him. "You'll hurt me."

"I ain't gonna hurt you." Nate gently put Harper's feet on the floor. She hid behind his leg, gripping him. "Why would I hurt you? You're a friend of my brother."

Corey paced, muttering to himself, his eyes darting between the floor and Nate. The duct tape he'd used on Laura and Crissy lay right to Nate's left.

"Put your hands behind your back!" Corey yelled, waving the gun.

Nate complied. "Okay, okay."

Corey picked up the tape and wrapped Nate's wrists, not noticing Nate was holding them slightly apart.

"Okay, now let's go," Nate said. "Let's go see my brother, Charlie. Let's give him his little girl back. C'mon, Harper. Hold onto my belt. That's a girl."

Nate knew he was taking a chance. Normally, going with a kidnapper is a terrible idea. But he wanted to get Corey out of the house and away from Laura. He for sure didn't want the man taking Harper alone. By going with Corey, Nate would be able to protect her. Get them both out of the situation.

Corey grunted and gestured for Nate to move.

For we battle not against flesh and blood ...

Nate could feel the evil emanating off Corey like heat. *God, help me.*

Nate set his jaw. *Take the helmet of salvation and the sword of the Spirit, which is the word of God, praying at all times in the Spirit.* He straightened his back, willing himself to trust. God knew where he was. He was stronger than any power of darkness.

But as they walked toward the kitchen door, Nate saw something that made his knees grow weak and his flesh nearly fail: a pipe bomb, wired to a cell phone, on the floor next to the back door.

38

"HITCH! HITCH!" Scott yelled, running down the rutted driveway. He reached out and touched the man's arm. "Talk to me."

Hitch shoved Scott, who fell back against a tree. Scott righted himself. "C'mon, man. What's going on?" He kept his voice calm.

Hitch turned and for a minute, Scott thought he was going to hit him. His hands were clenched, his face twisted in anger. "I thought he was in Colorado," Hitch said, turning away.

"Who? Your son?" A good guess. A great guess. Scott saw Hitch's shoulders drop, then his head.

"Yes. My son." Hitch started walking again.

"Tell me."

Hitch stopped.

Scott heard a noise and saw Mike approaching. He waved him off. "Tell me," Scott repeated softly.

Hitch took a deep breath. "My wife and I divorced when my son was young. She got custody. I didn't see him much. My job ..." He didn't finish that sentence. He didn't have to. "My son was diagnosed with schizophrenia in college. Such a bright kid. But he became delusional. Paranoid. We—my ex-wife and I—got him into treatment, tried to help him." He shook his head.

"Nothing worked. He missed appointments. Didn't take his meds.

"When he was twenty-four, he decided to go to Colorado. Started working, he said, as a programmer. He found a cabin off in the woods and lived there, isolated." Hitch shrugged. "I lost track of him. I didn't know where he was. Every month I put a thousand dollars in a bank account. I never knew his address, even what town he was near, or if he had a cell phone."

"And your wife?"

"She'd had custody of him. I assumed she knew what was going on with him. I didn't."

"So how'd he get here?"

"When I saw that first message, I thought it sounded like Corey. Too much like Corey. He's brilliant. Honestly!"

"I believe you."

"But he was in Colorado, I thought. Then, after we found that paper in the backpack, I called my ex-wife."

"Where does she live?"

"New York. A political science professor, also brilliant. Also wrapped up in her job. Apparently, at some point, she found out he was living here, 'either in western Virginia or West Virginia' is the way she put it. But she never bothered to tell me." Hitch shook his head. "Didn't care enough to tell me."

"What's he want? What's his endgame?"

"You read that paper. He's paranoid about the government. Thinks it's spying on us. He's worked up some weird political theory that involves mail trucks spying on us, messing with our brains so the government can control us. So he's using stuff I taught him when he was a kid about bombs to fight against the government, which his mother taught him was corrupt." Hitch took a deep breath. "He's here, in Virginia, and I didn't know." He slammed his fist into a tree.

"But now you know, Hitch," Scott said, "and you know what you have to do."

. . .

CALDWELL PUT Scott in charge of the investigation. The first thing he did was get investigators tracing James Corbin Hitchens. They called his mother, they checked with motor vehicles, they canvassed the neighborhoods and stores within fifteen miles of the trailer.

Hardly anybody knew him. But the pastor of a little church down the road had a little information. "Stuck to himself," the pastor said. "Didn't talk to anybody except Charles Lee, his neighbor. Charlie tried to help him. He'd take him food, groceries, supplies. Charlie told me Corey was mentally ill. Felt sorry for him. Said he was going to talk to social services about getting him some help." He shrugged. "Maybe that's what triggered all this."

Scott sent somebody up to social services and indeed, that department had visited Corey a month before the first mailbox bomb. Was he paranoid about the government coming to get him because of that?

Most importantly, where was he now?

He called Jess and asked her to send him her research on Corey Hitchens. She was out but promised she'd send it when she got back to the house. The Virginia DMV had no record of a driver's license or car registration for him. Investigators finally found an expired driver's license picture from New York state.

That's when Caldwell showed up. He'd driven from DC to make sure the investigation got back on track. "I've asked the pastor of the church down the road if we can use their building as a headquarters for the next couple of days," Scott told him.

"Did he agree?"

"Yes. There's weather coming in this afternoon, and we need to get out of it. We've about done all we can here," Scott said, nodding toward the exploded building.

"If Charles Lee was the one person helping Corey, why would he blow up his house?"

"We don't know."

Caldwell crossed his arms. "How long did Hitchens suspect it might be his son?"

"He said when we got the first letter a week ago he thought it sounded like him. But he believed Corey was in Colorado."

"He should have said something right away."

"It must have seemed far-fetched." Scott gestured toward a vehicle where Hitch sat talking to another agent. "He's telling Julie everything he knows about Corey. Unfortunately, he hasn't been around him, hasn't even communicated with him for eight years."

"We have no license plate, there's not a doorbell camera or traffic cam around, no neighbors nearby. It's going to be tough finding him."

"I told our people to find out what he's driving. Maybe it's a vehicle with stolen tags, or farm use tags, or no tags at all. But he's getting around somehow," Scott said. "There's no place to walk to. So he's got to have a vehicle, and somebody must have seen it."

"Right," Caldwell said.

Scott's phone buzzed. He answered it, then said to Caldwell, "The church is ready for us. I want to move us before those storms hit."

"Let's do it."

The small church had a separate education wing. The building held a large meeting room flanked by small classrooms. A kitchen and bathrooms completed the layout. Miraculously, the church had good Wi-Fi thanks to a rural broadband grant.

Scott was reviewing field reports when a tech employee approached. "Sir, there's a call for you. A 911 supervisor."

"Thanks." He took the phone she offered him. "Scott Cooper," he said.

"Agent Cooper, one of my operators has a 911 caller specifically asking for you."

"On the line now?"

"She is still on the line with her, but I can play the original recording if you'd like to hear it."

"Go ahead." He heard some clicking and then the recording began.

911 What's your emergency?
A man entered our home. He's kidnapped my husband and a child. He has a gun. I'm tied up and there's ... there's a bomb in our house. I can see it!

Scott's adrenaline raced through him. It was Laura's voice. Laura! He put his hand over the phone and yelled, "Mike!"

Okay, ma'am, I need you to stay calm. We're going to send help. Let's confirm your address.

Scott grabbed a piece of paper and wrote down Nate's address as Laura gave it to the operator. Then he wrote BOMB! underneath it and shoved it toward Mike. Caldwell came over, drawn by the intensity.

Okay, ma'am. Are you hurt?
I'm scared.
Is anyone else there?
My friend, Crissy, and she's ... he hit her and now she's unconscious.

The 911 operator told Laura to stay on the line until rescue workers got there. Laura interrupted her.

I'll stay on the line, but they can't come in! The bomb, it's right at the door. Look, I need you to call an FBI agent. I can't get to his number, but he needs to know.

Laura went on to give Scott's name and that he was assigned to Quantico.

Please call him. He'll know what to do.

"That's why we called you, sir," the 911 supervisor said. "She asked for you."

"Have you dispatched?"

"Yes."

"They need to wait for the bomb squad. It's critical. Do not enter the house. Wait for the bomb squad. Look, we're going to need to go live on this. I'll give you back to the tech so you can arrange that."

Scott handed the phone back to the tech. "Go live on that 911 call. I want to know any developments. Stay with it!" To Mike he said, "This is my friend Nate's house."

"Holy cow."

"Stay with me."

Caldwell's eyes widened. "He's your friend?"

"Not only my friend, but the victim buried in the pile at Deer Park. But I can handle it. I know his place. I lived there. I know the victims. Mike will keep me out of trouble."

Caldwell shook his head. "Okay. Do it."

Scott turned to the room full of investigators. "Listen up, folks. Now!" The room noise subsided. "We have a report of a kidnapping and a bomb, undetonated, at a house. Here's the address. Here's what we're going to do." He outlined his plan and passed out assignments.

Mike yelled, "Let's roll!"

39

Sprite followed them, barking, as Corey forced Nate and Harper to walk through the woods. Finally, Corey swung around like he was going to shoot the dog. Nate saw him and yelled, "Hold on, hold on!"

"Sprite!" he yelled. "Leave it. Go home!"

The little springer, unused to that tone of voice, dropped to the ground and looked up sadly at Nate.

"Go home," he yelled again. *Oh, God make her go home!*

"Move," Corey said, shoving the gun toward Nate.

He walked on. The next time he glanced back, he saw Sprite just barely in sight, slowly army-crawling toward him on the narrow path. *She knows this ain't right.*

Soon they came to a wider path running toward the road, and Nate saw an old windowless cargo van with bald tires and a lot of rust. Corey slid open the side door, metal screeching against metal and told Harper to get in. Nate started to follow.

"Wait," Corey said. He reached inside, grabbed some wire, and wrapped it around Nate's wrists. Then he put a bandanna around Nate's eyes and shoved him inside.

Nate had to scramble to right himself. There were no seats.

He sat on the bare metal floor, Harper next to him, as Corey drove. He wasn't sure how he'd get up when the time came. He couldn't let Corey know he had an artificial leg. If Corey made him take it off, he'd be hard-pressed to defend Harper.

Where were they going? The van bounced over ruts and rocks, then Nate felt the ride change as they emerged from the woods and turned left onto a paved road, probably the two-lane in front of his house. He tried to count the turns and estimate the miles, but he soon lost track.

Harper cried at first, whimpering like a puppy, but Nate comforted her, drawing her close as best he could with his hands tied. "You know how to pray, Harper?" He couldn't tell what her answer was. "Let's pray."

He had no idea where they were, no clue what Corey's plans were. He could hear thunder, and soon he could hear the swish of the tires on wet roads. "Hey, Corey, what's your plan, bud? Where we goin'?"

Corey didn't answer him. That was not good. Nate could hear the man muttering to himself. If he was delusional, Nate knew he could turn violent in a heartbeat.

I been here afore, Nate thought. He'd been immersed in chaos in Iraq, in Afghanistan, and even at home, growing up, when whiskey turned his father into a living nightmare. He had to have a battle plan.

And faith.

God had warned him about this with that black cloud dream way back when he was lying under the rubble. God knew it was coming. God was with him. God would help him. God would uphold him with his righteous right hand. Isaiah 41:10. One of his go-to verses.

He'd stand on that.

Thinking forward, Nate made three decisions. He'd try to stay engaged with Corey to keep things as low-key as possible. Maybe that would keep him from turning violent. He'd try to disarm him if he could. And if Corey tried to hurt Harper, he'd kill him, one way or the other.

He was working on getting his hands free. Duct tape wasn't the sure thing TV dramas made it out to be, but the wire wrapped over the tape, now that was another story. He'd need his hands free to execute his plan.

He worked at it for a while, got frustrated, then regrouped. He'd gotten Corey away from Laura. And he'd talked his way into staying with Harper. *Thank you, God.* Seeing that bomb right before he left chilled him, but honestly, there was nothing he could do about that. What could he do?

He had an idea. "Yo, Corey man, you gettin' hungry?"

Corey turned and yelled something. It sounded like he was getting frantic.

"I'll pay. Here, use my credit card. C'mon man. And you can get gas if you need to." He maneuvered his hands so he could pull his wallet out of his back pocket. He took the bills out, hid them under his leg, and laid the wallet on the floor next to him.

That worked. Nate felt the van move to the shoulder of the road and stop. He felt the vehicle shift as Corey got out of the driver's seat. He didn't anticipate the sharp blow as Corey hit him in the side of his head with the gun.

Harper screamed and scrambled away. Nate raised his arms and ducked to protect his head.

But the second blow didn't come. Corey grabbed Nate's wallet instead. Nate felt the van shift as the man moved back to the driver's seat. They started moving again.

Nate fought nausea. He could feel blood run down the side of his face. *I didn't lose consciousness,* he thought. *There's that. Thank you, God.*

Harper hid behind him. "It's okay," he said softly. "It's gonna be okay." Then he added, "Harper, if I tell you to run, you run, okay? You run and hide and then find a grownup to help you. Got it?" He felt her nod. "Good girl."

A short time later, he felt the van slow down, turn, and stop. Corey got out. Nate smelled gas. He was filling up.

Corey got back in and drove more, then Nate heard the distinctive sound of a drive-thru speaker: *What can we get started for you?* Corey mumbled something and moved around the building. Nate heard the rustle of paper bags, and then the van drove off. He could smell hamburger, fries, and his stomach growled.

After a while, it was clear Corey had bought food for himself and nobody else.

Never mind, Nate thought. He could do without food. The good thing was Corey had begun to leave an electronic trail.

40

As I walked up the ramp to Nate's back door, my phone rang. I pulled it from my back pocket and clicked it on.

Scott didn't wait for my hello. "Where are you?"

"Nate's," I said. "Just got here." I kicked something and looked down.

"Don't go in! Do you hear me? Don't go in the house."

Nate's pipe. Why was Nate's pipe on the porch?

"Jess, get away from the house."

I heard Luke growl. "What's going on?" A sudden surge of fear ran through me. I picked up the pipe, turned, and walked down the ramp. "Scott, what's happening?"

He told me, and everything he said and every step I took moved me further and further into Nate's dark cloud until I felt frozen, terrified, trapped. "He took Nate?"

"And a child, who I presume was Harper."

My head started spinning.

"I'm headed there now. Tell the first responders they have to wait for the bomb squad. Remember how the shed was rigged to blow up if someone opened the door?"

"Right!"

"I've got another call."

And just like that, he was gone, and I was alone. Alone!

Not quite alone. I dropped down, wrapped my arm around Luke, and prayed.

Thoughts marched through my head like troops mustering for the battle.

Perfect love casts out fear.

I could almost hear Nate saying those words.

Luke turned around and slurped me in the face.

I stood up. "God, I trust you."

I heard a vehicle coming up the driveway. A sheriff's deputy. Luke started pulling me toward the woods. "Just a minute!" I told him.

The deputy got out of the car. I told him who I was and what I knew. "Don't let anybody go in the house until the bomb squad clears it," I said. I told him about the shed that blew up.

My dog pulled me again. "I'll be back," I told the deputy. "Wait, Luke." He was pulling me one way, Emmy another. I could not handle this!

So I took Emmy to the barn, locked her in a stall with water, and told her to wait there. Then I turned to follow Luke as thunder rumbled in the distance.

Luke insisted we head into the woods. I followed him. He was tracking something, and he wasn't used to doing it on leash. I thought my shoulder would pop out of its socket. We were moving away from the house and down toward the road. We'd gone about a hundred yards when I stopped short. I could see vehicle tracks on a small path. Careful not to disturb them, we followed them to the road. The vehicle, whatever it was, turned left as it emerged from the trees, tracking mud as it went.

Luke drew my attention to something else—dog prints, small dog prints in the mud. He was sniffing them. Couldn't get enough of that smell. He looked at me. I followed the dog prints down the track and out onto the road.

The dog was following the vehicle.

I looked at Luke. "Is it Sprite?"

He went crazy.

I DIDN'T HAVE anything with me to mark the location of the tracks entering the road. I had no jacket, no scarf, no handkerchief. I was wearing jeans and a white T-shirt. With no other options, I stepped into the woods, took off the shirt, and ripped off the hem. I put the shortened shirt back on and tied the ripped-off hem to the tree closest to the place I wanted to mark.

I was convinced Nate had left in whatever vehicle made those tracks, and that Sprite had tried to follow him. Now what was I going to do about it?

The rumbles of thunder grew louder. I needed to head back to Nate's to get my Jeep. Which would be quicker? Retracing our steps through the woods or running back on the road and up the driveway?

I opted for the road.

Luke was sure I was going the wrong way. He resisted at first, convinced we should follow the dog tracks. I knew we needed my car.

At what point would Sprite give up and head back home? And could she find her way? Luke did, but then he's a big dog. Sprite was little and old.

I ran hard up the road toward Nate's, thunder chasing me, rain beginning to splat on my head. When I reached the driveway, I turned, ran through the woods, and I crossed the creek. Ahead of me, the yard and driveway were full of flashing lights and emergency vehicles. I didn't see any FBI raid jackets or anything that looked like Bureau cars, so I kept going until I got to my Jeep.

At that point, I faced a decision. Do I stay here and offer

support and comfort to Laura once they get her out of the house? Or do I chase after Sprite?

Was the bomb squad there yet?

I looked around and saw everyone was standing and waiting.

I'd chase after Sprite.

I put Luke in his crate in my Jeep. The original officer walked over as I was getting in the driver's seat. "No bomb squad yet?"

"Nope. We're just waiting."

"Look, I saw tire tracks in the woods. I'm going to go mark them."

"Okay. Be careful."

The driveway was completely blocked. I had to drive down the hill on the grass and cross the creek diagonally. When I got to the road, the heavens opened. Buckets and buckets of rain fell hard on the roof of my Jeep, on the windshield, on the hood. Was the storm drumming in anger or driving out demons? I didn't know.

I turned the wipers up high. I could hear Luke in the back moving around in his crate, restless. Once or twice he whined. I needed to call Scott, tell him what I'd found, but the rain was too loud, and it was too hard to see. I didn't want to take a hand off the wheel.

I had a hard time spotting the little piece of cloth I'd left as a marker where the vehicle left the road. I drove past it, my eyes searching for Sprite. One mile, two miles, three miles, four. That's when I saw her.

At first, my heart jumped. I thought she'd been hit. She was lying beside the road. I put my flashers on and jumped out of my Jeep. "Sprite!" The rain soaked me.

The little springer raised her head and wagged her stubby tail. She got up and staggered toward me. *Thank God!* I scooped her up in my arms.

She was exhausted. I opened the back door, rummaged around, and found a towel, which I wrapped around Sprite, who was shivering. Then I laid her in the front passenger seat. "You are a good dog," I said, stroking her head. "You just rest now."

I closed the front door, then found my SAR pack in the back, opened it, and took out a long-sleeved blue shirt that I wore on searches. My T-shirt, what remained of it anyway, was soaked.

Climbing back in the driver's seat, I looked around. No one was near me. I quickly switched shirts. I felt a lump in my pants pocket. Nate's pipe. I took it out and put it next to Sprite. "We'll find him, girl, don't worry." She licked my hand, nosed the pipe, and curled around it like it was a puppy.

Two police cars passed me, lights flashing. I picked up my phone and called Scott. No answer. I left a message.

What should I do next? I'd like to say I prayed and asked the Lord to lead me. I didn't. I thought it out "logically" as usual. "Logically" defined as what I felt like doing.

If I went back to Nate's I'd likely get trapped in there by all the emergency vehicles. Or Scott would see me and tell me to stay in my car. I couldn't do that. I was too restless. But if I was going to drive toward Nate, where should I go? How would I find him?

Just as I was about to head blindly into the storm, my phone rang. I didn't recognize the number. I answered anyway.

"Jessica? This is Mike Perez. Scott's friend."

Relief. "What's going on?"

"He asked me to call. He's up to his ears right now. Where are you?"

I told him I was out on the road. I told him about the vehicle tracks and about them turning north on the two-lane. "I marked the spot."

"How'd you find that?"

"My dog."

"Your dog."

"Trust me. He knows what he's doing. I'm going to park near that spot. I marked it, but it's hard to see with all this rain. I'm in a white Jeep Sahara, and I'll have my flashers on. Send a cop down, or somebody, so they can verify it."

Silence. Mike didn't believe me.

"Look, just tell Scott. He'll understand."

"Okay."

I turned my Jeep around and headed back toward the scrap of cloth I'd left. I pulled over and put my flashers on.

Five minutes later, a county deputy pulled in front of me with his lights on. I quickly exited my car, which is *not* the right thing to do because it alarms them. But I wanted to be sure he didn't drive over the evidence I'd found.

The rain had let up a little, but the thunder still rumbled. "I'm Jessica Cooper," I called out, keeping my hands clearly visible.

His hand came off his gun. "What have you found?"

We both had flashlights, and we needed them. It was already starting to turn dark, and the storm made it even darker. "Look here," I said, shining my light on the edge of the road. "The rain has washed the mud away, but you can still see tire marks in the gravel."

"Yes, ma'am," he said, squatting down for a closer look.

"And see, there are indentations going up into the woods. The weeds are knocked down. It looks to me like somebody parked there and then left, turning north on the road."

"Yes, ma'am," he said. "That fits with what we've got."

"Oh ..." I let my voice trail off.

He filled in the blank. "The victim's credit card was used to buy gas up the road."

I nodded. "Oh, right. Which station was that?"

"The Exxon up at North Ridge. It fits with the 911 call too."

"Oh? I didn't hear about that."

"A drive-thru worker at Burger King said this guy pulled up in an old white van. She said he was scary looking, and then she saw a handgun in plain view on the passenger seat. She freaked out, moved away from the window, and told her supervisor, who took over, finished the transaction, and then called 911 because the man acted so erratically."

"Well, that's something." *Thank you God for chatty deputies.* "Good luck to you guys," I said. He waved and went back to his cruiser. I got in my Jeep, waited for him to leave, then turned around and headed for North Ridge.

Now I knew what I was looking for. A white van, headed north, possibly northwest.

I went over what I knew about Corey Hitchens. He'd used drugs in the past. He knew how to rig bombs. If he was the crazy looking guy I'd seen in the woods when I was scoping out Charles Lee's house, he was certainly strange, possibly mentally ill. He probably lived off in the woods. He'd hidden in the woods near Nate's. If he had to hide again, my guess would be he'd do the same thing—hide in the woods.

Great. There were only several million acres of woods in the area where we were.

Why had he gone to Nate's? Was he after Nate because he thought Nate could identify him? Had his father told him Nate was beginning to remember the Deer Park bombing? That he had given a statement to the FBI?

It was hard for me to imagine an ATF agent volunteering information like that to a suspect, even if the suspect was his son.

The only other connection I could see between Nate and Corey Hitchens was Harper Lee. Corey would have seen Harper around Charles's house. Had he abused her? Is that why she stopped talking? Is that why he blew up the house? Was he now trying to shut up both Harper and Nate?

If so, why didn't he just kill them?

41

NATE'S SHOULDERS ached from having his hands tied in back. He tried stretching and shrugging to ease the pain, but nothing seemed to work. Steel hands gripped his shoulders, and no amount of shrugging or rotating released them.

Harper had gently pulled the bandanna down so he could see. "Good girl," he'd whispered, and he hoped Corey wouldn't notice. The rain, which had pounded the metal van for an hour or so, had eased up. Still, the vehicle was so noisy he could speak to Harper without worrying that Corey could hear him.

What did worry him was the fact that a few miles back Corey had almost lost control of the van, fishtailing because he went too fast around a curve on a slippery road. Now, with the bandanna down, he could see another gun, an AR-15 rifle tucked partially under a towel next to the seat. Corey was talking to himself, getting animated, shaking the steering wheel. And then Nate saw him take something from his pocket—some kind of pill—and pop it in his mouth.

He was losing it, Nate thought, and self-medicating to try to keep it together.

This would not end well. Nate started thinking again about

getting his hands free. He tried rubbing the wire on the rib of the van, but that did nothing. He tried stretching it and felt it cut into his wrist. *What can I do? What can I do?*

In the dim light, Nate saw Harper crawl across the floor of the van. There was a bag over there, a utility bag, and she started looking through it. He could hear metal things clinking together.

At the same time, the van started making a thumping noise, the engine jerking like something had broken. Corey pounded the steering wheel. He turned right off the road. In a flash of lightning, Nate saw they were at a power-line easement, a gap in the trees with a major power line running down through the middle.

The van jerked to a stop and Corey got out. With the dome light on, Harper scampered back to Nate. He tried to see what Corey was doing. Then he felt Harper behind him. He felt her hands next to his hands, heard a *clip,* and felt his wrists loosen. She was cutting the wires!

Nate looked at her quickly. She smiled at him. He kissed the top of her head.

Corey climbed back in the van. Nate dropped his head like he was sleeping, and Harper hid behind him. The van lurched forward.

Clip. Clip. Then one more, *clip.* A different sound as she cut through the duct tape. And he was free! He rubbed his wrists, although he didn't dare take his hands from behind his back. What a relief!

Thank you, God. Thank you, God, that there were wire cutters in the van, that she saw them and knew what they were and had the courage to use them. Thank you!

Gratitude—and hope—filled him.

The van rattled and shook over ruts and rocks and then *bam!* hit something hard. Harper gripped him. Corey accelerated, and Nate realized they were driving up the power-line easement.

Why? Maybe Corey had to rest. Or hide. Or maybe ... something darker?

He took a deep breath. He'd be ready. His hands were free. *God,* he prayed silently, *I know he is your creation, but I will kill him if he tries to hurt Harper. Please help it not come to that.*

42

As usual, I had more questions about Corey Hitchens than answers. If I followed the trajectory of the two locations where I knew he'd been seen, the gas station and the Burger King, I'd drive northwest toward Winchester, which made sense if he was going back to where he lived.

The rain came down hard again, dashing itself against the pavement and splashing in the ditches. I turned my wipers up to high and leaned forward, peering into the darkness. Night had fallen. Here I was, driving around in the dark and the storm, looking for them. I might as well have been trying to empty the ocean with a thimble. Catch the wind with my bare hands.

Soon, my despair grew, and my emotions bottomed out. My chest felt tight, and my heart ached. *God,* I prayed, *Nate needs you. He needs us. Please help us find him.*

My phone rang. I thought I recognized Mike's number. I was right.

"Hey, Scott wants to know where you are."

"I had to find Sprite."

"Okay, he wanted you to know the bomb was diffused and Laura's okay. Scared, but okay."

"That's great. Thank you."

"So, what? You'll be back at the house before too long?"

I should have said *yes*. Should have given up my solo efforts to find Nate. But I really didn't want to be sitting at the house while Nate was in trouble. I didn't think I could stand it.

I started to blow Mike off. Give him an ambiguous answer. Then I remembered I had a husband who loved me. Who cared about me. We were partners, and Mike was his guy.

"Mike," I said, "tell Scott I'm on 340, heading northwest. I just want to see if I can spot them. I won't approach them if I do. I'll call it in."

A long silence followed. I knew what Mike was thinking.

"He won't be happy, but I promise I'll be careful," I added.

That worked. Mike hung up.

I drove a little further and then, honestly, I had to pee. I mean, *really* had to. I was in the middle of nowhere—no gas stations, no fast-food places, no stores. The rain had let up, although I could see lightning to the west. I pulled over at a place with enough shoulder to park on near a big power-line easement. I went into the woods and did what I needed to do. As I came back out, two county cars blazed past, headed northwest.

They must be on to something, I thought. I got back in the car and turned on my headlights, intending to follow them. As I moved forward, preparing to get back on the road, I saw something odd. There was a broad access point leading from the road to right under the power lines and a fence with a big gate to keep people from driving up onto the property. I suspected dirt bikers and other off-roaders would have a field day there, and maybe there had been insurance issues.

The thing that caught my eye was that the gate was open. Not only was it open, but it looked like it had been rammed and run over.

Why would that be?

I started to drive off, then I remembered something. Corey

Hitchens' trailer was right next to a similar easement. I was still a good hour from where he and Charles Lee lived, but could he have driven up into the power-line property thinking it was his, or would lead to his? Or just because it looked familiar?

There were no houses around. None. What should I do?

I could call Scott, but I knew this would seem to him like a long shot.

I could drive up the power-line easement, but that would make me a sitting duck if Corey was up there, and my gun was locked up—at Nate's house.

I could forget what I saw and drive on.

I decided to forget it. Drive on.

But then I couldn't.

I parked a little way up the road. I took a small flashlight. And I walked back toward the gate.

And there I saw signs of recent entry, of mud disturbed like someone had lost traction, of weeds tamped down by two sets of wheels.

I had to do something.

My inclination was to walk up through the woods and see what I could see on my own. My inclinations just about got me killed when Luke went missing.

I was just about to say *oh, well* and start walking when another deputy's car came screaming up the road, lights on, no siren. I took my flashlight and stepped out on the road to wave him down.

He went right past me.

Forget it. I'll go by myself, I thought. Angry, I reached into my Jeep to grab my bigger flashlight. My hand brushed my cell phone. I picked it up and started to put it in my pocket. Something made me stop and do the right thing. I called Scott.

This time he picked up. "Where are you," he asked.

I could hear tire noise in the background. He was on the move. "I've found something. Up on 340."

"What?"

I told him. "I tried to flag down a deputy, but he just blazed on by."

"Are you carrying?"

"No."

"Tell me exactly where you are. I'll send somebody. Don't go up there by yourself!" He paused, but I didn't respond. "Jess, I'm serious!"

My jaw was tight. "I won't. But send somebody quick. I'm not waiting forever."

43

"HEY, man, I thought we were going to the hospital to see Charlie!" Nate called out. Corey didn't answer. He could see Corey shaking his head, talking to himself, hitting the dashboard and the steering wheel.

Corey rolled his window down and stuck his head out. Instinctively, Nate knew he was looking for a place to pull into the woods, a place to hide the van.

What would happen then? Would Corey try to fix it? Would he start them walking? What?

Nate knew his time to make a move was coming up. If Corey was delusional, there was no telling what he'd do.

Nate felt the van turn to the right, then begin to back up. He heard branches scraping along the sides. Then he felt it stop.

Corey threw the van into park and turned off the engine. Then he pulled something out of his pocket. A pipe. Filled it with something. And then lit it.

Nate's jaw tightened. Corey was smoking meth.

44

FOUR POLICE CARS right close together, lights flashing, went by me. I stood and stared as they disappeared into the night. Had the team found the van north of me? I started to doubt my disturbed mud theory. My heart beat hard. Part of me wanted to jump in my Jeep and follow them.

Then a sheriff's car pulled up in front of my car. Two deputies got out. One was huge—at least six four and maybe two thirty. He looked like a former football player. The other was shorter. He looked very young.

"Jessica Cooper?"

"Yes!"

"I'm Brady. This is Jim," the taller deputy said. "What do you have?"

"Grab your flashlights." I walked them over to where the gate was broken down. "Look at this." I pointed to where the mud had been disturbed. "That's just happened."

"What makes you say that?"

"Look at the ridges. If they'd happened yesterday or even earlier today, they would've been beaten down by all the rain we've had."

Brady took his finger and touched a ridge lightly. It was easy to flatten. He stood up and looked around. You think somebody drove up there?" He gestured toward the rising hill under the power lines.

"Look how the grass is tamped down. Somebody's been up there. And the gate is all broken up, so my guess is, it wasn't an official vehicle."

The two deputies looked at each other. "Want to go up there?"

"Wait," I said, "you should go through the woods. If Corey Hitchens is up there, you'd be sitting ducks walking through the field."

Jim dismissed me with a shrug. "We'll take our vehicle."

I didn't think that would work, but I shut up. I walked toward the edge of the woods and watched. Sure enough, a short way in, their cruiser got stuck. Then, to my utter amazement, I saw the two deputies get out and start walking up the easement. What were they thinking?

45

Some time went by. Five minutes? Ten? Nate didn't dare look at his watch.

Then Corey sat up straight, peering into the night. What did he see?

Corey grabbed the rifle and the pistol and left the van. Nate edged himself to his feet. "Harper!" he said. "Let's go."

Outside, Corey screamed and started shooting.

"Now!" The back door screeched as Nate opened it. He lifted Harper down. "Run! Run!" He put a hand on the door and jumped out. His leg buckled, he tried to regain his balance, then Corey hit him from behind.

"No, no, no!" Corey yelled. "No!"

The last thing Nate saw before he blacked out was Harper racing into the woods.

46

GUNFIRE! Four shots, followed by repeated rounds from a rifle.

My heart jumped. I raced to the deputies' cruiser and grabbed the radio mike. "Shots fired, shots fired!" I said I was a civilian and gave the dispatcher the location. I dropped the mike and grabbed the shotgun between the seats. Thankfully, it was unlocked.

The gunfire continued, but only from one direction. In my mind I imagined the deputies had found concealment but not cover. If they fired, the shooter would know where they were.

Either that or they were both hurt.

I ran into the woods and called Scott. I told him what happened. He told me to stay put.

"Scott," I said, "I cannot stand here and listen to those deputies come under fire. They're pinned down. I have their shotgun, and I'm going in."

"Jess. Jess!" I heard him yell. I clicked off the phone and heard a rumble of thunder. More storms on the way. Then more gunfire. I ran further into the woods.

47

I CREPT up through the woods, moving as silently as I could, thankful I'd grabbed my ballistic vest (a birthday present from Scott) out of my Jeep while waiting for help to arrive.

I chose to move parallel to the power lines and about thirty feet into the woods. I believed the cops were hunkered down. I hadn't heard any more gunfire from them. I was hoping they weren't hurt. The weeds in the field were thigh high—not high enough to shield them, so they were trapped. Would Corey go hunting for them? I wanted to keep that from happening if I could. Distract him. Draw his fire away from them.

A bolt of lightning crackled through the night sky. In that one-second flash I saw ahead of me a white van, backed into the woods perpendicular to the power lines.

I've got eyes on the van, I texted Scott, *about a hundred yards up from the road, in the woods to the left of the power line.* I could hear vehicles on the road—a lot of them. They were coming in cold. No lights, no sirens.

I wanted to get closer to the van. I wanted to find Nate. I wanted to spot Corey. I wanted to see Harper. I wanted to keep Corey from killing those cops.

I wondered how much of a survivalist Corey was. Did he have night-vision goggles? Was he watching me even now?

That thought made me drop to the ground. I grasped the shotgun and began to creep through the forest, angling to the left, moving farther from the power lines. In a flash of lightning, I could see the back door of the van stood open. Maybe Harper was inside. Lightning flashed again, and I dropped lower. That's when I saw Corey. He was looking right toward me. I buried my face and didn't move. When I peeked again, he was staring out over the field. He must not have seen me. I picked up a rock and threw it into the woods near the van. Then I hid my face.

Had it worked? Had it drawn Corey off the cops?

I kept moving until the van was between me and the field. During the next lightning flash, I saw Nate, lying on the ground to the left of the van. My heart skipped a beat. He wasn't moving. He honestly looked dead. I bit my lip. *No, God, no, God, no, God!*

Where are you? Scott texted.

I described my location. I told him where Nate was and what I could see.

A little later, I saw vehicles driving up the field, lights off. I figured they were in radio contact with the two officers. They'd evacuate whoever was hurt and use the rest of the vehicles as shields.

I could hear the rain in the treetops before I felt it. It collected on the leaves then fell through to me. Soon, I was drenched. A flash of lightning illuminated the vehicles in the field. Cop cars, Ford Interceptors, and big black SUVs, one of which I knew was Scott's.

Corey saw them too. He made a roar like an enraged animal. He shook his fist at them.

I heard a noise behind me. "Jess, it's Mike."

But I had my eyes on Corey. I saw him turn and kick Nate on the ground, kick him hard, again and again. And then he pointed his big pistol at my friend.

I stood up and ran toward him shouting, "Corey Hitchens! Drop the weapon!" in my best command voice.

Mike tried to stop me. I felt his hand on my foot, and I jerked it away. I stumbled and kept going. "Put it down! Corey, drop the weapon." He stopped kicking Nate and looked in my direction, stunned.

I took cover behind a tree and aimed the shotgun. "Put it down!"

Then he raised his gun and fired toward me.

The shot from the SWAT team rang out at the same time Mike dragged me to the ground.

MIKE COVERED me with his body. I could barely breathe. My heart was beating so hard I could feel in it my hands. Mike's breath felt hot in my ear. "Lie still," he said.

Finally, someone shouted "Clear!" and Mike rolled off. "Are you okay? Here, give me the gun." He took the shotgun and helped me to my feet.

Was I okay? I felt weak, jumpy, and out of breath. But all I could think about was Nate.

Scott ran up and grabbed me. "Oh, Jess!"

"Is he dead?"

"Yes, he's dead."

I felt my knees grow weak and my legs collapse as my heart broke. "No!" I sobbed.

Scott kept me from falling. "No, not Nate! Not Nate! Oh, Jess. The shooter's dead, not Nate. Nate's alive."

I struggled to stand. "Thank God!" I buried my face in his chest, relieved but exhausted.

Mike cleared his throat. "I can see why you say your wife terrifies you, Scott. I've seen tornadoes easier to manage."

Scott laughed.

"I want to see Nate," I said.

"C'mon." He put his arm around me and led me through the woods with Mike following. As we neared the cluster of agents and cops around the van, I uncoupled from him.

Nate lay on the ground. A couple of medics were assessing him. I knelt next to him and took his hand. He looked at me. "I'm okay. Find Harper," he said in a raspy voice.

"Where is she? In the van?"

"I told her to run. Hide. In the woods."

"These woods?"

Nate nodded.

I squeezed his hand. "We'll find her."

Scott immediately organized the cops to search. "Wait," I said. "She can't have gone far. Luke's in my Jeep. Let us try."

"You sure?"

"Yes."

Ten minutes later, Luke and I stood near the van. I told him to seek and pointed him into the woods, but I kept him on leash.

That did not work at all. He couldn't range back and forth. He couldn't follow the scents on the wind. He couldn't do what he loved to do, what he was trained to do, what he was made for doing.

The rain poured down. "Stop. Luke, wait." Lightning flashed. Thunder rumbled. All we were missing was a raging river. My heart drummed. My hands shook.

Luke stopped. I reached for his collar. My heart shuddered. I pulled back the clasp and released the leash. "Seek, Luke, seek!" My throat caught as I sent him off.

Scott touched my shoulder. "I'm with you."

Together we followed my dog into the dark night.

LUKE FOUND Harper fifteen minutes later, hiding behind a fallen log in the middle of a big patch of mountain laurel. I told Scott I would bet the human searchers couldn't have found her. She was well hidden and would not have responded to men she didn't know.

But she knew Luke, and she knew me, and soon we were walking out of the woods with her in my arms. Scott offered to carry her, but she clung to me like a barnacle. As we were walking, she whispered in my ear, "Nate?"

"He'll be fine, honey. He can't wait to see you."

The rain had lightened to a drizzle. Harper laid her head down on my shoulder. Scott held my elbow, steadying me as we made our way through the woods. Exhaustion made my muscles wobbly and my bones weary, but a deep contentment was mine as well. Nate was alive. Laura and Harper were safe. Soon, I'd get Scott back. And Luke and I were a team again.

Thank You.

48

When I was a child my father would occasionally rent a small sailboat from the marina near our Long Island home and take me out on the water. One time we were in a fourteen-foot daysailer, no keel, just a centerboard. The boat was, in my words, "tippy." The wind was blowing about fifteen knots, and we were cruising along, me in my life jacket, my hair tucked under a ball cap, my dad happily steering, one hand on the tiller, the other holding the main sheet. We came around a headland and *smack!* the wind shifted, hit the sail, and knocked us over hard. My hat blew off. Panicked, I grabbed for the gunnels, then shifted my weight to the center of the small boat to try to stabilize it. We rocked back and forth, back and forth, as my dad fought to regain control, my heart pounding hard.

He did, and we did not capsize, but for a long minute I thought for sure we were headed for a swim in the cold Long Island Sound. My dad laughed about it, but it scared me. Later, it became a metaphor for the seasons in my life, some long, some short, marked by instability and tumult. Like the one we'd just been through.

I told my friends that story as the four of us—Nate, Laura, Scott, and I—sat around Nate's ER exam room. We were waiting for the doctors to release Nate. He had a couple of broken ribs, bruises, and a laceration on his skull, but nothing that would require more time in the hospital, and he was anxious to leave.

"That's what I feel the last four months have been like," I said, "like I've been on a tippy little boat going back and forth, back and forth." I held out my hand, palm down, and tipped it to demonstrate. Everybody laughed.

Nate turned to me. "Sounds like the disciples on the Sea of Galilee."

"Yeah, but I didn't have Jesus with me," I said, making light of it.

"You didn't then, but you do now."

I blinked.

Nate. Always giving me something to think about.

Assured by the nurse that Nate would be released that night, we decided that I would stay and drive him home, while Scott would take Laura and start cleaning up the house. Laura, who was traumatized but otherwise unhurt, said the sooner the house was "reclaimed," the better. We'd already decided I'd stay with them a couple of days to help out. Scott had a ton of stuff to do to wrap up the Corey Hitchens case anyway.

Three days after he got home, Nate felt well enough to check on Charles Lee. Despite doctors' predictions, Harper's father, while badly injured, did survive. He told investigators that Corey Hitchens, his neighbor, had come to him asking if he could store a couple of boxes in his basement. Charles had no idea they contained explosives. "I was just tryin' to help a neighbor out," he said.

The doctors said Charles would be in the hospital about another week and then have a long recovery.

Trouble is he had no home to go back to and no other family

that could take him in, Nate discovered. So, true to form, after praying about it, Nate and Laura invited him to recover at their house. And once that arrangement was in place, CPS saw no reason not to return custody of Harper to Charles. Laura got her little girl, at least for a while.

Luke and I moved back to our townhouse in Manassas. We left Ember at Nate's. She had room to run there, and Nate said he liked the idea of having a big dog on the property. Her owner, Alex, was fine with it. He'd run into complications with his cancer treatments and was in no position to take care of her.

So our little boat was settled, sailing smoothly, running with the wind, I thought as I prepared dinner one evening in late September. Not tippy at all. I was trying a new recipe, a parmesan ranch chicken that I thought Scott would like, along with homemade bread and a salad. The house smelled great.

My phone rang. When I saw it was him, I braced myself for another cancelled dinner.

But no. "What are we doing tomorrow?" he asked.

Tomorrow was Saturday. "I don't know. Going to Nate's?" I thought maybe he'd want to ride his horse, Ace.

"Okay, great," he said. "I'll be home in twenty."

THE WEATHER in late September in this part of Virginia often warms up to the mid-seventies for a few days, a sort of goodbye kiss to summer. The next day, Saturday, followed that pattern. I'd put on jeans and a short-sleeved shirt, but I had a sweatshirt with me.

We were in my Jeep, headed south toward Nate's. Scott wanted to drive for some reason, so I was just chilling in the passenger seat, listening to Luke chomping on his squeaky toy in the back, while Scott and I talked.

He'd taken his daughter Amanda and her boyfriend Ethan

out to dinner earlier in the week. As a result of their conversation that night, Ethan had decided to move out. He said he wanted to marry Amanda, but wanted to do it right, in a way that respected her.

Amanda was furious.

About the time Scott finished that story, he turned off Route 29 onto a two-lane road. "Hey, where are you going?" I said.

"I want you to see something."

We wound our way up through the beautiful countryside, past Angus cattle placidly grazing and fields of drying corn ready for harvesting. Spontaneity is not Scott's strong suit, so I grew more curious with every mile. *This better not be another horse*, I thought.

He turned left into a curving driveway lined with trees, which gave way to pasture enclosed by horse fencing. A two-story white house came into view—a house with big windows and a wide front porch, with boxwoods and rhododendron and what looked to me like azaleas hugging the front.

My mouth went dry. "What is this, Scott? Why are we here?"

He parked under the shade of an old oak, turned, and smiled at me, his eyes shining. "Come see."

We left the Jeep open for Luke. Scott took my hand. We walked up onto that porch, and he removed the key from under a flower pot. Then he unlocked the front door.

The thick, oak door opened into a large foyer. Ahead of us was a hallway leading toward the back of the house and a staircase sweeping up to the second floor with a glossy brown banister. To the left was a dining room and to the right a parlor. The rooms were furnished, but it was pretty clear no one currently lived here.

We explored the house together—the three bedrooms upstairs; the two bathrooms; the study/nursery; the full, walk-up attic. When I looked out of a bedroom window and saw the stable, I was sure I knew what was going on, but I was afraid to ask. I didn't want to break the spell.

Back downstairs, standing in the quaint old kitchen, I found my courage. "What are we doing? Why are we here?"

Scott took me in his arms. "If you like it, I'd like to buy this place."

My head spun. "Can we afford it? I mean, Scott ... it's beautiful."

"We can afford it."

"How'd you find it? I thought you'd stopped looking."

"I had to stop looking, but I never stopped praying." He kissed me. "I was talking with one of the sheriffs who worked the bombings. We were wrapping some things up on his end. Somehow we got on to houses, and I told him we were looking to buy a place in the country. This was his mother's place. Where he grew up, in fact. She died and his wife doesn't want to live out here. He said he'd cut me a deal if he could come visit now and then."

"It's pretty far from Quantico."

"I won't be at Quantico forever. It comes with twenty-seven acres, and if we go through a lawyer, I think we can swing it."

I could hardly believe what I was hearing.

"You can have plenty of room for your dogs ..."

"... and you can do your horse thing."

"Equine therapy." Scott said. "A different way to fight evil."

A pickup appeared, coming up the lane. "Nate?" I said.

"He knows a lot more about houses than I do."

Nate got out of his pickup and lifted Sprite down, sparing her joints. He looked at his watch while he walked toward us. "Twenty-eight minutes. Not bad."

I let Luke out of the car, and he and Sprite began playing. Scott and Nate started going through the house, beginning with the basement. I took a seat in one of the rockers on the front porch, and caressed by a gentle breeze, I began dreaming.

We'd be twenty-eight minutes from Nate and Laura in the rolling foothills of the Blue Ridge mountains on twenty-seven acres, with a pond and a stream and a stable. Room to run. Room to roam. Green pastures. Still waters.

I closed my eyes. *Thank you, Jesus.*

ACKNOWLEDGMENTS

My sister, Karen Giorgis, in addition to being a wife and mother of three boys, taught preschool in her small, rural county in Virginia for over thirty years. What a legacy! By the time she was ready to retire, she'd begun teaching the children of her very first students.

There's no way to quantify the impact she's had, but I imagine it is substantial. By teaching generations of kids to share, by getting them ready for kindergarten, and, most importantly, by introducing them to the truth that "Jesus loves me," Karen's work helped knit together the fabric of her county, and, by extension, this nation. There are no hero medals for people like her, no accolades on the silver screen, no trophies, and no big retirement packages, but where would we be without them?

On a more personal note, Karen has read every single one of my books, from my first, faltering efforts in *The Tiger's Cage* to the most recent one. She is the only person who remembers one of my unpublished manuscripts, *The* 19th *Agenda*, a book about a bomber, and she has called, emailed, or texted me every year in April for over thirty years to tell me she remembers it.

When I chose the plot for this book, I decided the first bomb would detonate on April 19th. In addition to that being a significant date, it's a tip-of-the-hat to Karen, a thanks to my sister for her faithful, steady support since I began this journey in 1993.

The rest of my helpers are a line-up of the usual suspects and I am so grateful for them! Barbara Johnson and Jessica Burnside of DOGS-East and Retired FBI Special Agent Dru Wells checked the manuscript for their areas of expertise. Erin Unger read an early version and gave me some great feedback. Barbara Scott provided the final editing. My daughter, Becky Chappell set me straight on some things in the first draft, and then did the publishing honors. June Padgett of Bright Eye Designs crafted the cover art. Books & Such Literary Management's Janet Grant, as always, provided her support.

I've very thankful to the Lord for the way he touches hearts through these books and for you, my readers, who give me the gift of your time in reading them.

Linda J. White

Soli Deo gloria

ABOUT THE AUTHOR

Linda J. White has loved dogs and a good dog story since early childhood. Her current buddy is an eleven-year-old Sheltie, Keira, who patiently came out of retirement to do a "nose work" class so Linda could experience the beginnings of training for SAR.

Linda has been a government worker, a mom at home, a Bible study teacher, a freelance writer, and the assistant editorial-page editor of a daily newspaper. Her late husband, Larry, a graduate of the American Film Institute, made training films for the FBI Academy. She has three grown children and five grandchildren and lives in Yorktown, Virginia, where she enjoys watching birds migrate and grandchildren grow.

www.lindajwhite.net

ALSO BY LINDA J. WHITE

The K-9 Search and Rescue Series:

All That I Dread

The Fear That Chases Me

When Evil Finds Us

FBI Thrillers:

Bloody Point

Battered Justice

Seeds of Evidence

Sniper!

Words of Conviction

The Tiger's Cage

Made in USA - Kendallville, IN
77044_9781737235620
08.24.2022 1635